Edited by:

James Ward Kirk

Alternate cover by Jerry Langdon

Copyright 2013 James Ward Kirk Publishing

Copyright James Ward Kirk Publishing 2013
Internet: jwkfiction.com
Twitter: @jameswardkirk
Facebook: James-Ward-Kirk-Fiction

Cover art and design copyright William Cook 2013
Photography by Mike Jansen copyright 2013
Alternate art Jerry Langdon 2013

ISBN-13: 978-0615844992

(James Ward Kirk Publishing)

ISBN-10: 0615844995

All rights reserved. No part of this book may be reproduced in any form or by any electronic or mechanical means, including information storage and retrieval systems, without written permission from the publisher or author, except in the case of a reviewer, who may quote brief passages embodied in critical articles or in a review.

Contents

For Monica M. Kirk

Introduction

J. Daniel Stone

The idea of sex in horror fiction exploded upon the pages of Stoker's *Dracula*, a non-traditional novel about the love of eternal life and the writhing of human lust that plagues us all. Next up (naturally) is Howard Phillips Lovecraft, whose use of language (and general lack of the physical drug) inadvertently induced psilocybin imageries of mythology and vanquished gods unto his readers. Shirley Jackson's horrific visions still ache with a longing and deviant need for acceptance of alternate sexual needs due to her own repressed sexuality. And more recently, we're continuously awed and shocked by Clive Barker's *Books of Blood*, which to me was the first successful amalgamation of sex, drugs and horror rolled into one.

Sex is the sin that we all crave because the world blossoms anew after an orgasm. Drugs drown out all the realities we wish to run away from; they also help us mold reality into something ephemerally satisfying—which keeps us coming back for more. Horror is the seduction that allows us the freedom to delve into a state of mental masochism. We want to be scared; we want succumb to someone else's nightmare. We *like* it. We *need* it...much like drugs and sex.

Scapegoat or escapism?

We might never know.

J. Daniel Stone
New York City, 2013

Red in the Hood

Timothy Frasier

The red haired girl walked through the hood with rage
simmering inside
Catcalls and whistles stung her soul so she detoured down the
alley
Life so promising when she was young, there seemed to be no
limits
But her granny had her needs, she'd hustled for her since eleven

A black Caddy blocked her path, Red swore out loud
Out stepped Wolf, the Westside pimp who had killed fifty men
Hello Red, you sexy slut, then flashed a gold filled smile
You still trickin' for Granny, or independent now

Red lit a cigarette and regarded Wolf through the haze
I still work for Granny, but that could someday change
If only I could find someone who could make that witch go
away
Tonight her door might be unlocked, she's known to be careless

Wolf came near and whispered softly while slipping his hand
down her top
Red took a drag from her cigarette and then shoved it in his ear
She laughed as he rolled in the gutter among the condoms and
the trash
I'm off to Granny's you big bad Wolf; come claim your prize if
you dare

Red walked past Granny as she was getting it on with her pusher
Ignoring the sounds of passion as she got in and out of the
shower
Hey hot momma, wanna join the fun, there's room for another
That's my granny you perv, plus I'm off the clock; she gave him
the finger

Red dressed slowly in front of the pusher, just to make her
granny mad

But Granny paid no heed for she had no need, stoned out of her
gourd
The pusher stood up, then fell to the bed as his head exploded in
mist
Wolf stood smiling in the doorway, his silencer still smoking

Granny spit brains from her mouth, her red face framed in
horror
She flailed her arms and pissed the bed as Wolf slit her throat
Well Little Red, I'll collect my prize, are you glad now to see me
With a smile she took his arm and led him to the bloody mattress

She slipped down his pants slowly and watched his excitement
grow
Then severed his manhood with her razor, laughing all the while
Wolf cursed, screamed, and stumbled about as his life blood
gushed out
Red surveyed the carnage and said, *Now I can live happily ever
after*

The Witches

Roger Cowin

1.

The men call their wives
to the slaughter.
Under a lunatic moon
the crops run red,

Straw effigies are stuffed
with something
unspeakable.
Offerings are burnt.

The split footed god of the forest
summons the children
to join the rites.
Horns sprout from their heads.

They dance and feast and drink,
make the proper sacrifices,
speak the ancient, profane prayers
that make the crops grow
and keep the old gods sated.

What children born
of these unholy unions
will be fattened and prepared
as sacrifices for the next festival.

2.

Old Scratch,
lord of perfidy,
he of cloven hoof
and bifurcated tail,
holds sway
over the sabbbat.

His witches writhe naked
at his feet
covering him with kisses,
mosquito haired hags
gnash and snarl
at each other
for the chance
to lick his ass,
plunging clawed hands
into the foul
excrement
that drops from his ass
to shove iinto
their mouths
in unholy mockery
of the sacrament.
The men bend over,
spreading their
ass cheeks and plead
to be filled
with his goat cock.

Tomorrow, they will
dress in their Sunday
finery and worship
at the altar of Christ
and accuse their neighbors
of heresy.

3 Love Poems

Roger Cowin

1.

Lay your weary head to rest
My beautiful one, my lover,
Your hair like black damask
Spilling across my pillow
In intricate patterns.
I let the stylus of my fingertips
Trace across the surface of your face,
Bone white in the moonlight
That streams through the window.
How I ache for you, desire you,
How I want only to take you
In my warm embrace
And fill you with all my love.
Alas! If only I had kept your body.

2.

You stood with your back to me,
Facing the ocean as the wind
Whipped your hair about your face
And ignored my desperate pleas.
I promised you were the only one,
Pledged my eternal love and devotion,
I got on my knees and offered you
The moon and stars if only
You would be mine.
But you only stood there, mute and cold.
In desperation, I offered you my brain.
And as you bit a chunk
from my skull and swallowed,
I knew you truly loved me.

.

3.

"Love may be
Many a splendor thing,
But it is so cliché," you said,

"We must do something
To prove our love unique."
So as we kissed,
I took your tongue between my teeth
Ripped it from your mouth,
And placed it on a chain
Around my neck.

Love is a Gun

Roger Cowin

Love is a gun, warming my hand,
a hot smoking barrel oozing
seminal bullets.
Man, I really groove on all that
flesh and violence,
my loaded .45 humming
its sexy death song firing
round after round
into your moaning body
till my chamber's spent
and we both lie there,
side by side,
dead but more alive
than we've ever been.

My Sweet

Mathias Jansson

The rusty needle right in my vein
a mixture of blood
from a nymphomaniac insane
and juice from a zombie brain

I feel the drugs inside
like falling through
doors of nightmares
to the darkest hell

I can already feel
your rotten flesh
waiting for me
in the chamber of love

Where I will tear your skin
from your bones
and eat your meat
for you will be
the only Sweet
I will ever eat

Brothel of hell

Mathias Jansson

A soul is the price
you have to pay
when you visit
the brothel of hell

Passing throw corridors
with open doors
to every pleasure and perversion
leading to eternal damnation
I saw a leather faced man
fucking a woman with a chainsaw
and a monster ancient old
sticking its tentacles
in every hole
on the woman on the floor

But in the last room
was my own desire
an angel fallen from heaven
with broken wings
shackled in chains of lead

I heard her whisper in my ear:
Please release me
and heavenly pleasures
will forever arouse you fire

What a fool I was
falling for the temptation
to late I realized that I had
released the plague
of redemption

Flesh, Blood, and Bones

Shawna Bernard

It happens at night.
The thin, salty flesh crawls across your bones,
looking for its way home.

It finds, instead, too many mistakes—
grooves and speed bump calcifications,
a poor reward for living.

It doesn't fit.
If you think about it,
it almost makes sense. Almost.

You told him slowly, carefully,
as the blood drained in haste, that the doves flew away
too soon. The water

still rippled on the lake,
cool, blue steel
shook like a sheet.

The flesh stretches over your face,
holes left for you to see. Hear.
Breathe. Scream. Love. Lick. Lie.

Alone, wishing
you had reached deeper,
that the skin was more... forgiving.

Could you let it go this way?
Allow for a fall
from grace? From higher

up
than you knew they could fly?
Stand aside. It's moving again.

Dentist

Shawna Bernard

just relax
       as I drill into you,
              crushing the brittle shell
                     of your false existence;
                            exposing the raw nerves
                                   of your primal fears.

                                   and don't
scream
                            as I scrape away
                    your pseudo veneer –

              I know
          what's underneath.

I've waited so long
        to suffocate you,
            to bring tears
                to your eyes,
                      make you ache –

                      because I know you,
                        and because I
know how.

Nightwing

Shawna Bernard

Haunting thoughts deliver screams of silence through the soul
as nightwing creatures of the mind retreat to darkened holes.
Begging for repentance and to live in fear of sin,
the battling vengeance calls to hidden voices deep within.
The soundgardens of anguish strike a tune of empty lyre
upon the hour when images of heathens do appear.
Vague regions of reality await beyond the pale,
but in the lurking storm above, a horror does prevail...

She

Selene MacLeod

blonde stuck pale hair whore whorl
curled on cheek jaw ridge hard plastic – so hard
you could punch and never
shatter
she
curled in sheets splatter plastered white
like angel wings curve on shoulder cold, see
there where pulled back
thigh muscle smooth,
not silk or cream or butter,
only skin
-o
she squat onstage
onslaught sex all hot dance beat
canned latina smoke cigarette
bent over pussy pantomime
she
lit a smoke told me she -bi-
asked if i had any money -any coke- she broke -
rubbed her nose
blinked
all jumbled now, pulsedamp
-you're fucking crazy-
slit mouth gash lipsticked red slippery
-she laugh at me what i got her for
mouth
o mouth, she tongue fat worm
-o now-
she
soft gold cold curve nipple
hand-mine or hers?-
o hot
stroke throb pulse
she
sirenbell scream
-shut up just shut up-

she wet break snap bone gristle heat damp hard now
head back eyes closed breathe fast blood behind my eyes
                          o
              she still so
         much blood so
                    she
      what   want
                  she
                  one
        eye   stare
               blank
      vast   january
               sky

Corpus Delectable

Sydney Leigh

"Eat me," I whispered into your ear.

Your lips gently traced the sloping curves of my neck as I pressed into your body in the warmth of our bed.

"Do you really want me to?" you asked breathlessly, between kisses.

"Yes," I answered desperately. *"Please.* I *need* you to."

Your mouth found mine for one passionate moment before you backed down and your face disappeared into the darkness under the sheets.

As I moaned, I felt the gravel of your words against my skin: *I love you,* they said.

"I love you, too," I answered back, and closed my eyes.

When I woke from the dream, your oversized t-shirt clinging to the perspiration pooled in the swale of my chest, I noticed the blue glow of the computer screen stealing out under the door to your office.

I must still be dreaming, I thought – you'd been dead for a year now.

Sometimes, in the shadowy dread of inveterate nightmares, I'd roll over in bed and you'd be there, your back to me, the back of your head splayed open from the bullet and soaking the chambray sheets with shards of flesh and blood. In others, I'd close the mirrored door of the medicine cabinet after swallowing a mouthful of Prozac, and you'd be looking back at me; the smoke from the gun floating from your open mouth like you'd just taken a drag from a cigarette and didn't inhale.

But this was no dream.

I pushed open the door slowly, two prayers silently vying across my lips. In one, I yearned for you to be there, an invocation that your death itself was the dream – that waking now, I'd find you just as you'd been that night - before closing your lips around the cold steel of the handgun's barrel.

And one begged mercilessly that you would not.

But there you were, your silhouette illuminated dimly by the screen, your hands resting beside you on the arms of your executive leather chair. The smell of sulfur from the gunshot suspended in the small room grew sweet in comparison to what I knew could only be the senescence of you.

Stepping closer, my insides pitching from the efflux, I saw you turn slightly at my presence. My bare feet seemed to fuse with the taut carpet under me as I discerned the grossly flawed contour of the back of your head. The chair swiveled slowly, deliberately, as your anchored feet brought us face to *almost* face.

Your malachite skin hung in sallow, fleshy strips, your eyes grievously displaced amidst the once perfect symmetry of your features. Your smile revealed a black chasm from which tiny, legless creatures crawled, writhing luridly along the gangrenous points of your teeth.

I reeled and stumbled backwards, awakening with my back pressed against the wooden threshold of the doorway. You lowered yourself down as the words echoed deafeningly inside my head.

Eat me, I heard myself say, and felt the blessed agony of your first bite.

Fair Play

Brigitte Kephart

Things were a bit foggy at the moment for Dave Bogden. He remembered the bar, a little hole in the wall dive on the main strip from the night before. The luscious red head, oh yeah, he remembered her. Doctor, she said, Dr. Shelley. The way she leaned into him, sliding her leg between his legs, dropping her long red fingernails along the zipper of his jeans. She wanted him bad. The way he hardened against his jeans.

Tease.

It would be the usual, drop a little something into her drink, take her home, fuck her.

Maybe leave her in her shirt and drop her outside the hospital where she worked with no pants on.

What happened though? Dave tried to focus on his surroundings. Shelves were lined up against the far wall with jars of all shapes and sizes, equipment scattered about the room, some looking discarded and unused, while others seemed to pulse with life.

Where the hell was he?

A bright fluorescent light flashed on in the room and Dave searched for its source, unable to turn his head.

What the fuck was going on here?

A long lean finger came into view. Tink, Tink. A red fingernail tapped on glass three inches from his face. Her smiling face moved into view. Her long hair pulled back and secured in a ponytail. She was dressed in a long white lab coat.

"Hello, Lover," She coo'd. "Remember me? You are such a naughty boy."

He watched as she picked up a vanity mirror and placed it on the shelf next to him.

"I know you remember me," she said, "and I remember you. How long have you been slipping roofies into young women's drinks? Eh?"

She straightened the mirror, then her hands came down on the glass around his head and she turned so he could see his reflection. It wasn't his reflection he saw. It took him a moment, a few brief synapses firing through the brain, sending messages.

The glass tank and what appeared to him to be a brain floating in the fluid two brown eye balls still attached to the organ.

"I guess you won't be raping any other teenagers. And, I am so going to enjoy working with you."

He could no longer see her but the words were reaching him. He watched as a long thick probe dropped into the tank next to the brain and he felt a shock of electricity jolt his consciousness. It felt like every nerve in his body had just been set on fire. He saw the pupils drop to pinpricks and then dilate. He tried to blink, to scream. The impulse raced from his brain instructing him to open his mouth, but nothing came out.

The brain bobbed up and down, brown eyes floating in separate directions. Then he saw it, the familiarity of color, the small missing piece of the left iris. He was looking at his own eyes. His eyes attached to his brain, free floating in a glass tank. He tried to scream again, nerve impulses causing the brain to bounce again, and his eyes tracked wayward to the side.

"We're going to be very, very good friends. Isn't that what you once told me?" she said, and then she sent another bolt of electricity into his brain.

"Bitch, Cunt, Whore"
Dead Zoe zero

Chalk

K. Trap Jones

The whiskey isn't helping. I wish it was, but my emotions are hell bent on eroding whatever rational thoughts I have left. I find myself in quite the predicament. Boarded up in my hotel room, I can hear the police negotiator outside spewing pathetic attempts to ease the situation, but I cannot understand his muffled voice through the dresser leaning against the door. By now, the entire hotel is vacant with media helicopters flying overhead. It's all a game; a predictable game within an unstable environment. For fifteen years, I have been employed by the police department and now I find myself on the other side, within the boundaries of the yellow crime scene tape. The media will spin my crimes in a way that I am seen as a horrific person who tormented the city, but that was not my intention. Self-preservation served as my only guiding light within the darkened tunnel of my life. Chalk, it was always about the chalk.

The city was my studio, the pavement was my canvas. For years, I was employed as the only Chalk Outliner for the police department. Within the city, suicidal jumpers were a common practice. Almost every night, some poor sap was standing on a ledge trying to be talked down by police and family members. As others wept, I always hoped that they would take the leap of faith, knowing that once they collided with the pavement, my job would begin. Every corpse that splattered against the unforgiving cement was a creative piece of art in my eyes. The pools of blood, the shattered torsos; they were never identical amongst the dead. There is nothing that I had not outlined. I was a master for details. Like I said, chalking was art and I was the artist.

Coming upon the scene, I would also venture to the ledge where the person stood so that I could look downward at the corpse. From above, I could really appreciate the canvas. Only by doing that could I incorporate all of the pieces to the sadistic death puzzle. When a body slams into the concrete, the internal organs can be forcefully extracted from the shell and continue their momentum further away from the impact zone. Amateur outliners often miss those intricate pieces by not observing the scene from above. Not me, I had to capture and outline every morsel of the body; every drop of blood.

Without notice, the city saw a sharp decline in jumpers. I am unsure of the reasoning behind the reduction, but nonetheless, it did occur. There were nights when I was not summoned at all. Gradually, the nights became weeks without my phone ringing. It plagued my mind and toiled with my emotions. I sought shelter in the shadowy nightlife of the city; drinking heavily and seeking the company of prostitutes in order to numb the emotional distress.

One particular night, the whiskey was going down my throat so smoothly that I over indulged in the venomous liquid. With a prostitute riding atop me, I felt my erection decrease and she noticed the same. Annoyed, she unsaddled me demanding payment even though I was not aroused. The open balcony doors allowed the heat from the night air to barrel into the room. The wobbly ceiling fan provided no escape and could barely slice through the thick air during its rotations. She lit up a cigarette and walked out to the balcony. Naked and caked with sweat, I could feel the sheets clinging aimlessly to my body. My eyes stared at the ceiling, trying to count each white popcorn piece. Depression was sinking in as I wallowed mentally alone within a darkened pit. Huddled in the shadows of my own mind, I heard my phone ring. The custom ringtone was for the department. It had been weeks since I had heard the *Batman* theme song. The whiskey fled from my veins; the foggy cloud of depression vanished from my mind. Answering the call, I remained silent to capture all of the details, but the whiskey toyed with my mind as the location revealed itself. The same hotel I was in, the street out front. With the phone glued to my ear, I peered through the fluttering curtains and did not see her there. I crept slowly out on the balcony and could see the police lights gleaming in the alleyway. Over the edge I looked, straight down at the corpse of the woman shattered upon the pavement. My throat clamored and my forehead excreted pure whiskey from the pores. Any moment, the police would be at my door. I had to get dressed.

As the police entered into the room, they joined me on the balcony as I tried my best to suppress my slurred speech. In their mind, there was nothing amiss as they knew that I always began a scene by looking down at the victim. I excused myself from the balcony and surveyed the room for any of my belongings that I may have overlooked in my hasty cleanup. Satisfied, I made my way down to the street level. From the angle of the broken neck, she had rotated several times in the air before landing, which proved that she must have slipped over the railing and somersaulted. Her cigarette still burned near her bruised hand. Standing amongst the detectives, I found it difficult to swallow and speak. Just moments before, she was with me in the bed.

The following night, still high from the excitement, I laid face up in a different hotel room with another prostitute going down on me. Her mouth was warm and inviting, but all I could think about was how good it felt to hear the *Batman* ringtone. Not sure whether it was her doing or I reminiscing about outlining, but I ejaculated. The release eased my mind, but also conjured up a twisted thought that stretched my mouth into an evil grin. With the warm breeze slithering into the room like a snake in an overgrown field, I led my companion onto the balcony for a cigarette. I poured her a few shots of whiskey, so that the liquor would kill off any of my remaining DNA she potentially had in her mouth. Four stories up, the pavement was barely noticeable within the shadows of the alley. My hands shook uncontrollably; my mouth salivated out of control. In all of my years, I had never actually witnessed a person colliding with the street from an above viewpoint. It was like watching your favorite artist as they prepared to touch the blank canvas with the first stroke of color. I felt anxious, like a child unable to sleep on Christmas Eve. As her body toppled over the railing, I studied the motions of her as she fell. She randomly reached out with both hands, trying desperately to grasp anything that would assist her, but there was nothing to grip. When she passed the third floor, her eyes met with mine. A coat of fear invaded her pupils and clenched her retinas so tightly that her vision bled death before she even hit the pavement. I always wondered about that precise moment during free fall, when the mind copes with the idea that it is helpless; that key turning event where approaching death is understood and acknowledged.

From four stories up, I felt her bones break; I felt her internal organs collide with one another. A stream of blood flowed freely from every open wound that she had. The river of red siphoned through the cracks of the street and poured into a pothole like a waterfall. The portrait was complete. Dressed and ready to go, I eagerly held my phone; waiting for *Batman* to sing to me.

I heard the sirens from a few blocks over and checked my phone to make sure there was enough battery charge. It was only a matter of time before my phone lit up in excitement. As *Batman* played, the caller ID read *Police*. The detectives once again entered the hotel room as I stood on the balcony overlooking the deceased jumper. Her blood loss created a red sea around her corpse. Her eyes stared upward and chilled my spine. Her last vision was of me watching her fall. Thank God the embedded picture within her eyes could not be extracted for evidence.

On the street, I outlined her death with chalk, making sure to capture every essence of the suicide. Her skull had split into two equal parts; her arms were mangled by the multiple fractures. Through a small gash in the midsection, her intestines had forced their way out onto the street. I couldn't have asked for a more beautiful death to outline. I always carried a case of chalk with me to every crime scene. Most people think that there is only one kind of chalk, but there isn't. Certain terrain calls for a different density in the chalk so that the scene can be outlined correctly. Thicker chalk is used for heavier canvases such as roads. Wooden canvases are better outlined with a thinner chalk. The more porous the foundation, the heavier chalk is better as the powdery remnants can seep downward instead of widening the lines. It's similar to coloring as a child. A large crayon should never be used for the finer, more delicate coloring. Otherwise, the outline would simply be a huge disaster. Slowness is another key factor in whether the chalk outline is sufficient or not. The alleyways within the city provide the roughest of canvases. The numerous cracks and uneven pavement provide obstacles in attempting a straight line. If not precise in the methodology, the line will look like a jagged edge. Angles and different slopes of the pavement need to be accounted for prior to touching the chalk to the canvas. Anticipation of the inequality of the street can assist in the proper technique of chalk outlining.

Over the next few nights, the weather worsened and brought heavy rain to the city. Water and chalk are brutal enemies. Just like an artist never painting in the rain, I too could not accomplish much during the downpour. The waterlogged alleyways were not much help either, as the shadowy confines hid from the sun and extended the timeframe of the canvases becoming dry. The puddles were useless. They never added any good value to crime scenes. They displaced blood and contorted the true outline of the corpse. Not to mention, chalking on a wet surface was nearly impossible. However, the worst occurred when a fresh chalk outline was drawn only to be washed away by a rainstorm.

During the era of dampness, I scouted out new hotels in the city. I had only a few criteria when debating on whether certain hotels proved to be a match. One was a balcony that overlooked a secluded alleyway. The other one was that there had to be no obstacles in the way; no dumpsters, parked cars that would inhibit a falling person from landing on the street. I have been on crime scenes where a jumper had collided with an awning. It made it very difficult to chalk the victim as there were multiple points of impact. To avoid any such scenario, the balcony had to have a clear shot to the pavement. It was just a few things that I required before opting for a hotel.

With the absence of rain for a few days, the pavement began to dry and the nightly, warm air fed the wind once again. I opened my hotel room door as a prostitute walked in. She sat me down in a chair and proceeded to strip before me. My arousal was not from her bare breasts, but from the aroma of death spilling from the open balcony door. I could hear the moans of the awaiting street; I could smell the powder of the chalk grinding against the pavement. Her legs straddling me, I was deep inside her. I imagined the streams of blood excreting from her wounds. Her lifeless eyes stare up toward me; the sweat of my palms clinging to the rail as I looked down. Her mouth suctioned to my neck as her hips moved back and forth. I imagined her legs buckled from the impact; her knees shattered under the duress. My mind could not concentrate any longer; the bombardment of emotions overtook my rationale. I lifted her off me and pushed her through the doors onto the balcony. Still playing along, she bent herself over the rail and waited for me to continue having sex with her. Her skin glistened in the moonlight, but the shadows of the street below were calling my name. She flinched and moaned in ecstasy as I grabbed her from behind. Her pleasure quickly turned to fear as I lifted her over the railing and released my grip. Into the darkness she fell until her screaming mouth became silent upon the impact. Staring at the formation of her body, I had determined that she had broken at least one arm and was bleeding profusely from a neck wound. That sensation of soon hearing the *Batman* song once again flowed through my veins and gripped my pulsating heart tightly. That is, until I heard coughing coming from the street below. I squinted to focus through the steam rising from the alley. Her body was convulsing; her throat was coughing up blood. She was still alive.

Panic was always an unstable emotion for me. It was one of those emotions that I could easily live without as I saw no meaningful trait for its existence. Regardless, I found myself in a complete state of panic. My mind raced for some sort of method to the madness; any idea that could be portrayed before me.

Looking back into the hotel room, I saw that rationality within the form of blue vase sitting on the table. With my arms extended over the railing and clutching the vase, I tried to aim. In order to have it land directly on her head, I had to take into account the wind speed and the overall angle of the decent. The vase fell through the shadows and shattered against her skull, silencing the coughing. A brief sigh of relief excreted from my dried lips before the sounds of the sirens echoed through the city. With the addition of the vase to the crime scene, I thought it best that I not be there prior to police. Using the back alleys, I fled a few blocks before my phone began to ring. With a deep breath, I turned around, carrying my case of chalk toward the scene.

The next night, death filled the winds of the city and tempted me with another victim. I was in rare form; my outlining skills were increasing with every painting. I was in high demand by the police department. Everything was going according to plan until tonight. The familiar knock on the door led another prostitute to my room. She laid me down on the bed and stood over me while pulling down her skirt. Once again, my arousal came from the vision of her corpse helplessly lying on the pavement outside. The warm breeze of the serpent flowed freely in the room from the open balcony doors. Whiskey poured down my throat as she faced away from me and lowered herself down. I over indulged in the liquor as I watched her waist grind back and forth. I placed one hand on the back of her shirt to guide the motion, but felt something odd. Several wires were twisted underneath her shirt. At first I thought it was her bra, but she wasn't wearing one. Curious as to what it was, I couldn't figure it out until my phone rang. *Batman* greeted my confusion like the hammer of justice. She was wired; a plant, a mole. And my ringtone just filtered through the microphone and into the ears of God knows who was listening on the other end. The whiskey bottle shattered against the back of her skull as she fell off of me and onto the floor.

I had no time to think as a knock pounded on the front door. I heard the hotel key from the outside swipe, but it was denied access. Panicked and irrational, I pushed the dresser in front of the door to buy me some time. Another hotel key swiped followed by the sound of acceptance. The door became ajar as it struck the dresser. I pushed the cabinet closer so that the door could no longer open. I used everything that I could to blockade the door.

On the balcony looking down at the police cars is where I find myself with a cigarette in one hand and case of chalk in the other. They are speaking to me through the front door as well as using a megaphone from the street below, but I can't understand what they are saying. My mind has blocked them out and I am grateful for that. Leaning against the railing, I opened my case of chalk and selected the thicker density ones as the terrain below was a rough canvas for outlining. The three pieces I threw down were caught by some of the officers. With my hands on the rail, I once again wondered what goes through a person's mind when they are helplessly falling to their death. Is it fear? Is it a reflection upon one's life? The good and bad choices that we all make? It is clear to me that I will not ponder about any of that. As I stare down at the blank canvas before me, my only thought is that I hope that a clean and precise method is used to create my own chalk outline.

Jerry Langdon
Sex, Drugs & Horror

Skin Flick

Ken Goldman

WHAM

They met on midtown Manhattan barstools inside a crowded 5th Avenue pub. She exchanged ninety minutes' worth of the requisite lounge-speak with him over the several white wine spritzers customary for the Friday night ritual. When the time felt right he hailed a taxi to take them uptown, escorting her into his Park Avenue walkup where the young attorney went belly-on with the girl for over an hour.

Although one night stands were quickly becoming anachronisms, tonight fortune had smiled on Gittleman & Silvestri's star player. A small part of that fortune probably had hinged on the photo which had recently appeared in the Business section of the Sunday Times above a caption listing the man's name and credentials, a fact not lost among the bistro's more aspiring female patrons.

Another evening spent doing the bedspring hula was not a bad way to pass a wintry midnight. Still, Vincent felt the evening called for a little more creativity on his part than he had thus far demonstrated during their short time together.

BAM

At first Vincent did not believe Moira would go for his idea, especially not this quickly. But neither had he pictured himself sharing the covers of his brass bed alongside the new paralegal from Shengold and Roth three hours after they had exchanged introductions at Marabella's Alibi Tavern. Early impressions made from a bar stool's perspective were not always accurate given the sexual paranoia of the 90's, but black spandex tells no lies.

Moira had proved herself as enigmatic as a cheerleader with a bullwhip, even enthusiastically assisting him when he slipped the condom on. The raven-haired stranger gave him a surprising E-ticket ride without the traditional waiting period. Considering the evening's circumstances the suggestion Vincent contemplated sharing with her did not seem so out of line as it would have an hour earlier.

Typically, serendipitous sex amounted to little more than masturbating with a partner. But there seemed a rhythm to his encounter with Moira that went beyond sexual parameters. From the get-go the woman seemed completely in sync almost as if she had known him, and he enjoyed a good verbal sparring partner as much as he did an ebullient companion beneath his sheets. Still, holding her in his arms during those disquieting moments after such cavalier fucking felt vaguely ridiculous. He did not even know the woman's last name. Maybe she had told him back at Marabella's, but if she had he didn't remember it. His mind had been on other things, specifically on how much he would enjoy wearing Moira's long legs around his neck. The two lay beneath the cool sheets in a gray silence lasting the entire length of Vincent's Marlboro.

"You know, the first person who speaks after making love usually says something stupid." She slid closer to him. "Do you feel like saying something stupid, Vincent?"

He touched her cheek, turning her face toward his so he could look into her eyes. The gesture seemed almost tender, a strange counterpoint to what he was thinking.

"Can I be honest?"

"Oh fuck: Is your next sentence going to end with the words 'genital warts' or 'blood test'?"

He stopped her question with a finger to her lips, offering his most reassuring smile. "I've had my shots, okay? It's just that I don't often make a suggestion like this. So if you plan on turning indignant and smacking the shit out of me, tell me now and I can spare myself a lot of embarrassment, all right?"

Moira returned his smile, indicating that she might consider sharing this diversion. "Smacking the shit out of you? Is that what you're into?"

An audacious little piece of ass as well as an excellent lay; Vincent liked her. He pulled himself from the bed.

"We can negotiate that part later." Slipping into his jockey briefs he stepped inside the walk-in closet and returned holding a small video camera. "What I was thinking we might try is a little home movie. Watta ya say, kid? Ya wanna be a star?"

Staring at the camcorder she giggled, but her twisted grin revealed nothing of the cogs turning inside the young woman's head.

Moira climbed from the bed and walked to Vincent without covering her nakedness as so many women did on first nights. She squeezed her breasts into his ribs, brushing her lips against his ear while flicking her tongue at it with soft butterfly kisses. When she spoke he felt her warm breath heat his skin.

"That Sony's got video stabilization, I hope. You know, in the event of bumps or knocks on this casting couch of yours, that sort of thing? Wouldn't want that picture out of focus when you whack off to your video memorabilia, would you, Cecil B.?"

Vincent smiled, knowing that beneath their repartee Moira had discerned the uneasy demons lurking behind his pig-in-shit expression. Most nights the space alongside him in this bed remained empty, and even a videotaped remembrance of a warm body seemed better than that empty space. In place of the touch of a woman's flesh an inventive home video would see Vincent through those nights spent alone. The adage about Nature abhorring a vacuum proved especially true for single men. Whenever a woman's hand was unavailable, there was always his own.

Moira paused, contorting her face in mock concentration while she pretended to consider his suggestion. She was toying with him, but he expected that much. Women enjoyed doing that, as if false modesty were a coy remnant from some earlier age as tight-assed as the new millennium was in danger of becoming. Finally she answered, "Sure. Why not? But I've got a suggestion too. You want to set up that fancy shutter box while I share it with you?"

She did not have to ask him twice. He pulled a tripod from the closet and placed it beside the bed before the woman might have second thoughts. When he rejoined her Moira was holding her nylons balled in her hands.

"You ever play blind man's bluff?" she asked, tugging at the sheer material like a child twisting a long strand of taffy, hiding half her face demurely behind the extended nylon.

"Not since I was a kid."

"Well, Vincent, tonight you get to be a kid again. Shut your eyes."

Like an obedient child, he did just that. He knew this game, and playing it was going to make for one hell of a mind fucking video.

She tied the stocking securely around his face, covering his eyes and wrenching the fabric so tightly his temples throbbed. He forced himself not to wince with the sharp pain.

Blinded, he heard the young woman sifting through her hand bag for whatever paraphernalia she had brought along. Some object jingled and snapped, something metallic sounding like locks twice being opened and clicked shut again. In workmanlike fashion the woman secured his wrists to the supports of the beds brass head rest. She had handcuffed him, and the cuffs were strong suckers from what he could tell. Unable to pull free he yanked himself into a clumsy sitting position, preparing himself for a whole lot more action than, up to this moment, he would have had any right to expect.

"I'm guessing you've done this before," he said.

"Oh yes. That I have. Wipe that smile off your face, please, or I might become very cross with you."

"The stocking's a little tight. Could you loosen it a little?"

"I could. But no. I won't. You don't want to spoil the surprise I have planned for you, do you?" She kissed his mouth hard, her tongue playing hide-and-seek with his. Pulling away she shoved him into the mattress so abruptly he lost his breath. While he gulped for air she tore his jockey briefs from under him. He lay twisting naked before her.

Vincent felt the sudden rash of a blush heat his face. The reaction to his complete vulnerability first startled, then fascinated him.

"Got you where I want you, huh, Vincent? Excuse me for just a moment, will you, sweet cakes? I've some business to attend to."

A moment later Moira's voice came from what sounded like the kitchen. "Just getting a few things I may need. Don't miss me too much." Drawers opened and slammed shut as if the woman was searching for something, but Vincent could not imagine what.

. . . or maybe he could .

"Moira?"

Nothing. Not a word.

"What the fuck--?"

In the momentary silence a disquieting thought occurred to him. Had he been scammed? Was this woman playing him for a sucker, seducing him just to rip him off and leave his sorry ass tied here while she ransacked his apartment? Bar sluts stung wealthy schmucks all the time as a way of life. Christ, some made a living of it. He probably didn't even know this woman's real name. Maybe she had lied to him about working for Shengold and Roth too. How could he have been such a stupid shit not to see this coming?

He pulled at the cuffs that bound his hands to the posts, feeling the flesh of his wrists chafe against the tight metal shackles that scraped harshly against the brass supports. Moira had done a damned good job making certain he could not pull himself free. She was probably robbing him blind right now.

No, not blind.

Blind*folded* .

"Hey! Come on, Moira! Let me in on it, will you?"

Stupid . . . Stupid . . .

The attorney inside his brain told him that something didn't add up. There were easier ways to pull this off besides fucking him, and what would the woman hope to find in his kitchen anyway? Maybe this scenario was part of her game, meant to keep him anxious inside his darkness, intended to make him feel weak and vulnerable. It was a power thing, probably rooted in dated buzz words like penis envy. Moira needed this master/slave bullshit to get herself off. That had to be it.

Had to . . .

As silently as a panther she had returned to him. Probably she had been standing aside for a minute or two watching him squirm, savoring the moment.

"I'm ready for my close-up, Mr. DeMille," she said in a throaty whisper that was not an altogether poor imitation of Gloria Swanson. "I turned the camera on, okay?"

Before Vincent could respond she pressed her mouth against his with such breathy force the woman could have been administering CPR. She smeared his face with wet kisses as if tasting him, sucking and biting at his flesh as she progressed slowly down his neck, kneading his chest with her sharp nails as her tongue slid south in long serpentine streaks. Stopping at his inner thigh she teased him with her fingertips, thumping on his skin, then scratching at it. He could not tell if she had drawn blood, but he would not be surprised if she had.

"What were you looking for in my kitchen?" he finally managed, aware his voice had lost its wise ass edge.

"Uh uh."

Her mouth curled into a smile as her lips touched his warming inner thigh, and he could not help smiling too. Moira's open mouth continued its voyage upward. Her lips airbrushed his cock, then took it slowly inside her mouth while her tongue did a mad dance around it.

"Christ, that feels so good -"

The woman stopped his words by touching his lips with cold fingertips.

"Don't speak."

He felt a sudden freezing wetness between his legs and recognized at once what the woman had taken from his kitchen. Moira had slipped ice cubes into her mouth, and Vincent throbbed and swelled with each flick of her chilled tongue. Something bestial reawakened from deep inside him, some ravenous and unwieldy ogre taking its commands from the blood-gorged member pulsating between his legs. Forcing himself to remain silent he concentrated instead on the soft skimming of the woman's cold lips touching his balls with quick angel kisses. In his mind's eye he pictured Moira's lips blue with the icy chill of the cubes warming to the hot flesh of his prick, and he thrust himself at her so she could take him full into her mouth.

She did. Moira filled her throat with him, licking and biting at his cock like an insatiable animal finally come to feed. Her mouth became a living thing, moving in a rhythmic stop-action motion strobing inside his brain. He wanted to break free of the blindfold and cuffs, to tear his fingers inside his tormentor's snapping pussy and to fist fuck her raw, then to dine on Moira's dripping cunt until she begged that he shove himself inside her. In the same moment he almost spilled the volcanic ash bubbling within his groin, she stopped herself cold.

"Do you want to fuck me, Vincent?"

"Yes."

"Let me hear you say it. Tell me how much you want to fuck me ..."

"I want to fuck you."

"How *much*, damn you! Tell me how much you want to fuck me!"

She scattered a handful of ice cubes between his legs. The freezing sensation first numbed then excited him while she lapped at the icy puddles in his crotch like a thirsty cat. Vincent's body twitched and heaved almost against his will.

"I want to fuck you more than anything Ive ever wanted! I want to fuck you in your mouth, in your cunt, in your ass. I want to fuck you six ways from Sunday! I want to fuck you until your goddamned eyeballs explode!"

"*Do it!*" she screamed at him, sitting on his chest and pushing her damp vagina into his mouth.

"My hands?" he asked, his voice pleading like a horny teenager's. "Will you free my hands so I can touch your tits?"

She slapped him open-palmed across his face, slamming him so hard his front teeth came down painfully on his tongue. He tasted his own blood.

"No pleasure without pain, you bastard! Do as I tell you!"

And now her cunt came alive too. It rose and fell on his mouth, and Moira pressed herself so hard against his face he almost could not breathe. Despite the blood inside his mouth he crammed his tongue into her, eating her while grotesque animal noises escaped from deep inside his throat, eating every inch from inside the woman's vagina until his jaw throbbed with flashes of sharp pain.

She took his cock into her hands sucking it more vigorously than before, almost chewing on it. Vincent pictured his own blood dripping from her teeth into the reddened flesh surrounding his balls, blood she had swilled from his torn skin. Still he engorged inside the woman's mouth. She lifted herself on him, and as he slid himself inside his cock grew even harder.

Straddling him, she leaned and arched her back as if reaching for something above her, then heaved and swelled like an ocean wave breaking on him. The release of hot semen seared through his prick as if he had ejaculated battery acid.

He screamed. He had to scream. And just as quickly he stopped.

Because something hit his head hard . . .

Vincent had only enough time to feel the thick pain explode in his temple. He passed out that moment into a darkness blacker than what lay behind the woman's nylon stocking that he still wore tied to his face ...

...Thank You, M'am

Damn.

Vincent's head hurt. It hurt bad. He rubbed his temples to soothe the throbbing of the turbojet engines revving inside his brain. It took a moment for the realization to hit him.

My hands are free!

When he pulled the nylon stocking from his face the burst of sunlight almost blinded him. Squinting through the mixture of pain and daylight, he looked at his digital clock on the night stand. It was 10:32 a.m.

. . . and the girl was gone.

Maybe he had been right about that harpy all along, and he was not sorry Moira had left. There certainly was no kick in waking up with the Marquis de Sade. Pulling himself from bed he stepped on the cracked remains of what had been his Sony camcorder. She must have used the video camera to bludgeon him.

"Crazy bitch," he muttered.

He checked his belongings on the bureau. The Rolex remained where he had left it and seventy-three dollars lay untouched inside his alligator wallet. At least the woman hadn't taken anything expensive that he could tell. The videotape cartridge of last night's performance lay in the middle of the bureau as if Moira had cleared a space for it. Vincent knew he must look like shit. He stared into the wall mirror to verify it.

Moira had smeared four words in blood red lipstick on the glass.

Play the tape, Vincent

He felt genuinely curious now. Something seemed very squirrely about all of this. He snapped the video cassette into his VCR and sat on the edge of his bed to watch the Toshiba's monitor.

Moira came on screen standing in his kitchen. She wore the black spandex mini and was still combing her hair when the picture came on.

What the hell is she do-?

He leaned forward while she spoke to him with words uttered the night before.

"Hello, Vincent. You couldn't videotape this particular scene with me because at the moment you're chained to your bed post waiting for me. And I'll bet while watching this you're still wondering, 'Now just what the fuck was that lunatic bimbette doing in my kitchen making such a racket?'" She pulled a drawer open and quickly slammed it shut, opening it again to rattle the contents. "See, I didn't want you to hear what I was really doing in here when I let a very special guest into your apartment. Damned clever of me, wouldn't you agree, Vincent?"

He scratched his head. The woman was making no sense. Clearly she had come more unzipped than he had imagined.

He heard his own voice on the videotape call to her from the bedroom.

"Moira?"

On screen, Moira smiled.

"You were getting pretty antsy all chained up in there, weren't you, sweet cakes? I don't have very much time, so I guess I should explain what-"

He heard himself on the tape interrupt her again.

"Hey! Come on, Moira! Let me in on it, will you?"

"That I will, Vincent. That I most certainly will," the woman said directly into the camera. "Tell me, Vincent. Have you asked yourself who's been holding this expensive Sony while I've been making my little speech?"

Almost answering her aloud he felt like an idiot because the thought had not even occurred to him.

The video camera jiggled for a moment, and Moira's face lost its clarity. The camcorder exchanged hands and now Moira was holding it. The automatic focus kicked in. Once it did, Vincent's mouth came open as if his jaw had dropped a screw.

Some other woman was staring at him from the television's screen. She seemed a sickly imitation of Moira, and her emaciated image roused something sinister inside the shadowy caverns of Vincent's psyche as a distant memory struggled to be reborn.

"Vincent, meet my sister. You see, she followed that taxi we took here tonight. Look hard at her. I imagine the family resemblance might be difficult to spot now. But you already know her name. Think back a few years. You know my big sister, don't you?" Moira leaned closer to the camera lens. "You do know her, don't you, Vincent?"

He formed the name on his tongue without uttering a sound.

"See . . . Seena ..."

But the ashen faced woman staring back from the television screen was nothing like the Seena he remembered.

"I know I'm not very pretty to look at, Vincent," the woman said in a loathsome mimicry of her sister's voice. "But you once thought I was. During our one night together you told me I was the most beautiful woman you had ever seen. Is that what you tell all your women? Is that how you get them into that big brass bed of yours?"

Moira zoomed in for a close-up of Seena, enabling Vincent to take a more intimate look at the woman whose ulcerous skin hung in fleshy tatters from her face like a ruined patch quilt. He had to force himself to look at the screen.

"It's syphilis, Vincent. The final stages of venereal disease and extremely contagious, caught during one intoxicating evening back in those decadent '80's when safe sex wasn't even a part of a man's vocabulary. Certainly it wasn't a part of yours. But you always had Lady Luck in your corner, didn't you? Yours was a dormant form of the spirochete, making you only a delivery boy for the bug, so to speak. Lucky you. That's what my doctors told me can happen, since you don't appear to have been infected. Me, I wasn't so lucky, as you can see for yourself."

The picture jiggled as Seena reached to her sister for the camera. Moira came on the screen again while putting on her coat.

"But that doesn't mean Seena can't return the favor with

some of those micro-organisms you were so willing to share with the women in your life, Vincent. Still feeling lucky enough to roll those dice again? No pleasure without pain. Remember?"

Moira's smile evaporated. She finished buttoning her coat and walked out, closing the door very gently behind her. Vincent understood why.

He sprang from the mattress to watch close-up while the videotape's prologue played out. But already he knew where the rest of the previous night's documentary was heading. Elbowing the beads of sweat from his forehead he watched the remainder of the recorded drama unfold on the screen.

"I'm ready for my close-up, Mr. DeMille," the bony creature on the television's monitor joked to the blindfolded man handcuffed to the brass posts.

And Vincent gagged as he watched Seena crawl naked into his bed.

In your Dreams
Dead Zoe zero

Happy as Cotton Candy

William J Fedigan

Waiting for Nora to die is killing me. Killing me! It guts me open and guilt rolls out like fire. "I gotta see her, help her. I gotta do something good," I tell myself, but I do nothing but wait and wait.

It's four a.m. I'm sleeping, dreaming about Nora the way I do—*tossing, turning, soaked in cold sweat*—when the phone rings. I answer it—and the gates of hell open wide.

A woman at the other end screams: *"Puke! Puke!"*

Before I can say "Who the fuck is this . . ." she screams: *"PUKE! PUKE! PUKE!"*

Her voice is familiar, but I can't place it.

"Who the fuck is this, for chrissakes?"

"The monkey's off your back, motherfucker. Are you happy now?" She says.

It's Nora's mother. Calls me 'motherfucker,' figures it suits me just fine.

I have to ask "Is Nora all right?" but I know Nora's not all right.

"Nora died. She's dead. *Dead!*"

"God no," is all I can say.

"She choked to death on her own vomit. On her own *PUKE!* Nobody there to help her, to save her. She died alone, motherfucker. Are you happy now?"

"God no . . . No . . ." is all I can say.

"It was you killed her, motherfucker. You took the easy way out. You left her, and she died alone—*CHOKING ON HER OWN PUKE!* You shoulda been there. You coulda saved her . . . It was you killed her. It was you . . ."

"It wasn't me killed her. It was her! She killed herself! I couldn't save her! Nobody coulda saved her!"

I say it, but its bullshit, every word, *BULLSHIT!* I took the easy way out, and Nora died because I wasn't there. It was me who killed her.

"I pray to Christ it happens to you, motherfucker. I hope you choke on your own puke—and the last thing you see in this world is rats comin to eat your fuckin eyes."

She hangs up loud. My head explodes.

Nora's dead. She choked to death. She died alone. It's my fault. It's real now—as real as rats eating my eyes . . .

I go cold and numb. I hold the phone tight like it's a life jacket keeping from going under, but my hands shake badly, and I drop the phone.

I'm going under.

I need a drink.

I need a big drink. One I can swim in. One I can drown in.

I've been dry a long time, but I don't care now. I pour a deep one. I throw it back. It feels good. I throw another one back. It feels better. I wait for the flush to burn my guts and kill my brain, but I can't stop thinking about *Nora choking, Nora dying, Nora dying alone.*

I throw another one back, hard this time. I get dizzy. My head spins like a kiddy ride, then it stops dead. I'm twisted around and I'm looking backward. I'm looking at the past, *our past.* I can't breathe . . .

"I can't breathe," Nora says. Maybe she's lying again. I don't know. I do know she's drunk. I do know she's dying, and I do know if she doesn't stop drinking, she'll die for real—all the way dead.

"I can't breathe," she says. "I'm scared," she says. "Help me," she says.

I want to get the fuck out, but I stay. "Ok. Ok. Don't worry." I tell her.

Nora puts my hand between her breasts. I feel bones. I try not to think about them. Her bones are sharp, like chicken bones. I try not to think about them.

Her heart pounds too fast, lungs work too hard. She's not lying this time. She really can't breathe. I spread my fingers and press down. My fingerprints show white on her chest.

"Watch me," I tell her. I take a deep breath, let it out slow. "In and out. Slow. That's right. We'll breathe together. In and out. In and out. That's right. You and me together."

I'm tired. My fingers twitch. She stares at me. Her eyes are dying. I try not to think about them.

After a couple minutes, Nora breathes normal again. She still scared. I'm glad she's still scared. If she stays scared, maybe she'll sober up for good this time . . .

I'm drunk, pouring myself another big one, when the phone rings. I figure its Nora's mother again, screaming how it was me killed Nora, how rats are gonna eat my eyes, shit like that.

I let it ring six, seven times, then I figure "Fuck it," and I pick it up.

A man on the other says: "Turk Street. 2am. Quick, clean, cold."

It takes me a minute to clear my head, to recognize the voice. It's Benny Teardrop. He sounds happy. "Two guys," he says. "Two taps each," he says. "In the face," he says.

(Benny Teardrop shoots people. He's good at it.)

"Remember last Christmas, the way you smoked Sonny Bright and his sister, Twinkle. Same thing."

(I shoot people. Benny says I'm good at it. Benny says I'm gifted.)

"Are you listening to what I'm sayin?" Benny says.

I don't know what the fuck to say.

"Are you listening to me? Turk Street. Two a.m. Two guys. Two taps each. In the face. Quick, clean, cold."

I don't know what the fuck to say. I'm drunk.

"Say something, for chrissakes!"

All I can say is "Nora's dead, Benny . . ."

"Jesus fuckin Christ!" is what Benny says, pissed-off, breathing hard, like its Nora's fault, being dead.

"She choked to death on her own vomit—*on her own puke!* She died alone. I shoulda been there, Benny. I coulda saved her . . . It was me killed her . . . Me."

"Jesus fuckin Christ" is what Benny says, pissed-off, breathing hard.

"I took the easy way out, Benny. I left her and now she's dead. *DEAD!* And it was me killed her, Benny. Me . . . I killed her . . . I killed her . . . I . . ."

"Have you been drinkin" Benny says. "Are you drunk, for chrissakes!"

"Yeah . . ." is all I can say. No use lying to Benny. He knows me.

"Jesus fuckin Christ! What're you doin? You been dry a long time. I was proud, you stayin dry so long. Now . . . You're a worthless piece of shit again . . ."

"I'm sorry . . ." is all I can say.

"You wanna make it a double funeral, you and her? Is that what you want? She almost killed you when she was living. You want her to kill you now she's dead, for chrissakes."

"No . . . no . . ." is all I can say, but Benny words tear into me.

"She almost killed you, pushin you down the stairs the way she did."

"It was an accident. I told you it was an accident."

"An accident? She was drunk. You said something, pissed her off, and she pushed you down a fuckin flight of stairs. You were lucky that time, only broke two ribs."

"Ok . . . ok . . ." is all I can say, but Benny's words rip into me, and now I'm bleeding.

"Let me tell you something else," Benny says, loud and hard and cold. "It wasn't you killed Nora. It was Nora killed Nora. It was just a matter of time before she drank herself into the dirt. Face the facts, for chrissakes."

Benny shouldn't have said what he said about Nora. I was bleeding bad now.

"Fuck you, Benny. She wasn't always like that. You didn't know her before."

"Fuck me?"

"Fuck you for sayin what you said about Nora. It's not right, what you said."

"Ok. Ok. Forget I said what I said, for chrissakes. Just sober the fuck up. Make sure you're ready for tonight. Understand?"

Benny Teardrop hangs up loud. My head hurts. I hold onto the phone tight.

I'm going under.

This time, I don't give a shit . . .

"I don't give a shit," Nora says. "Go ahead. Watch me."

I watch Nora suck it down like its lemonade, and it's August at the beach, and she's dry as sand.

She walks toward me. Her legs give out, and she sits down hard. The bottle falls outta her hand. Vodka pours out and makes puddles on the floor.

She picks up the empty bottle. She looks at it. She looks at me. "Are you happy now?" she says. "Yeah. I am," I tell her.

She throws the bottle. It hits my shoulder. "Get the fuck out," she says.

She says it again and again, softer each time, crying now. She looks at me. I know the look. I know her. She wants me to stay, to hold her, to tell her something good. But I don't stay. I tell myself my shoulder hurts like a son of a bitch. I tell myself I'm mad as hell. I tell myself a lot of things.

Truth is, I'm tired of Nora's shit, and I leave because it's too hard to stay . . . And it's easy to leave.

I get the fuck out fast . . .

". . . Get the fuck out fast. Are you listening to me? When it's done, get the fuck out fast. Quick, clean, cold. Understand?"

Its Benny Teardrop calling me back, making sure my brain is still working, pretending nothing happened.

"Yeah . . ." is all I can say. I'm still drunk.

"Sammy's going through the door first, you behind."

"Sammy? I thought Sammy was in the Bug House."

"He's out. Clean bill of health," Benny says.

"Jesus fuckin Christ . . ." is all I can say. Sammy spends so much time in the Bug House it's like his home away from.

"Don't worry about it. All Sammy needed was a rest, clear up his head. He's ok now. In the pink. All you gotta do is back Sammy up. "

(Sammy shoots people, likes to give em a new asshole in the middle of their forehead. Sammy's good at it. Benny says Sammy's gifted.)

"Whatever you say" is what I tell him, but I don't like it, Sammy in front, me behind.

"It's your call, Benny. Sammy goes through the door first, me behind. You said there are two guys inside. Right?"

"Right. Two guys. Frank and Mike Cazzo," Benny says.

"Whadda they do?"

"They fucked up. Pissed somebody off."

(Somebody fucks up, pisses somebody off, Benny gets the call. Benny makes the plans. Benny calls me.)

"Everything's ok, then?" Benny asks, checking me out, making sure I'm ready for tonight, ready for the Cazzo brothers.

"Yeah . . ." is all I can say. Not the truth, not even close. I'm tired all over.

"Look, I'm . . . I'm real sorry about Nora. I want you to know that. What happened to her . . . It's sad, tragic even, dying the way she did. And I hate sayin this again, but it was just a matter of time before . . ."

"It wasn't supposed to happen to her, Benny. Not to Nora. Choking to death, dying alone, nobody to help her . . ."

"Thing's not suppose to happen, happen all the fuckin time. You know that. Face the facts . . . She's dead and gone, for chrissakes . . ."

(The kind of guy Benny is has ice growing in the middle of his heart. He says I'm just like him, but I'm not. I had Nora.)

"Are you sure you're ready for tonight. Can't afford you fuckin up."

"Yeah . . ." is all I can say. Not the truth, not even close. I'm tired all over. Dead tired.

"Good. Me and Sammy'll pick you up two am sharp. Get a couple hours sleep before. It'll do you good to rest up, get some sleep . . .

"Sleep is death's brother" is something Benny read in a book.

Benny reads books, tells me about them. It makes me think, but I can't figure out what the fuck "Sleep is death's brother" means, and I don't care. It sounds good to me. I'm tired all over. Dead tired. I want to close my eyes and I want to stop breathing.

But I don't stop breathing. I sleep and I dream. I dream about Nora, the way she was before—perfect—like she never cried a tear in her life.

"Are you happy?" is what I always ask her in my dream.

"Happy as cotton candy" is what she always says, like a kid at a carnival, thinking her life is sweet and light, thinking it'll always be that way . . .

I wake up, open my eyes. I'm empty and hurting and cold inside because Nora's life didn't go sweet and light. Her life went bad . . .

She died alone . . .

I shoulda been there, done something good, saved her, made her life sweet and light again, but I didn't. I took the easy way out because it was easy . . .

I was wrong.

I should have stayed. Nora would be alive if I stayed.

I close my eyes again. I want to sleep and I want to stop breathing. I think about what Benny read in a book. Maybe sleeping and dying are like brothers, sharing the same blood, going in the same direction, ending up in the same place.

I want to sleep and I want to stop breathing, but I can't . . .

I'm still breathing . . . I'm still empty and hurting and cold inside . . .

I think about Nora—Nora sweet and light—and I'm sad . . . So sad . . .

"Cheer the fuck up. You look like shit," Sammy says, smiling, laughing, happy like its Christmas morning. Sammy loves to shoot people. Give them a new asshole, middle of their forehead.

We're standing in a cold drizzle on Turk Street. Thee a.m. Benny's in the car, engine running, lights off, eyes peeled, looking left, right, front back—trying to look everywhere, trying to keep things in focus.

"You look like shit," Sammy says again.

I don't say anything.

"It's a beautiful night," Sammy says. He's tap-dancing in the puddles like he's Gene Kelly, and it's Singing in the Rain.

"I'm singing in the rain, just singing in the rain . . ."

Sammy's trying to piss me off. He knows I hate movies, with music. I tell Sammy, "Shut the fuck up."

"What a glorious feeling. I'm happy again . . ."

"Shut the fuck up, Sammy."

Benny gets outta the car. "What the fuck you doin, Sammy?" he says.

"I'm happy, is all," Sammy says.

"Calm the fuck down, Sammy," Benny says and gets back in the car.

Sammy's mad, feelings hurt. He looks at me.

"Just don't go hinky on me tonight," he says.

"What the fuck are you talking about?"

"When I was in the Bug House, I heard about it."

"Heard about what?"

"I heard about the Coyle job, how you went hinky."

"You heard wrong. It was a clean job."

"Why do ya think Benny wants me goin through the door first? Doesn't want you goin hinky again. That's what he told me."

You heard it wrong. It was a clean job. Benny even gave me a bonus, for chrissakes . . . Now shut the fuck up, Sammy."

But Sammy heard it right. I went hinky. I went hinky big time . . . It shoulda been easy . . .

Easy . . . four a.m., Eddie and Paddy Coyle—two fat fucks—sleeping in the living room. Nobody else in the house. TV on loud— playing kiddie shows, cartoons, shit like that.

I pull my piece, line em up, squeeze off four rounds. Pop-Pop Pop-Pop. Two guys, dead, heads like busted watermelons. Quick, clean, cold.

I pick up the brass, four shell casings, the way I do, being careful. I turn around and I'm getting the fuck out fast when a scream behind me, high and sharp, cuts me in half.

I know the voice . . .

It's Nora's voice. She's screaming.

"He's gonna kill me! Help me! HELP ME!"

I don't think. I spin around, start shooting blind, like its ghosts I'm trying to kill. I see a body drop, but I don't see Nora.

Where the fuck is Nora? Did I shoot Nora? Did I kill Nora?

I walk over to the body, slow and shaky. I look down. It's not Nora.

It's a little kid—a girl, maybe a boy, I can't tell. Head's gone.

The TV is flickering cartoon colors all over blood and brains and bone—like it's a rainbow in hell.

I start going hinky. I'm sweating ice. I'm shaking.

I step over the kid, and I look for Nora. Everywhere.

I can't find Nora. Anywhere.

I'm going hinky. I start to pray the only prayer I know . . . A priest said if I had a soul, it would help me find it . . .

"Something's lost and can't be found.

Please, Saint Anthony, look around."

I say it again. And again. "Please, Saint Anthony, look around . . ."

I'm on my knees, praying, sweating, shaking, going hinky . .
.

Hinky . . .

"Please, Saint Anthony . . ."

Then I hear Nora scream: "He's killing me!"

"Who's killing you?"

"He's killing me . . . Killing me . . ."

"Who's killing you?"

"You're killing me!"

"What are you talking about?"

"It's you killing me! IT'S YOU! You took the easy way out. You left me alone to die and now I'm dying, dying for real—all the way dead. Are you happy now? ARE YOU HAPPY NOW?"

I'm not happy. I run outta the house like it's burning down around me. I trip, I fall, I get up. I'm going hinky . . . Hinky . . .

Thunder rumbles loud in my ears, like its God screaming at me.

I'm crying now. I can't stop . . .

It starts raining, hard . . .

It's raining hard on Turk Street now. Sammy's excited, keeps saying, "I go through the door first, you behind. Two guys inside. I give em each a new asshole, middle of their forehead. Ok?"

"Yeah. I heard you the first three fuckin times, for chrissakes. Let's get the fuck outta the rain and get this thing done."

But I don't give a shit about rain dripping down my face, like its tears. Or Sammy. Or Benny waiting in the car. Or the Cazzo brothers waiting to get new assholes. I'm thinking about Nora. I'm thinking I shoulda been there. I'm thinking I woulda saved her. I'm thinking it was me killed her.

I follow Sammy up two flights of stairs. Sammy's happy, excited. Sammy thinks he's Gene Kelly again.

"Let the stormy clouds chase everyone from the place . . ."

I tell him to shut the fuck up. I figure the docs shoulda kept Sammy in the Bug House longer, much longer, maybe forever woulda been a good plan.

Come on with the rain . . ."

I'm telling Sammy to shut the fuck up when the gates of hell open wide . . .

LIGHTNING . . . THUNDER . . . SMOKE . . .

I remember standing behind Sammy. The hallway is dark and tight like a coffin. Then muzzle flashes light the place up. Then *BANG! BANG!* So loud I go deaf. Smoke fills my nose. Sammy moans, falls backward, lands on me. I'm pinned under him. I try to move. Sammy turns his head to me. He whispers:

"Come on with the rain.

I gotta smile on my face . . ."

Sammy smiles. Gene Kelly dies. *(I hate fucking movies, with music.)*

Through the smoke I see a guy—must be one of the Cazzo brothers, I figure—looking down at me, his piece pointed at my face. I tell him, "I wanna go to sleep. Shoot me. In the eyes. I wanna go to sleep. Please. I'm askin you. Please."

The guy laughs, figures I'm hinky, should be in the Bug House, so he doesn't shoot. He kicks me in the head, hard.

Everything goes black, and warm, like blood . . . Then cold . .
.

I'm cold all over. I figure I'm dead.

"Am I dead?" I ask Nora.

"You're not dead," Nora says.

"Am I dying?"

"You're not dying. I'm the one who's dying."

"Waddya mean?"

*"I can't breathe," she says. "I'm scared," she says. "Help me,"
she says.*

*Nora begins to choke. She grabs her throat. She chokes and
she pukes and she can't breathe. "God . . .no . . ." is all I can say.*

*Nora falls down. She's twisting on the floor, grabbing her
throat, making noises, like she's drowning. She goes limp, her
life spilling out. "God . . . no . . ." is all I can say.*

*Nora stops moving. "God . . . no . . . No . . ." is all I can say
because I know she's dead. I know Nora's dead . . .*

But Nora isn't dead.

Nora's laughing.

Nora's laughing at me.

*"See how it looks, choking to death on your own puke," she
says.*

"God . . . no . . ."

*"You left me and I died alone," she says. "I pray to Christ it
happens to you. And before you die, I hope the last thing you see
is rats comin to eat your fuckin eyes . . ."*

I look down. Rats are crawling up my legs.

Nora's laughing loud now.

*The rats are moving fast . . . Up my chest, face . . . Toward
my eyes.*

I start screaming. I can't stop screaming . . .

I stop screaming because Benny is slapping my face, hard. I open
my eyes, look around. I'm in Benny's car. "You're ok now," Benny
says. "What the fuck happened to you guys?

"I don't know. Me and Sammy are walkin up the stairs. We
get to the top. Maybe they hear us coming. Maybe they don't.
Maybe they're waiting for us. I don't know. Next thing, *BANG!
BANG!* Sammy falls on me. I can't move. Then some guy kicks
me in the head . . . That's all I remember . . ."

"Jesus fuckin Christ," Benny says.

"We fucked up."

"Big time," Benny says, scared.

Benny doesn't say anything about Sammy, where he is, how he is.

I gotta ask "What happened to Sammy?" but I know it's gonna be bad news.

"Dirt nap" is all he says, like it's not important now, Sammy being dead and gone.

"What the fuck are we gonna do, Benny?"

"We're gonna get the fuck outta her fast. Find a safe place. Hide."

"Hide?"

"Hide. And pray."

"Maybe we can find them, the Cazzo brothers . . . Make it right, so nobody gets pissed off."

"Too late . . ." is all Benny says, his face is turning gray like cement. He knows we fucked up . . . And somebody's gonna get pissed off about that, real soon.

It's four am. We leave Turk Street in a hurry. Benny drives fast. It rains hard. Sewers overflow. Rats run for their lives. Waves of brown water cover the car windows. *"Shit,"* Benny says. "I can't see a fuckin thing. *Can you see anything?"*

My eyes are closed. My head hurts. I'm thinking about Nora, something she said a long time ago . . .

"If we were on a boat and it was sinking," Nora said. "I'd give you the last life jacket to keep you from going under."

I laugh, thinking it's a joke what she said.

But it's not a joke. She looks at me, hard. She waits for me to tell her what I would do . . . Boat sinking, one life jacket left . . . What I would do . . .

I lie. It's easier that way, lying.

"I can't see a fuckin thing. *We're driving blind,"* Benny Teardrop says, not liking it, driving blind, scared of it, driving blind, going hinky, driving blind.

It rains harder. Benny's scared shitless, screaming, *"I can't see! I can't see a fuckin thing! I can't see! I can't see!"*

I tell Benny slow down, pull over, take it easy.

Benny doesn't listen, drives faster, screams louder.

Then Benny goes hinky big time . . .

He pulls his piece and fires four rounds through the windshield.

Rain and glass come in sharp. Benny stops screaming, starts crying. The ice growing in the middle of his heart melts. It leaks out his eyes and down his face.

The car slides sideways, bounces off another car, like we're in a giant pinball machine or playing bumper cars, *having fun . . .*

I'm happy. The rain's pouring in. *We're driving blind.* And I'm happy about that, *driving blind.* It's a good thing, *driving blind.* Not seeing where I been or where I'm going, it's a good thing. I'm happy about that.

I'm happy as cotton candy about that.

"Fish"
L. A. Spooner

Sex Demon from Hell

Max Booth III

Paul desperately wanted to fuck.

He was seventeen years-old for Christ's sake. Everyone he knew was fucking except for him. It didn't make any sense. Statistically speaking, there were more girls at his high school than boys. He should have been chosen by now. He didn't even care by whom—anybody would do. If all the girls at his school were getting laid, then why was he still a hopeless, pathetic virgin? Were the girls sharing dicks? What was wrong with his? It worked perfectly fine and he wanted to prove it.

He *needed* to prove it.

He couldn't explain it. Maybe it was a feeling of inadequacy. Everywhere he looked, people were fucking. On the TV, on the Internet, in school; people fucked there too. He had caught Shawn Callahan and Nancy Hiaasen in the football parking lot the other week; her legs stuck out the windows, her white tennis shoes still tied to her feet. Her panties were hanging from her ankles, and all you could see in the car was Shawn's bare, hairy ass thrusting into the car seat like an animal. Paul remembered her panties had been red. Silky, he thought.

He wanted to be the wild animal in the car, releasing all his animalistic urges once and for all. He had them just like everyone else—animalistic urges. He wanted to fuck. Everyone wanted to fuck. He was the only one who couldn't seem to, though. No one wanted him. They would take Howard Larsen over him, and that was really saying something. Howard Larsen worked at Burger King after school. His face was covered with zits the size of those mini bouncy balls you'd get out of a quarter machine. You would take one look at those things and just want to thwack it as hard as you could until it exploded hamburger grease all over the place. Plus he had glasses—huge, black framed sons of bitches that he constantly had to push up the bridge of his nose on account of sweating so much. That was Howard Larsen for you. It was also the same kid that had been gotten a blowjob from Cindy Grace in the Burger King public bathroom. At least that was the rumor. It might have just been a handy.

Still, though. Paul would have killed for a handy. He would have killed for anything.

He needed a release, and jerking off just wasn't doing it anymore. It was too lonely and depressing, hiding away in his bedroom, playing the Rolling Stones to drown out the noise, and just whacking away over muted sex videos online. Even the sex videos were depressing. Watching these women whom he would never meet in real life, knowing that deep down, they didn't give a single shit about Paul. They were just there for the money. Most of the time he wasn't even able to come because he'd sit there imagining what they were thinking. Sure, they were moaning and doing a convincing enough job of enjoying getting pounded in the ass, but he was sure that in their heads, all they could think about was how a thousand creeps would be watching this, touching their pathetic small cocks, and drooling. It must have creeped them out. In return, it creeped Paul out.

No, he couldn't do the sex videos anymore. He wanted his own movie star just for himself.

He needed to *fuck.*

It was Bobby Wilburn that first told him about the woman living on Rosewood Boulevard. They were in the woods behind the high school, sharing tokes off a badly wrapped blunt. P.E. class would not miss their absence.

Bobby was probably Paul's best friend, and they weren't even that close. Bobby just still hung out with Paul because they'd been thick as thieves back in elementary school. So maybe it was a kind of pity thing, Paul guessed. Bobby had sex all the time. They were nothing alike, anymore.

Paul inhaled on the blunt a little too strong and became lightheaded as a result. He worried about falling down and embarrassing himself in front of his pseudo-friend, but then decided he didn't care. He kind of hoped he did fall.

"Have you done it, too?" Paul asked, trying to take his mind off the fact that the trees were swirling around his face like kaleidoscope-vision.

"Done what?" Bobby took the half-smoked blunt and puffed like he'd been doing it for years.

"You know," he said. "Visited her. That woman."

"Oh. No, I haven't. Lucy would cut my nuts off if I ever did something like that. But like I was saying, Steve did. He told me about it last month."

"What happened?"

Bobby laughed. "What do you think happened, man? They boned. He said she was the best lay he'd ever had in his life, but between you and me—I doubt that's really saying much, considering who we're talking about."

He stopped and gave Paul a look similar to a look Paul had given a schoolmate when he'd made a suicide joke to her in math class, only remembering afterward that her mother had hung herself the previous summer.

"Oh, shit. You're a virgin, aren't you?"

"*What?*" Paul squeaked. He'd been caught. The charade was over. "Of course I'm not a fucking virgin. Jesus Christ."

Bobby looked at him suspiciously, not fooled. "Who have you been with?"

Paul didn't have to think hard. He simply recalled the image that came to mind whenever he didn't have Internet access for his sex videos.

"Morgen Summers."

"You're full of shit," Bobby said, laughing louder than necessary.

Paul shook his head. "No, really. Last fall, at that Halloween party. We both got wasted off spiked punch and did it in the backyard."

In reality, however, he had gotten drunk at the party alone, wandered outside, and found Morgen fucking the captain of the football team on the grass. He liked to imagine it had been him, though.

Maybe one day it would be.

Bobby stopped laughing and gave a serious look; impressed. "Damn, bro, I actually heard about that. But I thought that'd been with Ronnie."

"That was all me," Paul confided, smiling at the idea.

"Wow. Never thought I'd hear that one. Hot damn."

Paul finished off the blunt, and flicked it into some leaves. It was most likely a huge fire hazard but he was simply too high to care. "So anyway, about this woman."

"Yeah."

"What do you know?"

"Well, Steve told me that he'd found out about her on account of some dumbass cousin of his or something. She's just this prostitute, man. Some whore. But I guess she's amazing. Like, from out of this world. Cheap, too, apparently. Real cheap. He told me she suffers from nymphomania or some shit so it's not really like she's doing you a favor, but the other way around."

"On Rosewood Boulevard," Paul said.

"Yeah."

"Where at, though? What house?"

Bobby tried to think but his face made this scrunched up look like he'd swallowed a lemon. "I don't know. I think it's the one with that crazy tree out front."

The crazy tree was indeed crazy.

Paul stood out on the sidewalk staring at it. There were no leaves on it, emphasizing the stripped branches springing from the base like dying hands sticking out of the grave. Arms twisted and curved at impossible angles. It made him sick to his stomach just to look at it.

Yet he couldn't look away.

Beyond the tree was the house. It looked like every other house on Rosewood Boulevard; the only differentiating feature about the place was the tree. Beyond that, it was basically identical to the rest of the houses.

But inside this house, there was something new. Something Live Oak was not used to. This was a town of high standards. It prided itself on its football team, on its politics. It did not tolerate filth.

It did not know about what was living inside the house on Rosewood Boulevard. It did not know about the prostitute.

The whore.

Paul brought twenty-five bucks with him. He wondered if it would be enough. Maybe he should have just gone back home; do it another day. One of his favorite television shows would be starting soon, anyway. Plus his mom was making tacos. They'd be cold if he didn't leave soon.

No.

He mentally punched himself in the face. If he didn't do this— *right here, right now*—then he would forever hate himself. Every night he laid in bed, depressed because he never got chances like this. And now he had one of those chances. A chance to change everything. This was his moment. He wanted to fuck; well, this was where you fucked.

Paul rang the buzzer and waited on the porch. He waited a good five minutes. The day was quiet, the day was still. Just when he was about to give up and go home—tacos once again on the brain—the door swung open, revealing a tall, strong woman standing behind it. Not a girl, but a woman.

Paul gave her one look and forgot all about tacos and TV and everything else. She was a little taller than Paul, with red hair that dropped all the way to her ass. The outer edges of her eyes were shaded purple, as were her lips. She wore a black dress; kind of see-through and silky, but it didn't reveal much skin—like a dress you'd wear on Halloween, Paul thought. But that was all he thought, for his breath had been stolen.

The woman stood there at the door and looked Paul over slowly, then smiled a smile that made his heart skip a beat.

"Hi there," she purred.

Paul continued to stand there on the porch not saying anything. All he could do was look.

"You gonna say anything, stranger?" she asked.

Paul coughed. It had gotten very hot all of a sudden. His skin felt like it was in a microwave. "Uh. Hi."

"Can I help you with something?"

"Uh, um, well. I . . . uh."

The woman smiled. "Yes," she said, "yes I can help you with something. Come on in, boy."

Paul did what he was told without saying anything. It was almost dream-like, how he followed her through the darkly lit house. There was a long hallway, then they were in the kitchen. She told him to have a seat, and asked if he wanted a glass of ice tea.

"Yes," he mumbled. "That would be nice, thank you."

"Sure thing, honey," the woman said, bringing two tall glasses of ice tea to the table and sitting down next to him. She handed him one of the glasses and watched him take a drink. It was good. Very good.

"My name is Lilly. What's yours?"

"Paul."

"Well, Paul, would you like to tell me who told you about me?"

Paul gulped, suddenly feeling like he was in trouble. Jesus, what had he been thinking? Stupid, stupid!

"A kid at school," Paul said, finally.

"What's his name?" Lilly asked.

Not wanting to squeal on one of his only friends, he said, "Steve, Steve Luntz."

The woman nodded. "Ah." She took a drink of her ice tea and said, "I know Steve. Steve was a bad apple. He didn't listen to what I said. Are you a bad apple too, Paul?"

"No, ma'am."

"That's good," Lilly said, "because I like my apples to be good." She gave Paul a playful squeeze on the knee and he flinched. He had to adjust his legs to hide the sudden erection rubbing against his jeans.

Lilly smiled. "You ever have sex before, Paul?"

"No, ma'am."

The kitchen was becoming very, very small. He wanted to leave. This was wrong. But it was right, too. He didn't know what to think, so he took another drink of his ice tea.

"Mmm," she said. "That's good, that's real good."

"Ma'am?"

"I like 'em when they're innocent like you. They give me their all."

"Oh."

"That's why you're here, yes?" the woman said. "You want to go to bed with me."

Paul hesitated. "Yes, ma'am."

"Tell me."

He decided to stop thinking. It all felt so much like a dream, he figured he might as well treat it as a dream. A dream, which is like life, only without consequence.

"Tell me, Paul," the woman said again, leaning closer. Her hand traveled from his knee and rubbed up his leg, stopping at his crotch. She gave it a soft squeeze. "Tell me."

"I want to go to bed with you," he whispered.

"How bad?" she asked, leaning closer than any female had ever been to him. She nibbled on his ear and he felt his whole body tighten.

"Bad!" he said.

"What will you do for me?"

"Anything!" he shouted. "Anything you want!"

"Good," she whispered. "Because I'll also give you anything *you* want."

It felt like the buttons on his jeans were going to pop off and go shooting across the room, like the cork from a wine bottle. "*You!* I want *you!*"

"Well, then. Let's go."

They had to walk through this impossibly long hallway to get the bedroom. The whole time Paul followed behind, his eyes remained glued to the curves in her ass, watching it bounce back and forth with each step. He was bewitched.

The bedroom itself was dark. Very dark. The woman wasted no time in pushing Paul on the bed. She carefully stripped him of all clothing while he lay there helplessly. This was really happening. Jesus Christ.

Then she took her own clothes off, the thin rays of sun from the closed blinds revealing pale, white skin. She got on the bed with him and slowly crawled up his body. He felt her nipples rubbing against his skin the whole time and it made him insanely hard. He didn't know what to do. Then they were face to face, and she was prying apart his mouth with her own mouth, and penetrating his face with her tongue. It welcomed itself among his teeth and gums and tongue and flicked at him like crazy. The woman was hungry and she was feeding. He was her meal. Paul could only lay there, arm on either side of him, and let it happen. He wanted it badly; he wanted it more than anything in the world. He didn't know what to do about it though, but this woman knew exactly what to do. And that's what she was doing—taking charge.

Then he noticed the smell.

It hit him like a ton of bricks. Before he'd been too distracted to notice. But now, in the dark with her tongue going nuts in his mouth, all he could think about was the smell.

Like fish, he thought. Like a bucket of dead, half-gutted fish left out in the sand all day under the sun.

It smelled *warm*.

It made him want to vomit.

Then she sat up, straddling his lap, and slid down his painfully hard cock. It was entirely wetter than he expected. Almost sickly wet. It reminded him of that time when he was a kid, and his parents had taken him to that haunted house for Halloween. There was this special attraction there where they blindfolded you and made you feel all these different horrorish sensations. They were all supposed to be body parts, according to the haunted house. Like the meatballs were eyes. The egg foo young was a heart.

And the bowl of spaghetti, that was supposed to be guts.

He remembered how old and stale it felt, and how much sauce they'd dumped in the bowl. His hands slid in that bowl and he was instantly greeted with this warm, disgusting sauce. He wanted to pull out right away, but there was so much goddamn sauce, his hands slid even deeper, until they were rubbing against the bottom of the bowl, nearly elbow-deep in the stuff.

It was the spaghetti he thought about now.

The woman, Lilly, rocked her hips back and forth on top of Paul, moaning louder than he expected. It was all very exciting and frightening. The smell grew stronger as the sex continued. He almost started gagging, but stopped himself by reaching around and squeezing her ass, pulling him closer against her. He felt completely trapped underneath her, and he loved it.

"Yes, oh yes," the woman moaned. "You are a good one. Yes, you are going to be very, very special. Oh yes."

"Yes," Paul moaned back. Then he came. Hard. His whole body convulsed and he wrapped his arms around her, squeezing her tight like she was the only thing stopping him from freefalling a thousand feet. Everything went dizzy, and he heard her moaning softly next to him, breathing just as heavy as he was.

"We are going to do wonderful things together," she whispered.

"Yes," he said.

Afterward she turned on the nightstand lamp and went into the bathroom next to the bedroom, leaving Paul laying flat on his back in bed. He didn't move. He felt completely content. No wonder everyone did this. He couldn't imagine anything better. This . . . this was the meaning of life, right here. For as long as he lived, he would simply need no other answers.

He sniffed and grimaced. The smell still hadn't left. Jesus, what the hell was that? It was awful.

Like fish. Old, rancid fish. Gutted and left in the sun.

He followed the smell and glanced down his body.

His eyes widened at the sight of him.

What the fuck.

This wasn't normal. This never happened in the sex videos. What the hell was this?

Blood. It was blood.

All over him. On his stomach. On his thighs.

On his cock.

The head looked like it'd been dipped in a jar of pasta sauce. Only this wasn't pasta sauce. It was fucking blood.

"Oh, my God," he cried quietly, and jumped off the bed. He ran into the bathroom with Lilly, almost to tears.

"*WHAT THE HELL DID YOU DO TO ME!?*"

Still sitting on the toilet, the woman took one look at him and frowned. "Yuck. That was a lot messier than I thought it'd be."

"*WHAT ARE YOU TALKING ABOUT? WHAT HAPPENED TO ME?*"

She shook her head dismissively. "Nothin' happened to you, honey. That's all me. Sorry, should have told you. I bleed."

"You bleed."

"All women do, honey."

Paul paused. Looked at Lilly, then back down at his cock. Blood was running down his leg. He sniffed. The smell made him want to kill himself.

He turned and stepped into the glass shower and turned the HOT faucet all the way to the left. He only managed to vomit twice before he was finally clean.

Over the next two weeks, Paul visited Lilly a total of nine more times. He couldn't help himself; it was like an addiction. She was the heroin and he was the pathetic junkie, totally lacking a will of his own. Even when they were in the middle of fucking, he'd be craving the next time they'd be able to do it again.

And the best thing was, she didn't even charge him money. Whenever he asked how much she wanted, she would just smile and kiss him and tell him that he was enough, that she just wanted him. Nothing else would compare.

Every man wished to hear those words. He couldn't have been luckier.

The only thing he didn't wish for was the blood. And, of course, the accompanying smell. He had always thought that it was only supposed to last like a week, and then go away for the rest of the month. Yes it still persisted—if anything, she bled more as they continued the sex.

The thought revolted him. It'd make him gag just thinking about it, and afterward he would swear never to do it again, not until the menstrual cycle finally passed. But then a day would pass and he would find himself running back to her house on Rosewood Boulevard, knocking feverishly and taking off his clothes before he was even all the way through the front door. He would completely forget about the blood until they were in the bedroom, and she was sliding down his dick, that smell of rotten fish raping his nostrils.

One afternoon, a month or so after their relationship began, Paul was in the bathroom wiping his cock off with a towel. Lilly was standing in front of the mirror fooling with makeup. Paul couldn't take it anymore. He felt that he'd had enough sex by now to begin questioning things. Sure, he was by no means a pro—but he felt like he at least knew a little bit, now.

"Lilly," he said, trying to breathe out of his mouth.

"Yes, baby."

"I want to ask you something."

"The blood," she said. It wasn't a question.

"Yes."

She nodded in the mirror. "I know, you're probably confused. You think I should have stopped bleeding by now."

"It's been over a month."

"I know. But here's what you don't understand, baby."

"What?" Paul asked, not sure if he wanted to know what she was about to say next.

"It never stops," she said. "I always bleed."

He paused, not knowing what to say. "How? Why?"

"It's my curse," Lilly said. "Some women, they're only cursed once a month. Me, I'm cursed for life."

"I don't understand."

"Neither do I," she said, "but that's just the way it is. Always has. I hate it just as much as you do. I wish it would go away. Do you wish the same?"

"Of course," he said, then added, as an afterthought, "But I still want to be with you regardless."

Lilly smiled. "That's sweet, baby, but it doesn't have to be so bloody, you know that? We can make the blood go away."

Paul was confused. If she could make it go away, why hadn't she before? "How?" he asked.

"I would need your help."

"I don't understand," he said, "what would you need from me?"

She closed her eyes and sighed. It was obvious she didn't want to talk about this no more than Paul wanted to hear it. But these things couldn't be avoided.

"I would need your total devotion," Lilly said at last. "I would need you to be mine, and myself to be yours."

He could feel his dick shriveling up into his body as he stood there in the bathroom, the coldness of the tiled floor sending shivers up his legs. "I thought I was yours," he said, confused. "I thought you were mine."

She reached over and touched his cheek. "Not yet, baby. You have to really mean it. You have to tell me that you would do anything for me, that you give me your soul, and promise to devote the rest of your breaths serving my needs."

Her hand trailed down his naked body and cupped his balls. She squeezed gently.

"Anything you want," Paul whispered. "I am yours forever."

"Good," she said, and kissed him.

Paul felt a chill zap through his whole body. He suddenly became much lighter than he was used to—he almost felt *weightless.*

She led him back into the bedroom and pushed him onto the mattress. Despite having just ejaculated, Paul had no trouble growing erect again. She straddled on top of him and went wild. Paul watched in awe, stuck in a dream-like state, studying her face as she moaned. He didn't move the whole time; even when he finally came again, his facial expression did not alter from the same drugged, monotonous look.

Then she lay down beside him, breathing heavy, and the trance broke. "Jesus Christ," he sighed, ready to pass out from exhaustion.

"No," she whispered in his ear. "He has nothing to do with this."

When he went into the bathroom to shower again, he noticed that his cock was completely bloodless. It had worked. What he'd said, he'd fixed her. She was better now. Normal.

He looked at his cock for a long time before returning to bed and falling asleep. This was the start of something new.

Paul heard the words but he didn't quite understand what she meant. Of course, deep down, he knew damn well what she meant, but another part of him found the words she spoke completely alien. This just didn't make any sense.

It shouldn't have been a surprise. Not once had he used protection when they fucked. They warned you about these kinds of things in sex education all the time, but . . . he didn't know. Once she pulled him into her house, the thought just never crossed his mind.

But now . . .

Now she was pregnant.

"How is this possible?" he said. They were sitting at the kitchen table, drinking ice tea. He couldn't remember the last time he'd been home.

"I think you know how it's possible," she said. "Last night, you gave yourself to me, and I accepted. These are the consequences. Now, are you man enough to accept this new responsibility?"

He didn't think he was. Then she kissed him, and suddenly he felt like he could take on the whole world. "Yes," he said. "I'm ready."

"Good," she said. "Because we're going to have babies, and I need a man who will be there."

"I'll be there for our baby," he confided.

"I'm going to need someone to protect our family," she said.

"I'll protect our family with my last dying breath."

He realized he couldn't remember his mother's face, and wondered if she was worried about him. Then he decided he didn't care. He had a new family to look after now.

"There's someone you need to deal with."

"What?" Paul said. They were lying in bed a few weeks later. They'd just got done fucking again, and now he was cuddled up next to her, rubbing her swollen stomach. He could already feel their baby kicking at them. Everything he had learned about pregnancies no longer voiced itself in his head. This was what was real. The woman on Rosewood Boulevard was his only reality now.

"Do you remember that boy, Steve?" Lilly asked. "The one who told you about me?"

He didn't like where this was going. "Yeah. Of course I remember him."

"Well, he used to visit me, like you. But he wasn't good enough. He left me, he called me names. He called me a whore."

"No."

"Yes," she said. "The other day when you went out to the store, he came back. He was mean to me, Paul. He said he was going to tell the whole town about me, about what I'm doing."

"What do you mean?" Paul asked.

"He knows about me and you, honey. If people found out about this, there would be hell to pay. People wouldn't approve; they'd hate me and make sure I burned. They'd make me and our baby go far, far away. Do you want that to happen?"

He felt the baby kick again.

"No," he said seriously. "Nothing bad will happen to you. I promise."

"Will you take care of this boy?"

"Yes."

"You'll make sure that he'll never be able to hurt us?"

"Yes."

"Promise me, Paul. For our baby. For our family."

"I promise."

He had never been good friends with Steve, but they'd talked on occasion. He'd been to his house a few times to play videogames.

It wasn't that far of a walk from Rosewood Boulevard. The house overshadowed his presence like the sun over the earth.

He didn't know what he was even doing here. But he had a feeling he would know when the time came. Right now he was just going with it.

He tried not to think about the knife sheathed in the back of his pants.

The doorbell rang, and after a few moments Steve's mother answered the door. She took one look at Paul and grimaced, taking a step back.

"Oh my God," she said, "are you okay?"

"Yes, of course, thank you," he said. "Is Steve home?"

She gave him another doubtful look and said, "Uh, yeah, him and Bobby are in his room. Go ahead."

She left the doorway and allowed him entrance. He walked down the hallway to where he remembered the bedroom being, and pushed open the door.

Steve was sitting on the ground playing his PlayStation. Bobby Wilburn was next to him, also gripping a controller. They both turned their heads at once and gave Paul a look of absolute horror.

"Jesus Christ," Bobby said, "what the hell happened to you, Paul?"

Steve jumped to his feet at once. "You were with her, weren't you?" he exclaimed. "I fucking knew it! Everyone was saying you'd skipped town, but no, not me. As soon as Bobby told me he'd told you about that whore, I knew right what happened. Holy shit. She really got you bad. Are you okay?"

"Don't call her that," Paul said, sternly. He took a step forward.

"What?" Steve said. "Listen, you need to sit down, I'll call the police. This time they'll believe me. That fucking bitch . . . I don't even know what she is. I'm just glad I got out before it was too late. I was there the other day, trying to find you . . . and I swear to God, I thought she was going to kill me. That whore is evil."

"Shut your goddamn mouth," Paul said again.

"Hey, uh, Paul, relax," Bobby said, standing up and putting a hand on his shoulder.

Paul reacted almost instinctively, reaching behind his back, pulling out the kitchen knife and thrusting it in the side of Bobby's stomach. Bobby let out an unnatural gasp and bent over. Before anyone could even react, Paul took the knife out and slammed the blade down in the back of Bobby's neck. A dozen droplets of blood splattered on Paul's face.

Bobby fell to the ground, still.

Steve just stood there on the other side of the room, dazed. The crotch of his blue jeans had turned dark.

"No," he whispered. "Please don't do this."

Paul took a few more steps forward. He did not blink.

"You threatened my family," he said.

"What?" Steve groaned, pressing up against the wall with no chance of escape.

"You want to kill my baby?" Paul asked him, holding the knife up against the boy's throat.

"No! Jesus Christ, no. I don't know what you're talking about. Please, don't do it. Oh my God."

Paul cocked his head and growled, like a dog on the prowl. "My family is all I have, and I must protect them. I have no choice."

Steve tried to push him away then, but Paul was too powerful, as if overwhelmed by supernatural strength. Paul countered with a head-butt, breaking Steve's nose instantly and sending him flying back against the wall. He leaped on top of his prey like a hungry animal.

"Oh, shit, get off of me, no, please."

Paul drove the knife into Steve's stomach, pulled it out and stabbed him again. Then again. With each stab, Steve let out an exhausted breath. It excited Paul, and made him wish he was back home with his woman. His family.

Paul paused, looking Steve in his dying eyes. He held the tip of the blade up to his neck, panting.

The last thing Steve said was, "Jesus, that smell, it's all over you," and then the knife slit his Adam's apple to shreds and he said no more.

"Oh, my God," said a voice from behind him.

He jumped up and spun around, spotting Steve's mother in the doorway. She was shaking something terrible, looking at Paul like he was a monster.

"What have you done?" she cried.

"What was necessary," he whispered.

She turned around and ran down the hallway. Like a lion, Paul took off after her, the knife gripped in his fist. His eyes stung of the blood caught in them. He didn't let it bother him as he ran through the house, chasing after the woman.

The front door swung open, and Paul's heart sank.

He couldn't let her escape. She would tell everyone, and his family would be ruined.

He had to protect his family.

Paul sprinted outside and leaped off the porch steps. Steve's mother was already in the middle of the street, screaming bloody murder. He had to silence her before it was too late.

She made the mistake of assuming he wouldn't follow her outside. She stopped running.

Paul ran up from behind and punched the knife into her spine, causing her to bend at an odd angle and collapse to the ground. The street was empty save for the two of them. No cars were in sight. The neighborhood was theirs.

Paul got on top of her, screaming that he had no choice, he had to protect his babies, there was no other way. Then he began to stab the knife in her cheek and he didn't stop until her face was the equivalent of a gutted jack-o-lantern.

"I'm sorry," he whispered again, dropping the bloody knife on the street. "My family . . ."

And with that, he ran.

Back home, in the house on Rosewood Boulevard, Paul lay cuddled up to his one and true love. They couldn't have been more content.

The bed sheets were soaked in blood but it didn't bother him so much this time. It wasn't the same kind of blood.

Paul smiled at the sight of his new babies. Just a few hours old, and they were already scuttling around. He watched them climb up the walls, then onto the ceiling, looking back down at him as they explored this new world he and his darling had brought them in.

They were beautiful.

The woman kissed him softly on the lips and he kissed her back.

His family was safe for the moment. And the next time a new danger threatened them, he would not hesitate to do what was necessary.

He would protect them with his last, dying breath.

"Addiction"
Stephen Cooney

Smoke and Mirrors

J. Daniel Stone

We drove to New Orleans, the city of Lestat de Lioncourt, juju dust and hurricane ghosts. A cradle of fears blossomed like carrion plants in the Deep South. No feedback, no black static, just the frightening smell of midnight kudzu and the shimmering galaxy above our heads. There's no better way to understand how infinitesimal life truly is compared to all that universe . . . to gaze into a puddle of stars.

Three thousand miles would pass us, three thousand miles laced with a fear and loathing that there would be no craft beer passed the Maryland border, and certainly no infectious, viral music. But I liked speed, and that affinity took Dex and I fast out of New York City. I-95 South was a lonely bastard road that glittered like ribbons pulled out of a cassette tape. We were only three states south of New York when Dex pulled out his favorite short story collection, *Smoke and Mirrors*. He read *Snow, Glass, Apples* aloud in the dark as I beat the radio for any lazy FM rock station I could find, hearing only the southern song of white noise.

The words swirled. Without Dex's wonderful voice the ride would've been lonely and maddening; to be without the sight of his sand colored hair drifting like a flag through the southern wind and the glare of his intoxicating green eyes focused on the words was a reality I wasn't able to face.

"'I think of her hair black as coal, her lips, redder than blood, her skin, snow-white,'" Dex said.

He loved that tale. I couldn't help but to imagine the evil protagonist, her dry bones rising to live again, her mouth wet with all that blood. But there was no greater story than that we already lived. It wasn't many moons ago that we were a band who sketched songs in our own blood and then inked the dried notes on our skin. We burned lyrics into the souls of all our listeners by the light of three suns and one star. Needs became a passing memory; desire haunted us long.

We were unstoppable: Dex, Tiff, Geri and I. Tiff played a wicked bass; Geri was on drums and mad as a hatter; I was lead guitar and Dex the ferocious vocalist. Our music was the avenger of nights veiled behind the calm sweet seduction of liquor and creation. It weaved tapestries of beat poetry throughout lower east side dives filled to the brim with the art-punk-poets of the city, kids overwrought by the desire to express one's self freely. Sinister music attracts the wastes of society, but those wastes come with money. And so they became drunk on our music, on lyrics written from the bowels of temptation and the dark fragilities that lived in us all . . . long after the chords had been pulled and the electric was cut off.

Devil doll stool pigeons crooning over my spoon and dropper. Gilt and red plush, the air is decayed with an evil substance like honey.

CAN I DRIZZLE IT ON YOU BABY?

Dex sang with a great pink mouth, howling his words like a voodoo spell running from brain to lips; his melodies were acid thrown into the faces of anyone who dared to listen. The riffs I wrote were inspired by beat poetry and the gritty crescendos of drop D tuning; my fingers teased every inch of the custom Warlock I built, allowing me to shock life into every single note that I imagined when I wrote my songs. Length is a plus when you're a lead guitarist; the hands that control the guitar are chiral mad.

Dex and I were temperamental lovers. We drank champagne from the bottle and never had to pay for one another's sex. Our tolerance to needle poisons was never capped off and the local hallucinogenic only strengthened our love of music and each other. He sung to me like he did our fans, spit in my mouth when I begged him, and bit my nipples until they were swollen and red as cherries. We did this to a soundtrack as always, an up-tempo thrash or a metal disaster. Dex liked to leave bite marks on all of his lovers; his teeth weren't sharp so a flowered patch of bruising littered my body after sleeping with him.

But of all the ephemeral lusts that plagued the city, Tiff was his one true love, his favorite out of us all. Rainbow hair covered the maddened face, the glowing eyes like one of Carter's wolves. Tiff was unseasonably feral, unable to conform no matter how experimental or fringy the trend, unable to sit still or be monogamous. But above all else she was a gifted, wicked bass player. The distortion pedal she used pounded like the death march; her fingers bore the calluses of natural born talent and determination.

Dex was unnaturally attracted to her. Perhaps it lay within the way she composed herself, as if all the problems of the world were always on her shoulders, or how she showed off her new talents as she took Henna art to new heights: a dastard skull on her calf, caskets ripped from their muddy beds across her torso and pirate ships crowding her biceps. But for all the strengths she had, there was but one weakness. One could see through all her macabre tattoos where the marks of poison began and ended; the needle scars had disintegrated her great vein.

So we lived the rock star lifestyle that most kids can only dream. But good things always come to an end. The old dog must learn new tricks or the next one will be on him, and it was that sick sense of reality that drew us out of the New York club scene. The fans gave up on us to new trends; the nights of music and mayhem were over. Dex claimed I was a useless hack, a distrustful lover (he was under the impression that I'd stolen Tiff from him). She'd toyed with his head so badly, had left him in such a state of lunacy that I once saw him back-hand her hard enough to draw blood from her nose, but then fuck her until she begged him to never stop. Dex often gloated how Tiff bit his foreskin and left him bleeding for days. Still bleeding? I didn't know. I wanted to unzip his pants and find out, to stroke the sopping red snake that nested between his legs until it threw up happy baby batter in my hand. The batter would be swirled red.

But by that time Tiff had left without notice, newly infatuated by a photographer boyfriend whose medium was to incorporate insects and nude girls into scheming black and white portraits. One day she returned out of the blue with clean bright eyes and the photos in her hand: she'd lost her lunacy in music, the dull glow of an artist. Dex tore the photos up and attacked Tiff with a jealous rage. I saw his eyes flush red, his face scrunch into madness; the ragged leather Tiff wore was torn to scraps in his grip.

"You're a fucking clown!"

Those were the last words I ever heard Tiff say, but they weren't the last of her memory. The knowledge that another man had spread Tiff naked all around the city like Dex did her clit drove him mad-insane. He could not bear the thought of another man running his tongue along the tiny nubs of Tiff's spine, her back suspended in midair like a flower stem, her legs open, and a heavily veined penis sliding into the honey of her vulva. Dex held foreplay on a pedestal of his sexual life, and for another man to take that away from him drove him insane. This thought would plague him and guide his heinous life from that day on.

Geri was gone by that time too, sick of Dex's whining and not convinced by my assurance that he would change. She never partook in our love triangle, our drug parties. Geri was best focused on music, constantly writing, not sold on the idea that being under the influence can liven up the creative process. She was stubborn in her own way.

As the club was getting ready to drop its last withering petal, Dex and I were left breathing in the last of its smoky life, thrashing our tunes for the sake of notoriety and nostalgia, even if only one or two tragic faced numbskulls showed up in support. So we played to empty dives and received enough payment to cover the cost of the craft beer we drank. It was worth losing the money to beer because at least those nights ended with a blast, whether bad or good.

After a while we lost the will to write, to live. Breaking into new territory just couldn't be done; the memories were too comforting. Mars Bar was gone, CBGB's lay a dried leather corpse, and The Knitting Factory wouldn't even book us because our turn out had thinned so badly. It was then Dex swore that he might never leave home, might never see the sun again. Without Tiff the world as he knew it could rip from its gravitational orbit and roll into a solar storm. Nothing mattered. He sung himself into a frenzy, destroying his throat until it was as raw as rug burn speckled across pale skin. He wrote his anger across the walls of our loft, *SO ALONE* and *BeTrAyEd* as he ripped the posters down and sat around drunk for days. I often came home to find him passed out and drooling on the couch, waiting for twilight I assumed. But before his eyes met the world again I'd run my fingers through the dyed oily mat of his hair, sniffing his alcohol breath just so I could taste him once more, remembering our nights of complete and utter youthful happiness. I loved him, and often dreamed of the day when we'd be close again.

Months later we tried to focus our minds, clear our heads and channel the whimsical muse to write again, tried so hard. I read *Naked Lunch* and *Souls on the Road* a dozen times. Dex read *Snow, Glass, Apples*, tortured by the memory of Tiff, in lust with the snow-white skin of the main character, and the snowflake that never melted when it landed on her cheek. *A cold heart. A blood-sucker.* When I realized that we managed to scribble down nothing, I offered the idea that we ditch what we knew and move around the boroughs. We took shelter in whatever vacant place was to be found. Dex would not speak with me directly, but he followed me everywhere I went and crawled into bed with me at night, kissing my neck and running his tongue down my stomach, into my crotch. Something in his touch drove me to love him more, even if I knew he was only dreaming of Tiff. Every morning I woke there was a new bite mark in some secret place. My shoulder, my left hand, and even my foot. I suppose that was the way he showed that he loved me without words.

It was enough to suffice. Words hurt; actions prevail.

Without the safety net of music we sat around and collected various insects and tossed them to be caught in the bell of cobwebs that decorate condemned buildings. Watching the arachnids suck ants and beetles dry of their gooey life made me almost want to do it too. Was this what Dex wanted to taste, the rich red life within us all? Was the blood of insects even red? Dex would often talk about how Geri was into the occult, a lover of ghosts, ghouls, goblins and tarot cards. But then again that's how he always talked after he topped off the bottle of one-fifty-one.

His voice had grown hoarse by this time, and he couldn't keep a note going for longer than a few seconds the way he howled like a hopeless hound about Tiff, about music. Me? I wouldn't dare touch my guitar. My fingers had betrayed me; my love for Dex had betrayed me. I realized that I'd become my own worst enemy; my perverse mind had trapped, squandered and squashed any chance of our band moving forward, in becoming better musicians. All I wished was to cradle the needle point bones of Dex's face and kiss the wretched curve of his throat forever. His blood would be sweet water beneath that moonlight skin. But that could never be. Dex decided that bisexuality was just part of the process of sex, drugs and rock n' roll.

I didn't know if living in the city prepared us for this kind of darkness or made us surreptitiously frightened of it, but when I looked out the window I saw the swamps of the south: murky, depthless, patrolled by arrogant gators and huge mutant fish with eyes that sparkled like coins dropped down a wishing well. I heard a symphony of frogs, crickets, and the whisper of oncoming rain, and then like some living nightmare the trees came at us with gnarled limbs and deep voices of warning.

My Prelude took us fast through the wilderness. Truck stops passed like Halloween attractions; the air was rank with the smell of the heavy ocean, boat fuel, and dead fish. We dared not challenge the peering eyes of the night like fallen southern stars as Dex kept the window down to let the melody of the southern wind flow like saliva over our skin, through his dirty glossy hair.

"The city of hurricanes and Mardi Gras," Dex said reading from a map and snapping open a warm can of Pabst Blue Ribbon.

"Drinking that shit again, Dex? I can't stand it."

When I saw the lights in the distance I thought about the city scene we left. I thought about Tiff, of insects and photography; I thought about the greedy kids, the seeping blowjobs, the arid stench of hangovers and the parties that never stopped. A familiar darkness enveloped my thoughts. I touched my body forgetting Dex was even there and opened the slick portal of my whiskey laced dreams. I imagined Dex's mouth opening, his lips wet with blood as they wrapped around my shaft, his throat a tunnel of warmth as he took me into it.

"The only way I'll ever live that life again is when I'm dead and cold. I dream of a bitter end," Dex said.

We invaded New Orleans at sunset and began to tour the city without a care in the world, the horribly haunted streets. Decatur, Bourbon and Canal were packed with tourists, the smell of beignets, coffee and exotic incense. We drifted passed the slimy brown snake of the Mississippi river; our hands sailed along the murky wrought iron fence that stopped us from taking a swim in the water that still stunk of bones and slave blood. A slimy muffuletta sandwich slipped from an old black man's hand and splat beneath a veranda. He picked through it with crooked fingers and wide yellow eyes.

The French Quarter was alive with the nightly bustle. Galleries swarmed above our heads; a garland of Mardi Gras beads hung like strips of meat and gleamed all the shades of blood under the warm sliver of moonlight. In Jackson Square the local art scene was in full blast. Paintings were strewn across spire gates; the poets were spitting prose and the street musicians were creating blasphemous sounds. A scrappy saxophonist with lightning fingers played his song of jazz and blues; an acoustic guitar whiz sat next to his case asking for chump change.

Further south were the nightclubs, dark little places where bourbon and absinthe flowed fresh as spring water. But then there came a sign, block letters faded to a dusty orange by rain and sunlight, wood slimed green by evil kudzu that wrapped around it like hunting snakes. An arrow pointed east toward the swamps. *SMOKE & MIRRORS*. Not the sideshow freaks or the aberrant, but an ambiguous phrase that lets the mind play tricks on itself.

"Wanna check it out?" I asked Dex.

"Just like the title of the book."

The path we took was muddy and unforgiving, the air thick and salty as soup. How could people live here? Human population: negative. Wildlife population: overcrowded. Plant life: swarming. Creole cottages spread vastly, dilapidated and torn, still trying to overcome the effects of Katrina. Who knew what skeletal hand was waiting to claim you behind a bush? Who would watch if I decided to run my tongue into Dex's pink gummy mouth? What happens in the south stays in the south.

"Here we go with the hocus pocus shit," Dex said.

"No ideas for months now," I said, taking a drag of a clove cigarette, smoke like grey snakes invading my throat.

I saw it then, a shadowed land built upon a swamp. A billion lights came rising in the black: Welcome to the Show. Neon swords slashed the night air; tendrils swirled. What better fun than sinister obscurity? I saw the remains of a graveyard arranged like sore thumbs, flecked with the dust of loneliness. A collapsing shopping district was long since abandoned; concrete succumbed to scourging wetland as if an island drifting into a vast green slime to nowhere. When I looked up I saw a churning metal colored patina of clouds that glowed the deep twilight of the city, but on ground level it was a dustbowl flanked by a ticket booth with a rusted money sign.

Pantomime ghosts lollygagged; ghost-mouths stuffed with cotton candy and corndogs choked until doom. Lights cued as if a song and a cryptic rollercoaster soared in the distance; twisted metal pierced the sky and rows of games rattled to life by phantom electricity: balloon darts, water guns, a wraithlike beaver stomp machine and a petting zoo of bones. There were eyes that watched us too, eyes of a beast or a child that had grown too fast to fit into its skin.

But it was then I saw the stage gloaming, beautiful stage that I imagined playing upon. One mic, one amp, and a pruned corpse lying across with sand colored hair, green skin and red lips. Dex became transfixed, immediately addicted. The lost artist within him was coming out of the closet.

"Ya'll came to my swamp," she said

Absinthe colored shadows moved like hummingbirds as she came out from the thicket of trees. A top hat covered straggled grey hair; skeleton features lined the haggard southern face pruned by old number seven. I noticed than that the carnival land I imagined was gone, was never there. It was a trick of the night.

"Saw what'chu wanted to see?" she said again.

"A stage," Dex said. "A stage to play."

"I usually charge for out of town folks. I know that Yankee filth accent when I hear it."

I saved my retaliation and let the scraggy old bat board us on a small boat and take us through the swamp. The Louisiana night drummed like the final standing ovation before we gave up on music. Dex drank the rest of my Magic Hat beer, a seasonal Oktoberfest; the red label had a picture of maddened monsters cheering beer mugs across a beat up wooden table. It was quite ironic.

We were in the heart of the American South. The swamp was a vast and lonely river of slime glowing against the moon. I looked across the water and saw the deep sea fish glimmer of scales and tentacles, the gentle explosion of swamp gas. *This is all Smoke and Mirrors*, I thought. *Tricks.* I touched the water and sniffed my finger, repulsed by the smell of moss and algae. We passed gators sitting atop signs that said *SwAmP ToUr!!!* and *MaRtIn LaKe*. Black bears scaled the trees until their limbs bent back toward the water. The insects were as big as vampires and they came right at my face looking for sweet blood.

"In the heart of the swamp you can find your desires," the lady said.

There came the sad sight of a tiny house sitting upon a dune of muck. The windows were dusted in swamp dust and pricked by a billion dots of green amoeba light from a candelabrum. I saw rows full of jarred spices and sinister herbs that sold for a penny. Swamp Magic was offered in long necked Stoppard bottles. One bottle was labeled *THE BLAZE OF A HURRICANE!*; another *GATOR DROOL!*. The color seeped into the crevices of our tour guide's face, revealing her crimson smile.

There was a girl chained to a wooden chair. Murky light shone upon her face. Her corkscrew curls were black as sin and her eyes were taped open and dazed, empty. I knew the bones of that face, had tasted those lips before. It was Tiff alright, and I nearly jumped from the boat as a scabbed hand came down like a gavel and shoved live butterflies into her mouth. Pictures were taken too. *Insects.* As she chewed a morass green goo slimed her chin, but she smiled maniacally with pleasure.

He'll make me famous, she had said. *I've been in every gallery in New York!*

"The butterfly QUEEN!"

I heard Dex's hopeless laughter as we rowed along. There I saw a cragged little person with a sunken face concealed behind a thin black veil. When she spoke her voice was high pitched; her words were the alien gibberish of a poltergeist language. Geri had once told me she had a fascination with Ouija boards and ghost hunting.

"Her eyes be glowing into you. She's wantin' to tell yeh something."

I never paid attention. The next few miles were like riding inside carnival mirrors. I saw a million fans waiting for us to play, a million gators. The mirrors were in the sky and within the swamp, and they made me think of the Ice Queen and The Dwarf. If I smashed those mirrors I was sure to break myself free, but I knew Dex didn't want to leave, didn't want to escape.

"The grand finale."

We were at the end now. The stage was all that was left to see. Dex and I knew exactly what to do.

The chartreuse stars were embalming . . .

It was as if we awoke from a healing sleep we were so ready to play. Dex clutched the microphone and I the Warlock. It felt like old times, like nothing had changed. The night air cooled our necks; the liquor went down like ice incinerating our guts. Dex's eyes were so black they glittered even in the dark. They were the eyes of the young man I had met in junior high, the boy who could sing worms out of their holes, who loved music more than himself. I dreamed of his penis again, dreamed the day I would taste the bleeding scrap of skin.

"On three," Dex said.

The warlock howled, sending a shock of reverb through the PA system, and Dex had no trouble edging his voice into the song. An all-out war of static ripped into the southern hemisphere, burrowing into the still swampland beneath our feet. Dex claimed everything with his voice, raping the wind and the waters, melodies gushing forth like lava with no remorse. He could wake ghosts with his tones, could influence the devil. There was no reason to stop.

I knew then that we never would as the first song cued and my fingers took charge, bringing us straight into the next one. It was one of our oldest, a song written by candlelight and too many Jäger bombs. Suddenly I smelled cough syrup, felt Dex's body lying next to mine, his birdcage torso sprawled drunk on my bed, the smear of my blood after he'd bit my ear, my tongue.

"Feels too good to stop drizzling that honey on you!" Dex sang.

Another lick thundered through the swamp. I closed my eyes and saw a cornucopia of notes thrashing, glass breaking. After the first twenty songs or so my fingers began to bleed, my mind grew numb. Dex ran his hands against his body, ripped off his shirt and scratched his torso until blood sparkled within the passionate tracks. He sang with a horrible throaty voice and bit the microphone until his lips were sore and bulging. Dex had found a new life in playing again. It was beautiful.

When he collapsed I held his quivering body close to mine, closed his eyes and kissed his cold red lips. *I'll never live that life again until I'm dead and cold.* I wanted to taste the true essence of Dex; it was time to leave my own mark upon his flesh like he had done mine so many times. And so we kissed as I pulled apart the flaccid scraps of flesh in his pants; my teeth deep dived into his neck. There was no blood, no sperm . . . already gone.

He was an x-ray hanged for the entire world to see.

That's when I threw the guitar away and jumped into the teeming swamp. I didn't care about being eaten or sucked down into the summer mud. When I came out on the other side I was wet, tired and alone, but defiant. I would not play until my fingers were bone dust and ash; I would not bear the ruins of deceit through Dex. His dry bones were a riddle of regret. A bitter end? Nothing more bitter than the taste of his spit, or how I'll remember his hair like Mediterranean sand, his lips redder than blood, and his skin, green as the southern moon in the swamp.

"You Shouldn't Have"
Stephen Cooney

My Dead Celebrity

Shaun Avery

"My best friend is running free
"Thanks to Mr Simmons and some taxidermy
"Now we're close as two great chums can be
"That's My Dead Celebrity and me."

That was the jingle that started things off, one of those maddeningly catchy ones that burn their way into your mind and won't get out until you've bought something.

The brain in question this time belonged to a sixteen-year-old girl called Lisa Higgins.

"Daddy," she said, turning away from the screen that had shown the advert to where her father sat in his favourite TV-watching chair. "Did you see that?"

He hadn't, actually – he had been drifting away somewhere, imagining what he and his wife would be getting up to when the lights went out. "See what, honey?"

Lisa found one of the many remote control devices lying around the floor and hit the "rewind" button. "This, Daddy," she replied, "Watch."

"Well, I'll be damned," he said when the advert, complete with infectious jingle, had played through again. "What *will* they think of next?"

"I don't care what they think of next," Lisa replied. "I want one of those," she added, pointing to the cavorting corpse on the screen.

"Oh, I don't know," her mother said, entering from the kitchen, an oven glove still covering one hand. "Where would we keep it?"

"It wouldn't be an "it," mother," Lisa insisted. "He'd be a he, and I'd look after him. Honestly."

Then she turned her gaze back on her father, doing her best to look lovable and sweet. "Can I get a My Dead Celebrity, please?"

And mother and father just looked at each other.

How could they refuse such a heartfelt plea?

It seemed that a lot of other children in the local area possessed the same manipulative skills as Lisa. For when the three-strong family arrived at the specially built "Designer Morgue" section of the mall, they found the place completely packed.

Making his way out of the exit, shop assistants pushing the My Dead Celebrity he had bought to his parents" car for him, Dave Walsh, a boy from Lisa's class, beamed proudly.

Lisa stopped to admire his purchase.

"Car crash," Dave explained. "They cleaned her up a little, though, put stuff in to rebuild her face." He grinned. "And other parts."

"Wow," Lisa said.

"The car crash aisle is pretty good. You won't be disappointed there." He patted her on the shoulder. "But have a look around. The overdose section is pretty fun, too."

Then he was gone.

This encounter made her more eager than ever to get her own My Dead Celebrity, and Lisa raced into the mall. But there were so many other browsers around that it was hard to get close enough to really check out any of the corpses in detail.

So she looked around and eventually found an aisle that was deserted.

Almost eerily so.

And asked the nearest assistant, "Hey, what's down there?"

He looked her up and down and up again like someone examining an alien species. "Oh, no one wants to go down there, little miss. You see, that's natural causes."

"Ooh," her dad said, coming up behind her. "Want to take a look?"

She didn't, not really; the recommendations Dave had made to her sounded cool, and she wanted to check those out. Besides, *anybody* could die of natural causes – she wanted to see the deaths that were usually reserved for the rich and famous, like "heart attack in a room full of hookers whilst strung out on designer drugs" or "bizarre helicopter boarding accident."

But both of those aisles were full.

And she'd rather go home with a My Dead Celebrity that died of natural causes than none at all.

So she headed down the aisle.

They found a more helpful, less judgemental, assistant this time, and he talked Lisa through the whole process.

"It's a new stipulation that famous folk can have put in their will," he explained. "When they die, they can have a funeral, priest jabbering, people crying – you know, all that boring stuff. Or . . ." and here he pushed open a door to lead them into a large storage area – "they can have their organs removed and their bodies stuffed and put on sale to fine fans like yourself."

Lisa looked. All of the bodies were mounted on wheeled planks of wood, their feet bolted to these bearers for ease of movement.

Lisa's mother was looking around, too. "Why are all these bodies back here?" she asked, indicating the vast array of My Dead Celebrities on display. "Why aren't they out there with the rest of them?"

The assistant answered the question, but he directed his words and his gaze at Lisa, perhaps sensing that she was the one he needed to impress. "Why, out there's the showroom," he said. "You can *buy* those, but then you wouldn't have had a chance to really look around."

"These all natural causes?" Lisa's dad asked.

"They are indeed. Every type of death has its own aisle and showroom."

He was rubbing the cheek of a pretty red-headed body. "They look so peaceful and at rest."

"The range has some brilliant make-up artists to work on the bodies before they're made available for sale," the assistant told him, and then winked at Lisa. "No one wants an *ugly* celebrity, am I right?"

She giggled.

Then her eyes fell upon someone.

"Hey," she said, "wasn't he a famous musician?"

"He certainly was."

"And he died of natural causes?"

"So the death certificate says."

"Brilliant," Lisa said. "I want that one."

Her mother came to stand behind her. "Ooh, he's a pretty one," she said, then looked at the assistant. "Would we have to do anything to him?"

The assistant seemed confused. "Do. . ?"

"You know: wash him, clean him, that type of thing."

Lisa rolled her eyes. Trust her mother to ask something embarrassing like that.

The assistant, though, took it in his stride, saying, "No, ma'am. Just a little dusting here and there, now and then, should be just fine."

"That's lovely," Lisa's mother replied. "I *like* dusting." She glanced over at her husband. "Amongst other things."

"Yes. Quite." The assistant smiled at Lisa. "Have you made up your mind?"

She laid a hand on the cold, dead arm of her choice. "Yes."

So they made the transaction.

And Lisa took home her very own My Dead Celebrity.

They were the sole topic of conversation when she returned to school the next week.

"Mine died in a fire," Nick Gunderson said. "He's all burnt and crinkly and everything."

Lisa frowned. "Aren't they supposed to make them up to look attractive?"

"Yeah, but I wanted mine to be more authentic – so I put his face in the fire for a bit when I got him home."

"I never thought of doing that to mine," Dave Walsh said.

"What'd yours die of?" Nick asked.

"Car crash."

"Big deal," Sandra Cross chipped in. "Mine was stabbed by one of his mistresses." She paused before adding the most impressive thing of all: "and for an extra couple of hundred, they let me buy the knife that killed him."

"Wow," Lisa said.

Then Dave nudged her, saying, "bet I know who *doesn't* have one . . ."

They all looked up at that.

Saw the shambolic form of Blinky Collins coming toward
      them.

"Hey, Blinky," Lisa said. "Got a pen you can lend me?"

He stopped. "So, so funny, Higgins. You didn't have a pen once. I offered to lend you one. And you're still making jokes about it, what?" He pretended to check the time on his watch. "Two years later? Really hilarious. Not ridiculous at all."

Sandra rolled her eyes. "Oh my God, he's swallowed a whole bunch of words again . . ."

"Equally hilarious, Sandra," Blinky said, then walked on past them.

They watched him go.

"Geek," Dave said.

"Bet he really *hasn't* got a My Dead Celebrity," Nick added; "Those weird parents of his."

Then all eyes turned back to Sandra, her friends remembering her earlier words.

"Can we see that knife?" Lisa asked. "Later on, I mean?"

"Why wait?" she asked, and that was when she pulled the knife from her inner coat pocket.

"That's awesome," Lisa said. "You can still see some of the blood on it."

And she went to take the weapon from her friend.

Which was, of course, when a passing teacher saw what was happening and decided to sentence them both to detention.

Detentions here were boring – the teachers made you hand over your mobile phone and personal organiser and social networking devices and all the other wonders of technology that no teenager could be without. Today, though, Lisa was fine with making conversation . . . something she did in hushed tones with Sandra.

"What's your called?" she asked.

"Teddy."

Something about the name and the fact she had said that her celebrity was stabbed rang a bell in Lisa's mind, and she said, "Teddy Barrington?"

"That's him."

"The actor?"

"Yep."

"Cool."

"What about yours?"

"Frank," she said, and the name made her proud. Made her eager to see him.

But detention dragged on and on and even talking about their new best friends could not make time speed up.

Then finally it was over, and Lisa raced home.

But when she got there, something was wrong.

"Mother," she said as she entered the main room, "have you moved him today?"

Busy with her furniture polish and duster, her mother replied, "Moved who, dear?"

"Frank."

"Frank, dear?"

"My Dead Celebrity, mother," Lisa said. "The one Dad bought me last week. Remember?"

"Oh yes," her mother said. "Him."

Then carried on dusting.

"Well, did you?"

"Did I what, dear?"

"Move Frank!"

"Oh. Yes." Her mother put the duster down, looked at Lisa. "Just for a few minutes."

"Why?"

"Just to dust the wall behind where he stands."

Which, Lisa supposed, was fair enough. They had given the stuffed star pride of place in their main room; he not only dominated *inside* the house, but you could look in from outside and see him, too. That had actually been her father's idea – like he said, "I spent enough on it, I want *everyone* to see it."

Lisa had agreed, at the time. Now, however, though she wanted everyone to *hear* about Frank, her Frank, she didn't really want them to *see* him.

Or touch him.

Like her mother had done earlier.

Lisa watched the older woman.

She had heard her parents.

She knew what they got up to when they hoped she was asleep.

So who was to say that all her mother had done was *move* Frank?

What if she had run her hand along his chest?

Placed her lips against his cheek?

Told him how much she loved the songs he had recorded when he was alive?

As Lisa wondered this – as images she did not want to see ran through her mind – her mother looked at her.

"Something wrong, dear?" she asked.

Lisa looked back at Frank.

"No," she said. "Everything's just fine."

Elsewhere in town, Blinky Collins was just arriving at his home.

A home that – just as predicted by Dave Walsh and Nick Gunderson – did not have its own My Dead Celebrity.

He could have asked for one, of course, and having heard how much everyone else at school had been talking about theirs, he certainly wanted to. But there was no point. He knew what his parents would say.

Still, he was a sucker for punishment, so he went right ahead and asked.

"Dad," he said, "can I get a My Dead Celebrity?"

His father looked at him over the top of a book – never an entertainment gossip magazine, like the parents of other kids read, but always a book – and replied, "Get a what?"

Luckily, there was an advert playing on the TV that very moment. So Blinky just pointed and said, "One of those."

"Heavens, Brandon," his dad said. "Why would you want one of those?"

It took him by surprise, being called by his real name, just like it always did. This house was pretty much the only place he ever heard it. Even the teachers sometimes accidentally called him by his unwanted nickname – an event that was always met with sniggers by Lisa Higgins and her chums.

Entering the main room from the kitchen, his mother provided the answer to the question just posed by his father. "Don't tell me," she said. "Because everyone else has one. Am I right?"

"Well, yeah," he replied. "Mom, why do you always make that sound like it's such a bad thing?"

He knew the answer, though. His parents were weird, they were different. They liked books more than TV and they wrote online essays and reviews of poetry and theatre instead of using social networking sites. How they'd produced someone as desperate to fit in as Blinky was a mystery to all concerned, but he knew they loved him, and they, in turn, hoped he would grow out of his need to conform.

But they would not give in to his demands today.

So he remained without a My Dead Celebrity of his very own.

Which meant that the other kids would continue to laugh at him – Sandra Cross would say, "Which one *you* got, Blinky?" and they would then all collapse in fits of hysterics. And Lisa Higgins would make the gag about him offering to lend her a pen again, even though he was pretty sure that if Nick Gunderson or Dave Walsh or pretty much anyone else had made the same offer it would have been all right. That was just the way things were for him – he had some mark that classed him as "different" and nothing he did would ever be seen as normal. Same with the "Blinky" thing – he was pretty sure that Dave blinked a hell of a lot more than he did, being too vain to wear glasses or contact lenses. But Dave was normal. He was "in." He had no nickname that defined him. That destroyed him.

But still Blinky tried to fit in. He still carried around a spare pen inside his pocket, in the hope that someone would accept his offer to use it. But like Lisa, no one ever did. And each new failure to belong, every time someone laughed at him or did not call him by his real name, was like a fresh new dagger in his heart.

These were the troubled thoughts of Blinky Collins as he logged onto the Internet that night.

Unlike his parents, he *did* do the social networking thing.

But no one ever accepted his friend requests.

So he found something else to search for online.

And had an idea that would change everything.

Friday night came.

The end of another week and Lisa was sleeping over at Sandra Cross's house.

A whole bunch of the girls were.

But it was no ordinary get-together.

They all had their new best friends with them.

And they were all watching the TV.

As with most new crazes that swept the nation, The Church were quick to condemn the success of the My Dead Celebrity scheme, though whether this was a serious protest or just another desperate attempt to appear relevant was uncertain. Whatever the reasoning behind it, though, a priest was appearing on a popular debate show, and the man facing off against him was Gilbert Simmons, the man immortalised by an advert jingle, the man who had invented the concept that had put a corpse in nearly every house in the country.

The host of the debate, a well-known enough sort who had already made a pact with Simmons about his own dead body, kicked things off by asking the priest, "what are your concerns about My Dead Celebrity being such a hit?"

"They make a mockery of death!"

Gilbert Simmons sighed. "You people are always trying to control what people do with their bodies when they're alive – is it *really* any surprise you're trying to do the same when they're dead?"

This got a laugh from the studio audience. Most of who were seated beside their own Dead Celebrities.

Trying to ignore the fact that the dice were loaded rather heavily against him, the priest said, "You can talk big with your scripted lines, Mr Simmons. But not everyone is a fan of what you're doing. Numerous members of my parish have signed a petition against your work."

"Oh, members of your parish don't like My Dead Celebrity, do they not?" Simmons grinned, playing to the audience. "A bit hypocritical, don't you think?"

"Hypocritical?" the priest replied.

Simmons shrugged. "Aren't their houses filled with pictures of a guy who's been dead for at least a couple of *thousand* years?"

Which, naturally, got the biggest laugh of all from the audience.

Even the host struggled to contain his smile.

The priest shook his head. "You have no shame at all, Mr Simmons."

"Hey," Simmons replied, deciding to get serious for a minute, "I'm just giving the public what they want. Everyone loves their movie, TV, music, reality stars, but they can't get close to them in life. So what's so wrong with letting the fans get close to their heroes when those heroes pass on?"

"Indeed," the host said, chipping in. "Playing devil's advocate –"

"You certainly are," Simmons interrupted.

"Playing devil's advocate, however, it must be said that the . . . star quality, shall we say, of some of your range has dropped since the line was launched. Dead actors have become dead people who once cleaned an actor's swimming pool."

"Hey, culture was heading that way *long* before I arrived," Simmons protested. "Besides, you know how hard it is to keep coming up with corpses when the demand is so high?"

"Why don't you start killing them yourself?" the priest offered. "You're breaking just about every other Commandment already."

"Half of me thinks that's slander," Simmons replied. "The other half thinks you sound like one hell of an ideas man." He winked at the priest. "Want a new job?"

"Really?" the priest said, suddenly bright-eyed.

Lisa and the girls missed the end of this exchange, however.

They were all asleep by then, curled up in the dead, stiff arms of the new loves of their lives.

Child-free for the night, Lisa's mother and father were indulging in some fun.

But he sensed that her heart was elsewhere.

"What's wrong?" he asked.

"Oh, I don't know," she said. "It just feels a little . . . strange without Frank in the house."

He knew what she meant. Ever since Lisa's new pet had entered the house, a fresh burst of energy had seemed to revitalise them all. With no celebrity here now, though, things seemed dull and static.

"Well," he replied, "I was going to surprise you with it, but . . ."

Then he stood and left the bedroom.

Unlocked his office and entered it.

And returned a few seconds later with . . .

"Oh, darling," she said. "My favourite!"

"Yep – Arnold Ralph Anderson. I know you've always loved his movies, and they just found him dead last week." He presented the corpse to her. "Happy Anniversary!"

"Oh, he's just beautiful. Thank you."

Then the glint appeared in her eyes.

One her husband recognised well.

"Let's put him on the bed," she said. "And make love on top of him."

Which Lisa's father thought was a great idea.

So they did it.

Sunday morning.

The manager of the mall watched the limo pull up: watched two people emerge from the back, the other one a glamorous but rather dead-eyed woman, the other a huge, beast of a man with legs like stilts on steroids and grizzly facial hair.

"Hello, Rita," the manager said. "It's an honour to have you in our small town."

Rita Rogers looked around. "The place looks a bit deserted. What's going on? I thought you said there'd be lines queuing up before I got here."

"Ah, yes . . . well, people are slow to rise today," he told her. "But they'll be here. Honestly."

"They better be," she said, and sauntered past him and into the mall.

"Yeah," the huge man reiterated. "They'd better be."

The manager was starting to get a pretty bad feeling about the way things would turn out today.

He had no idea.

Somewhere else in town, business was booming.

Every single seat in the cinema was taken up – though not all by the living.

Down in the front row, Sandra Cross pointed up at the screen and said, "Look, Teddy – that's *you* up there!"

And it was.

In the back, the manager of the cinema was pontificating at length about the depth of his genius to an off-duty usher.

"The best idea I've ever had," he was saying. "You know how many of those little pipsqueaks bought dead actors and actresses to be their best friends? Hundreds! And you know what I did?"

The usher did indeed. He, and everyone else that worked here, and probably every single person the manager had met in the last few weeks, had heard this all before.

"I got a list of all the names from a source at the mall," he went on, "And got the rights to show the entire backlist of each and every one!"

The usher stood. "Ah, I'm due back on now, boss . . ."

"Sit down, sit down – someone else can cover for you. I'm not done telling you how smart I am yet."

Sitting, sighing, the usher wondered if his pay – *any* pay – was worth this.

The manager of the mall was looking out over all that he surveyed.

His assistant had joined him.

"Kind of quiet today, boss."

"Yeah. No one's interested in celebrities today." The manager sighed. "Not living ones at least."

He looked down at the record store.

Rita Rogers, country music/pop crossover star, was supposed to be signing copies of her newest album today. Booked long before the My Dead Celebrity craze had swept the nation, she was now looking very bored, whilst her huge security guard was looking very angry.

"Going to end badly, boss," the assistant commented.

"You're telling me. Don't even ask how much I'm paying her to sit there looking bored."

The manager started mentally compiling his last will and testament.

But then saw something.

Who was this single, solitary figure walking through the store towards the singer?

"Knew they'd all want to come see their heroes in action," the manager of the cinema went on, much to the usher's displeasure and disappointment. "Knew they'd all want to bring their dead heroes with them. But dead or alive, breathing or not, if you take up a seat, you're going to pay for it."

The manager laughed.

"So they buy a seat for themselves, then another one for their dead buddy!"

He wiped a tear from his eye.

"Man, I just love this world we're in . . ."

Back at the mall, Rita Rogers was saying, "I have a twin sister, you know."

The bodyguard replied, "So?"

"So I was just thinking, I could have her killed, pretend the body is mine, sell it as a My Dead Celebrity and pocket the money."

She surveyed the empty record store.

"Beats doing *this* for a living . . ."

That was when someone entered the store.

 Stood before her.

"Signing, sugar?" Rita asked.

The figure nodded.

"Pen," Rita said to the bodyguard.

"Don't worry," the figure said. "I brought my own."

And Blinky Collins rammed his pen into the singer's throat.

"Oh my God," Lisa said, walking around the back of the gym area, "have you heard the news? I –"

Then she stopped.

When she saw that Sandra was cutting Teddy Barrington's hair. Using the knife that had killed him to trim the corpse's locks.

"They let you bring your guy to school?" Lisa asked.

"They had to," Sandra said. "Told the teachers I couldn't work without him being nearby."

"Damn," Lisa said. "Wish I'd thought of that."

Sandra looked up at her. "It's true. I don't like leaving him at home."

Lisa sat down across from her. "Yeah, I know what you mean."

Sandra raised an eyebrow. "Do you?"

Actually she did, or she was starting to, at least. Although her mother now had her own My Dead Celebrity, Lisa was still plagued by images of the older woman trying it on with Frank, her Frank. All that time alone with such a sex-god . . . who *wouldn't* have inappropriate thoughts about him?

Not inappropriate because he was dead, of course.

Inappropriate because he was *Lisa's* property.

Putting the knife away, Sandra said, "What's up?"

"Oh," Lisa replied, getting back on track, "just coming to tell you the news."

"The news?"

"Yeah," Lisa said. "We got another My Dead Celebrity. Dad bought my mother it for her anniversary."

"Wow," Sandra said. "Your family is so cool."

Lisa was pleased to hear envy in her friend's voice.

"Oh yeah," Lisa said, "and Blinky Collins killed someone."

It had all come to a head the night he had asked his parents for a My Dead Celebrity.

All the years of mockery and name-calling, all the laughter and torment, the faces of Lisa and Dave and Sandra and Nick floating around him infecting the ether of his room and he had finally had enough and when he had logged online and saw that Rita Rogers was coming to town to do an album signing it had all bubbled over and seeped out and he had decided to make a famous corpse all of his own.

To show them all.

To teach them.

Looking back, maybe he had gone temporarily insane. He supposed he must have done, for the thought of what he would do next, when the murder was committed, had never actually occurred to him.

Now he was on the run.

But before he disappeared, he had to face his tormentors one last time.

So Blinky Collins reached for the phone.

Ah, Lisa's father thought, lying back on the bed, is this not the life?

His wife may have been a dusting obsessive during the day, but at night she was transformed.

Especially since he'd bought her Arnold.

They now didn't – couldn't – have sex without him being in the room, and Lisa's dad was fine with that. Nothing wrong with a little fantasy, and besides, did he really have anything to fear from a dead man?

She was using him now to pleasure herself, sticking dead fingers up inside herself and moaning softly.

Whilst he watched.

It was like a whole different kind of porn.

That was when the phone rang.

"Lisa," he shouted, "get that will you, honey?"

"I'm busy!" she called back from her room.

He was sure she was . . . hanging out with Frank, her new best friend. Normally he'd hate to interrupt that, knowing how important it was to his girl, but the wife-and-Arnold show was just starting to get interesting as they both lost their clothes, her tearing at his garments with her teeth.

"I'll buy you some new accessories for Frank if you do!"

"Okay, daddy!"

He knew his daughter oh so well.

They had raised her that way.

"Come here," he said to his wife.

She did.

And Arnold, he came, too.

Lisa recognised the voice on the other end of the phone, but she was surprised all the same.

"Blinky?" she said.

"That's right."

"The police are looking for you."

"Yeah. Must be in all the wrong places, because here I am."

Lisa recoiled a little.

Had this little twerp just been *witty* with her?

She was sure he had.

Trying to reassert her natural control over him, she said, "so why are you calling me, loser?"

"I want to see you."

Lisa almost gagged.

Was Blinky Collins coming onto her?

"All of you," he said. "You and those three clever friends of yours."

Then he gave her a location.

"What makes you think I won't bring the cops?" she asked, when he was done.

"You won't," he replied. "But I know what you *will* bring."

Then he hung up.

Lisa looked into her room.

At Frank.

"We're going out," she told him.

And then she called Sandra.

It had become so common to see teenagers lugging around dead bodies that nobody batted an eyelid as a bunch of them headed onto a dusty, dirty field.

Some sort of weird get-together, they assumed.

"Look," Blinky said, waiting for them in the middle of that field. "Knew you'd all bring your new toys."

"They're not our toys," Lisa told him.

"They're our friends," Nick Gunderson added.

"Our heroes," Sandra concluded.

"Heroes?" Blinky said. "Why?"

The teens all looked at each other.

"Well . . ."Dave Walsh began.

"Because they've all been on TV," Lisa finished.

"Right." Blinky was nodding his head. "And that's all that's needed, right?"

"Where are you going with this?" Sandra asked.

"Apart from straight to prison," Nick added. Normally this one-liner would have had them all howling at Blinky's expense, but the tension of the situation had robbed the teens of what little sense of humour they possessed, and his witticism went unrewarded.

"Right," Lisa said, looking at Blinky. "And why did you call me?"

"I had to," he replied. "I wanted this one last chance to show you how deluded you all are."

"Um, excuse me," Sandra said, "but wasn't it *you* that just killed someone?"

Which kind of shut Blinky up for a second.

Because he *had*, after all, committed murder.

"I still can't believe you got away with that," Dave said, one arm around his My Dead Celebrity. "Didn't she have a bodyguard or something?"

"Yeah." Blinky waved the question away. "He was a roid-head. Slow and stupid. By the time he got moving I was out of there."

"Freak," Lisa said.

"You're standing there with your arm around a corpse and you call *me* the freak?"

"We're *all* standing with our arms around corpses," Sandra pointed out.

"Yeah, but *famous* corpses," Nick insisted. "Nothing weird about it if they're famous."

Again, his words were ignored by all.

"Right," Blinky countered. "And when you *all* do something, it's cool, isn't it? It's normal."

"Exactly," Dave said.

But now it was *his* turn to be ignored, as Blinky just kept on going. Gushing out words that had been building and festering inside of him for years.

"This year it's dead celebrities," he said. "Last year it was putting funny colours in your hair. Before that, wearing your jeans down low. Next year – if there is a next year – the TV will tell you all to do something else to be fashionable."

"What do you mean?" Sandra asked. "If there's a next year?"

"Look at yourself," he said. "You're all hanging around with corpses. You really think you can go back to normal after that?"

"Famous corpses," Lisa put in. "That makes all the difference."

"Hey," Nick protested, "that's what *I* just said."

But no one was listening.

100

Least of all Blinky.

He was vanishing somewhere deep inside of himself, realising he was just as guilty of following fads as these four were. Only trouble was, the clothes had never looked right on him, or he'd bought them – bought them himself, with money he'd saved up, as his parents wouldn't fund his fad-following ways – just that little bit too late. But his parents had been right. It had taken killing someone and then going on to the run to prove it, but they had been right. He *shouldn't* have tried to fit in. He should have just been his own person. And now he was suffering the consequences.

But then a thought occurred to him.

"What do you guys think would happen," he said, "if I turned myself in?"

"We wouldn't have to see your ugly face in the school hall anymore," Sandra replied, and high-fived Teddy standing next to her.

But Lisa shushed her.

Sensing that Blinky's next words would be ones that she needed to hear.

"I think I'm a pretty interesting guy," he went on. "Wish I'd seen that sooner, but there you go, that's life."

"Interesting?" Dave said. "How?"

Blinky shrugged. "Pretty interesting parents, pretty unconventional upbringing. Plus, you know, I *did* kill someone."

He smiled.

"I used my pen to do it."

His eyes met Lisa's.

"Remember that pen, Higgins?" he said. "Remember how I offered to let you use it, and you just laughed in my face?"

He came closer to her.

She had to struggle not to flinch.

All her friends here with her, the mighty Frank at her side, and still she felt his words infecting her.

"How do you think it'll make *you* look, when I tell that story?"

"They'll still hate what I did to that singer," he said. "They'll still know I'm a killer."

He looked around them all.

Feeling, for the first time in his painful life, something close to victory.

"But don't you think they'll feel a little bit of sympathy for me when they hear how you guys have treated me?"

They looked around each other nervously.

All except Lisa.

She had eyes only for Blinky.

And behind those eyes, her mind was racing.

Filling with images of Blinky being a star. Blinky being a hero.

As if aware of her thoughts, he said, "I could be a hero to all the other little Blinky Collins's out there, getting them all to stand up against the likes of you."

That was when she lost it.

The thought of someone like this getting famous – *being* famous the way Frank and Teddy and all the other My Dead Celebrities out there were – was just too much for her.

So she leapt at Sandra and grabbed from her the knife that had killed Teddy and rammed it into Blinky's chest.

Then watched him fall and spoke just one word.

"Loser."

Whilst from the other side of the field, unseen eyes watched.

It was early morning by the time Lisa got back home – it had taken a while to grab shovels from Dave's house and then bury the body, and as gorgeous as they were, four Dead Celebrities weren't much help when it came to digging.

So they'd had to do it themselves.

Dave, Nick, Sandra and her.

Then they'd sworn a pact with each other.

The call from Blinky had never happened.

They had never seen him.

A freak like him would never become famous.

But this endeavour had left her tired.

Oh so very tired.

So tired that when she hit the floor, she thought she had just passed out.

But then she looked up.

Saw her mother standing over her.

The woman was completely naked.

A savage look on her face.

"Whore," her mother said. "Little whore."

"What?"

"Don't try to deny it, bitch. He told me. He told me what you've done."

"What are you talking about?"

"You've been sleeping with my Arnold, haven't you?"

"What? You think I'd touch *that* old guy?"

"Don't you dare insult him!" her mother said, and went to stamp down on her face.

But Lisa grabbed her ankle.

Pulled it down toward her mouth.

And sunk her teeth into the flesh.

Teeth bared, mouth bloody, she looked up at her mother.

And realised something.

She was sure somehow she could taste Frank on her flesh.

She knew the old bitch had been messing around with him!

"Slut!" she shouted.

And then her mother fell on her, and they kicked and scratched and bit and tore at each other, ripping flesh, spilling blood, and then Lisa was on top and smashing the back of her mother's head against the floor again and again and then she was screeching, "Who told you that? Who told you I'd even *dare* touch something as old as him!" She slammed again. "Tell me." And again. "Tell me. I'll *murder* the cunt!"

"Why, *he* told me, dear," her mother said, and pointed.

Lisa looked.

But too late she sensed the trap.

And before she could see a thing, her mother had rammed fingers deep into her eyes and gouged them out.

"No!" Lisa cried. "I can't see him! Frank! Where are you, Frank? Help me please!"

Then as her mother coughed and spluttered and kissed goodbye to life she felt a strange presence behind her.

"Nice show at the field before," it said.

And then she heard no more.

"Pretty brutal."

"I'll say. But, you know, I think that Collins boy was right – murder *can* make a person famous.

"And matriarchal two-way murder?"

Gilbert Simmons looked down at the two battered bodies.

"I think these two will fetch a pretty high price in the showroom."

"Shouldn't we at least try to clean them up a little before the father gets home?"

"Are you kidding? The more freaked out he is, the less of a cut he'll want."

"I . . . I still don't know what I'm doing here."

Simmons sighed. "You're doing the new job I hired you for. At least that's what you're *supposed* to be doing. Now go and stand watch by the window and let me know when he pulls into the driveway."

His assistant – who had once opposed him on a TV show – did so.

"We shouldn't have let that boy die, Mr Simmons," he said.

Simmons rolled his eyes. "Come on. Be reasonable. We weren't to know she'd wind up killing him."

But he was grinning as he said it.

His back to his assistant.

"So how did you know to come here just in time for all of this to happen?"

"Market research," Simmons said. "Was here to investigate some recent successes of my business line." Hiding his smile, he looked back at his assistant. "It always pays to know your customers."

Silence descended for a few seconds.

The only sound the dripping of blood.

Then the assistant asked, "was it you?"

"Was what me?"

"She said someone told her that her daughter had been sleeping with her My Dead Celebrity. Was that even true?"

"How would I know?"

"So it wasn't you that told her?"

Simmons looked again at the bodies.

"It wasn't you that made this happen?"

And inside his suit, beneath the skin he wore, the thing that called itself Gilbert Simmons just laughed and laughed and laughed.

"Vagina Woman"
Dead Zoe zero

Blood Soaked

Jason Hughes

POLICE LINE – DO NOT CROSS tape was stretched across the perimeter of the old house on Sixth and Austin Street. The paramedics showed up quickly to the scene. Deputy Rogers and Sheriff Milford inspected the backyard and questioned the neighbors outside that gathered on the street for the macabre spectacle.

"Well, usually it would be my professional duty to tell you guys this type of thing, but they're both dead as you can obviously see," the Coroner, Jeff Talley, said as he looked at the decapitated bodies of Jennifer and Maxwell Parton. Both were lying on their crimson drenched mattress. Their half-mummified heads were impaled on the large posts at the head of the wooden bedframe. Maxwell's hand and Jennifer's foot were nowhere to be found. "They've been dead for a while," Jeff said as he glared at the heart that was scrawled in coagulated blood on the wall overlooking the room. "Jesus . . . *Christ*," Deputy Rogers said as he walked into the fly infested room. He gagged from the stench that consumed the small space. "Do you think this is a crime of passion?" he asked after a drawn out inhale.

"If that *is* the case, there was no passion for these two, I can tell you that much," Jeff replied. Sheriff Milford walked in behind them as he put a small notepad in his pocket. The neighbors didn't see or hear a thing. There are no signs of forced entry. Nothing is missing or out of place. No signs of a struggle as far as I can see," he said as he looked around the room in extreme disgust.

"By the looks of it, there was no time to struggle. The lividity is so bad on them, I don't know if I'll be able to find a primary C.o.D, unless a bullet is lodged somewhere under this mess," Jeff stated.

"You seriously have no compassion for your clients, do you?" Deputy Rogers asked in a dead serious tone.

"I've been doing this for two decades now. It may be a little unethical to some, but I have to find a little bit of humor in my job," Jeff replied.

"Even if the humor you choose to use is jet black?" Deputy Rogers inquired.

"I like to think of it as more a Hertz black humor. Get it . . . *Hertz* black?" Jeff said with a chuckle.

"You can be pretty sickening sometimes. Deputy, call in Forensics to do a three-sixty of the room in Luminol for saliva, finger prints and anything else you can possibly find," Sheriff Milford said as he left the room.

"Yes, Sir, I'm . . . on it," Deputy Rogers replied as he looked over to the empty doorway. A few seconds later, Sheriff Milford could be heard in the bathroom down the hall. He was gagging and regurgitating the lasagna casserole that he had for lunch into the toilet. "He isn't supposed to touch anything at a crime scene. I hope he uses something to cover his hands while flushing the toilet," Jeff said. Deputy Rogers shook his head as he waited for someone at *Elite Forensics* to answer the phone.

The forensics team showed up shortly and covered the room. The paramedics waited patiently to load what was left of couple into the black body bags and ship them to the morgue for the inevitable autopsy that would soon follow. "We could have a serial killer on our hands. This doesn't seem like a normal home invasion," Deputy Rogers informed Sheriff Milford as he reentered the room.

"That's what I'm afraid of. I was thinking the same thing," Sheriff Milford replied.

Dax Anderson met Delilah Edwards at a bondage club on the east side of New Orleans, Louisiana. They knew from the first night they laid eyes on each other that they were made for each other. They had blindfolded, tied up sex with whips and chains on the first date.

Dax was a twenty - six year old aspiring film maker at The University of New Orleans, Louisiana. Deep in the heart of voodoo and the United States' most haunted city. There were hauntings recorded and documented all over this state. St. Francisville was home to one of the most haunted plantations and motels in the United States. It had a share of curious visitors on a regular basis, had been on television shows and was a couple-only stay. Dax and Delilah had stayed there quite a few times. It gave them a rush to know they were not alone in the mortal world.

Delilah was twenty - three years old and unlike Dax, she did not believe in God, holy ghosts, holy spirits or anything of the sort. She was raised on religion by her family. She had attended a private catholic school for girls, where she was molested by the head priest her senior year. This diminished all of her faith in God and his followers. Soon, her mother followed the same path of deception in the Catholic beliefs right after Delilah told her of the molestation. She did not inform her until thirteen years later. She and her mother were very close.

Dax and Delilah got along great for the first few years. The situation began to grow very different. They were still together, but had a strong love for hating each other. Delilah beat Dax to a pile of blood and bruises on a regular basis. Dax would never hit a woman. He did not swing back, nor raise a finger. He just blocked himself. Dax verbally and most of all mentally abused Delilah, and his spewing words caused as much pain as her contacting knuckles. He brought her to tears as she beat him half to death. She also criticized him for believing in his so called "God," that she had been battered and abused by in the past. She had no faith and was out to destroy what faith he held . . . and embraced so dearly. Although he believed in this God, he was shallow and did not follow the hollow hallway of commandments he was given to reach the light. Not a single one. He was and forever remained Christian and soulless to the core.

Dax killed his parents when he was sixteen, two years before he met Delilah. No one knew who committed the heinous act, but Dax himself. After he cut their throats in their sleep, dragged them out of bed and committed the rest of the act on the bedroom floor. He left his mother headless in the hallway corner, cut into ten pieces. His father was on the kitchen floor. There was a trail of blood leading into the bathroom. No one knew what was behind that door. It was closed . . . and locked. He stole all of their money and drove across the country in his father's truck, from New Hampshire to Texas, to California, to Maine and back to New Hampshire. While on a detour to New Orleans, he met Delilah. They had been together since. He had cheated on her several times. Sometimes, he was very honest about it, more honest than she would have liked him to have been. She flew into fits of violent rage over this. On one occasion, she held a heating iron to his face and burned a huge, pus filled, red, purple and white, blistering whelp into his cheek. She once found one of his cold lovers in bed with him. She saw red, as her emotions, along with her heart faded to black.

They had been into and on drugs most of their lives. It started out with marijuana, LSD and Heroin soon became their drug of choice. They eventually cut back on the LSD. They just stuck to Heroin and occasional joint. They injected the needle on a daily basis. It mostly caused them to stay awake for days and sometimes weeks on end. They would hallucinate while they were wide awake. This sometimes set of LSD flashbacks and made them even more delusional and crazy. Not to mention violent, among themselves and others around them. Sometimes even within a good distance from them, miles. The whole city knew who they were, yet didn't have a clue. The population had seen what the couple had done when they are together for a night on the town, but had never laid eyes upon them. This was the way they wanted it. It had to be this way, for their nightlife to continue. Delilah mostly slept during the day and had a nocturnal relationship with the moon and stars. Dax had college and worked at the local movie theater to make ends meet. He had been there for six years now and was the manager of the theater. He made his own schedule. He usually worked in the morning then would go to school and go out, with very little sleep or none at all.

Delilah's birth given name was previously Dahlia. Her religious upbringing drove her in the opposite direction as she began to reach blooming adulthood. She always liked the name Dahlia, but wanted to rebel. She knew who Delilah was in the bible from having it drilled into her head for quite some time growing up in her household. The name meant something to her . . . rebellion and freedom. Dahlia was a strictly raised servant of the lord and Delilah wanted that part of her dead forever. She still loved and respected her mother, but wanted nothing to do with a religion that once abandoned her faith in a most horrible manner. She wanted all past memories of what seemed like a false hope to fade away. Even driving by a church or sign of praise would make her stomach turn. The unspoken voice in her head would curse the foundation as she passed. She knew this upset Dax, so she tried to hold in the retribution.

Dax and Delilah were sitting on the couch. They were watching a film project Dax had put together a few months before he started college. The movie was on a blank VHS cassette with no label, title or credits. Necrophilia turned them both on quite often. They sometimes made their own porn while watching this film or others on the taboo subject of post-mortem sexual intercourse. They inter-locked their arms at the elbows like they were getting ready to walk down the aisle. They wrapped their arms around each other's as a tightly bonded tourniquet and injected each other with a sharp, dirty needle, containing their shared stimulate of choice, heroin. This was some of the quality time that they spent together. They lied there for a moment. Delilah got up and disappeared into the bedroom. Dax could hear her from the living room as he watched television. In some ways, it added to the viewing experience. They had a date that night, and needed to get ready for a night on the town.

"Get in here! Bring the shit for tonight!" Dax yelled to Delilah as she touched herself in the bedroom. She was pleasuring herself after shooting up with Dax. Sometimes, he did not get her off in the way that she could herself. She heard his demand and got dressed. She got out of bed and kicked her ex-boss' severed head out of the way. She opened a dresser drawer and grabbed handcuffs, blindfolds, a couple of ropes and a knife. She walked into the living room with Dax. He pointed the video camera at her. "You ready?" he asked in a dead tone. She nodded her agreement. The two gathered their belongings, got into their car and drove off into the darkness.

They pulled into a local bar, called *The Final Resort*. They exited Dax's car and walked up to the bar. The slogan on the outside sign, under the bar's name read *YOUR FINAL DESTINATION FOR the NIGHT*. Some should have taken this as a warning and not a warm, friendly welcome.

Dax and Delilah walked into the bar and looked around. Many pool players and bar flies glanced at them. Some of the men's eyes were on Delilah. Meanwhile, Dax's eyes were on their wives and girlfriends . . . and so was his mind. Dax sat down at the bar and ordered a drink. Delilah looked over at the pool area and saw a couple playing pool. She looked at Dax with a seductive smirk of obscure malevolence. "I'm going to make some new friends," she proclaimed with a slightly devious smile.

"Take your time," he replied as he glared at the bartender, twenty- year old, Trishelle Davis. "So, do you come here often?" She gave him a strange look and proceeded to ignore him.

Delilah walked over to the pool area and up to a random couple. She strutted straight up to twenty - three year old, Mindy Lindsay like another male, fixing to take her away. "Hey, what are you guys up to?" she asked.

"Nothing, just hanging out and playing some pool," Mindy replied.

"Haven't I seen you somewhere before?" her twenty - seven year old boyfriend, Scott Taylor stated.

"Probably not, hi, I'm Cassie," she said with a smile. She reached out her hand to the both of them for a friendly introduction shake," Delilah replied.

"Hi, Cassie. I'm Scott and this is my girlfriend, Mindy," Scott said as he glanced over at Mindy.

Delilah repeated, "Minnnndyyyyy," in a playful tone. She looked Mindy up and down slowly with a smile that could melt through steel. Dax walked up behind her. "Delilah, are you ready?"

"I thought you said your name was Cassie?" Mindy asked in confusion.

"It is, Cassie is my middle name, I sometimes go by that," Delilah replied. She looked at Dax and continued. "And this is my boyfriend, Victor. Hey, we were thinking about hanging around somewhere else. Why don't you guys join us . . . what do you say?" Dax smiled as Scott and Mindy looked at each other. As they were leaving the bar, the television news reporter said, "Escaped convict and serial killer, Gordon Drake, may be in this area. Police say two bodies were found headless, matching his M. O." Dax and Delilah looked at each other and smirked as they exited.

They went back to Dax and Delilah's house to have their favorite poison. Their drink of choice for guests was J. D. on the rocks. The drink was mixed with Dax's favorite poison, cyanide, straight up. It was a cocktail of deadly proportions. Cyanide could usually be detected if one would take a whiff. It smelled like burning or toasted almonds, but they could not smell a thing. The liquor drowned out the fatal stench. The thirst for liquor drowned out the caution and awareness that they once had. Dax only put enough to make Mindy sick. Not to kill her. He had other plans. Mindy was knocked out cold.

Mindy eventually opened her eyes. She was very dreary and unaware of where she was. She looked around and started to scream. She choked and vomited as she gasped and shrieked for help. Scott was tied up right next to her, but could not hear her. He was already dead. She looked over and noticed that not only was he dead . . . he was gutted. His throat had also been cut from ear to ear and he had a hammer sticking into and protruding from his damaged skull. She began to feel a sharp pain. She looked down and blood was pouring all around her. Some of the fingers on her left hand had been cut off. One of her toes was also missing. She was growing weaker by the minute. Delilah walked up to her and started to lick on her face. Dax came up with a razor blade. He put it to his own arm and cut all the way down, applying little pressure. At this point, Mindy could barely scream. She was almost obscured into the afterlife. Dax untied her and laid her in her ex-boyfriend's blood. She tried to speak. "Why are you . . . ?" she uttered, but could squeeze but three words from her mouth. She was vomiting and bleeding her life away right before her own eyes and her boyfriend's decaying body. Dax turned on the video camera and aimed it at here with a smile. "Please, can I go home?! I just want to go home!" she incoherently slurred in tears. Dax just kept smiling and proceeded to undress her as Mindy's life drained, along with her tears, blood and bodily waste. As Mindy had become a motionless memory of humanity, Dax inserted himself deep into her lifeless shell. She could no longer scream. She could no longer move. She was no longer breathing. She was no longer alive.

Delilah caught him in the middle of his act of infidelity with the dying victim. This upset her, even though she was not fully satisfied by him on some nights. She saw this as cheating. She knew he would always do it. She decided to get her another partner of the living persuasion. She was very good at the subtle art of luring persuasion. That was half of the game she played on Dax, as he played her.

Dax was never faithful to anyone to begin with. His ex-girlfriend before Delilah, Jaime Norway, was his third victim. She caught him cheating on her with her best friend, Rachael Blackwell, which was Dax's fourth unlucky encounter after the affair. In his own mind, Rachael was a witness to a murder that he committed, naked and in front of her. She had to be eliminated.

Delilah sometimes wondered how someone who believed in a higher power could do the things he had done. In Dax's mind, God was forgiving and he knew that because he believed, he would have a secure place beyond the golden gates of Heaven, even if he *had* broken just about every commandment in the "good book." The two somehow meshed well together. They had their moments, as any other relationship or couple, but they somehow looked past the minor turmoil as their eyes connect. Still, the act of cheating disgusted her, even if the back door woman was a freshly deceased corpse.

Delilah drove to the local drive-in grocery store. She subtly scoped the domain and spotted a young man. He looked at her and smiled. She diabolically grinned back at him and motioned for him to come to her car. He could not refuse or resist. His name was Philip Johnston. He was twenty - nine years old and he was also married . . . with one child and one on the way, or "in the oven" as he and his wife of six years, Tonya put it. On the surface, they were a happy couple, or at least they seemed to be to Tonya. Philip wanted to taste what else was out there, and he usually did. He walked up to Delilah's car and put his arm on her roof.

"Hey, how's it going?" Philip inquired with a smile.

"Stare much?" Delilah replied. Philip started to choke on his words and cool.

"Oh, uh . . . I was just . . . ," she cut him off with a brick wall of halting seduction.

"Yeah, I know," she said with a calm and cool smile. She had a voice that could melt anyone's will power. Her tone already had Philip's curiosity peeked, and his will power turned to lava. He knew exactly where he wanted to take her, which room number and what he wanted to do with her, and her soft body. He could feel the blood rushing to the wrong head and she could see it. She loved every minute and inch of it. She was going to get Dax back, if he liked it or not. She knew one thing right away . . . she was going to love it. Philip's feelings were mutual for her. Delilah continued to charm him like a black kitten.

"So . . . what are you doing tonight," she asked.

"Picking up some shit for my girlfriend," Philip replied.

"Your girlfriend . . . hmmm . . . Wanna have some fun?" Delilah asked with a smile.

"Sure," Philip replied quickly, with no hesitation.

"Hop in," demanded Delilah with a subtle, blinding tone and head jerk. Philip got in and she took off with a skid down the road.

"So, this . . . girlfriend, does she know you jump in cars with random girls . . . *women*?" Delilah asked.

"No, but she can be a fucking bitch sometimes. Besides, what she doesn't know won't hurt her, right?" Philip replied with a flirtatious smirk.

"Riiiight," Delilah replied. Philip gave her a huge, glowing smile. They pulled up to Delilah's house. Philip was expecting a cheap motel, but this would surely do. Anywhere was fine to him. As long as he "got him some," as he put it to his friends. He called it "haunting her honey holes" to his friends and two year old son that was just learning to speak.

They pulled into the driveway and exited the car. As soon as they entered the house, Delilah stopped him dead in his tracks. "Wait here . . . I'll be right back." He waited in the living room. She returned with a blindfold and put it over his eyes.

"Here, put this on," she said as she tied the scarf around his eyes.

"Do I have a choice?" he said playfully.

"No," she replied.

"Ahh, I see," he whispered in a flirtatious tone. . .

"Do you," she replied in a dead serious response.

Dax suddenly stormed into the living room with a hammer. He was screaming in bloody rage. "Who in the fuck is . . ." Before Philip frantically spouted another word, Dax violently and viciously began bashing in his head and face with the hammer. At the same time, he was yelling in anger at Delilah. "You fucking two – timing, cheating ass whore! I *hate* you! I . . . fucking . . . hate . . . *you*!"

"You fucking hypocrite! You can have your fun and I can't! Fuck that shit! *Fuck* you!" she roared in furious repulsion and retaliation. As Dax continued to beat Philip's face with the hammer, the phone rang. Philip was convulsing and twitching on the floor in his own blood and urine. Dax pounded his face a few more hard times, before Delilah answered the phone, silencing Philip forever.

Delilah answered the phone. Her best friend of most of her life, twenty - three year old, Holly Jarvis, was on the phone. "Hey, what's up . . . *now*? I don't think it's such a good time . . . or idea," she replied to an unheard voice on the other end of the line as she looked over at Dax. She sighed and continued . . . "Okay, bye." She hung up the phone as Dax ignored her, gazing at the lifeless body of Philip . . . Delilah's would - be lover.

"That was Holly, she's coming over," she said.

"You didn't stop her!?"

"She didn't give me any time. Hurry, get him out of here and clean up this blood and shit," she said as she ran into her room to dry her tears. About thirty minutes went by. Holly arrived and rang the doorbell. Delilah answered the door. "Hey, Delilah," Holly said, as she walked past her and into the house.

"Hey," Delilah responded timidly.

"Where's Dax?" Holly asked curiously.

"He's . . . cleaning," Delilah replied. Holly looked down and saw a stain of blood. "What happened?" she inquired in a slight pinch of shock.

"Dax had a little . . . accident," Delilah replied.

"Oh . . ." She then spotted the blood drenched and brain caked hammer. "What in the fuck, Delilah . . . What in the fuck is going on?" Holly asked in a frightened sense of wonder.

"Holly, just leave, now . . . Just *go*!" Delilah blurted out, as she started to cry.

"Delilah, just tell me what is going . . ." Dax ran in behind

Holly and grabbed her by the arms, restraining her from moving. "Delilah, kill her now . . . She'll narc us out!" Dax demanded.

"No, Dax! She won't tell. I can't kill her . . . I c-can't!" Delilah screamed in tears.

"What are you . . . I'm your best friend, Delilah. I'll never turn you in. Please . . . don't," Holly pleaded in a frozen mask of dread and fear.

"Delilah, fucking *kill* her now! Do it!" Dax demanded once more. Holly tried to talk Delilah out of this horrible act on her by pleading with all of her life and screaming with all of her energy and lungs. "Please, Delilah! I love you like a sister! We've been through everything together! Please, you can't do this to meee-hehehehehheeee!"

"Don't lie to her . . . or *us*! We can't trust you! You would say or do anything to save your own life! Delilah . . . *kill* her . . . *now*!" Dax snapped in ferocious anger. Delilah started to cry harder, as she walked slowly into the kitchen. Holly watched her as she struggled with Dax and fear for her life. "Pleahehehaeaase dohohohohohooooon't!" Holly screamed. Delilah slowly walked back into the living room, staring her in the eyes. She walked up to Holly and Dax, and a sharp, silver steak knife to her side. "I'm sorry, Holly. I have to . . . I'm so sorry. " Delilah and Holly cried harder. Delilah started stabbing Holly repeatedly in the stomach. Delilah started crying harder out of disgust for herself and her present action. Dax let go of her arms, as she slid onto the floor, grabbing Delilah the entire way down to her knees. Holly fell to the floor, choking up blood. Delilah crumbled to her knees, crying. "I love you, Holly. I love you," Delilah uttered. She started to vomit all over Holly as she pronounced her love that they once had.

Dax put his hand on her shoulder, trying to comfort her. "I'm sorry, Delilah. She would have turned us in, both of us. She would have gotten scared and ran to the pigs," he said in a soft and comforting tone. Delilah wiped her eyes and pushed Dax with force and anger. "She was my best fucking friend and we trusted each other! She would have never gone to the cops . . . You *fuck*!"

"I thought you only trusted me. Remember? We only trust and love each other . . . no one else," Dax lovingly replied.

Dax and Delilah were kissing romantically. They grabbed a pair of knives and cut into the nameless, screaming victim that was tied up next to them. They sliced and diced until blood was gushing from the blue and battered teenage girl. They started to roll around in the crimson pool that was soaking the concrete floor, like red oceans of gushing ecstasy. Suddenly, Delilah pulled an axe from behind her. There were quick flashes of Dax and Delilah angry, in despair, alone and in rage and war with each other spinning through her mind. Delilah was kissing Dax. Now, they were covered in blood. Delilah firmly planted the axe in the back of Dax's head. Delilah woke up in a cold sweat. She was dreaming the entire time.

Delilah looked next to her and Dax was missing. She sat up and looked around in confusion. She heard something outside of the bedroom. "Dax . . . Dax . . . is that you?" she called out in wonder. She got up and stumbled out of the bedroom, in the direction of the noise. It directed her to the basement.

Delilah opened the door and walked down the stairs. She looked around and saw Dax, on his knees, with a bloody saw, and a Holy Bible. He was surrounded in blood, severed body parts, needles and syringes. He was wearing the freshly made, dead skin mask of an earlier victim from the prior week. He was also shaking and sweating in madness and paranoia. He was crying so hysterically that he did not notice Delilah as she stood there, looking over him with her arms crossed. "Why, God . . . why have you pissed on me? Why have you pissed on *us*? This entire fucking earth! This fucking life! Where are you . . . you *fuck*! Where in the *hell* are you? Do you really hate us all this fucking much!" Delilah started to laugh at him as he cried in despair. He was breathing heavily. "Having a little loss in faith there, babe? Even if there was a fucking God, Do you think he would forgive you for all of this? All of you hypo-Christians are the same. You think that that merciful fuck will forgive you for anything. You think that just because you are one of his so-called *children* . . . that you can get away with bloody fucking murder. You hypocritical bastards of Christ make me fucking sick! You don't believe in God, you believe in fucking pain!" Delilah snarled in a wretched sense of sarcastic sorrow.

"I see what you are. Your mask of faith is your mask of sanity!" Dax looked up at Delilah, as she stood before him. He stared at her for a moment and removed the mask made of flesh from his face. It was covered in blood that bubbled with every deep breath from his mouth. He looked at her for one last moment and threw up all around himself and the cadaver. Delilah's face went from disgust, to a diabolical, yet somewhat sexy smirk. "There's your God . . . a cold mass of puke and blood . . . a- fucking- *men*. If you want to fuck, clean up . . . I'll be in bed . . . and clean fucking good. I don't want that shit all over the bed. " She walked back up the stairs, as Dax sat there alone. He started to look around. He threw up again and stared up to the ceiling.

Delilah was in the bedroom. She was reorganizing things, cleaning and putting her clothing away. The phone rang. It was Delilah's mother, Mary Lou Edwards. They were still very close. Dax killed her father. Mary still did not know how he died, neither did Delilah. She picked up the phone. "Hello? Mom, hey. How are you? I'm great. Yeah, Dax and I are doing wonderful. He's in the shower. Long day at work today . . . Well, listen mom, can I let you go? I need some rest . . . okay, I love you too, okay . . . bye."

It was very easy for her to lie, until she hung up the phone. She started to cry after sitting there for only a few seconds, in disgust of herself and lying to her mother. "I'm so sorry, mom. If you knew how I really am, you would hate me. I hate myself. I've killed my best fucking friend and now I've lied . . . to you, the one who means the absolute most to me. I'm so sorry." Delilah sat there for a minute, while thinking in a disturbed silence. She thought of and vividly saw the past murders that she and Dax had committed in her mind. She thought about lying to her mother. She started to feel alone, in despair and angry. She had mental images of she and Dax making out She thought of the dreams and the blood drenched romance. It was like a real life Horror movie that would never stop playing in her head. She then snapped out of her dreamlike state and looked at the clock. It had been almost an hour since she talked to Dax in the basement. She left again to go find him.

Delilah walked back to the basement. As she entered, she saw Dax with a severed head. He was orally pleasing himself. She saw his actions of unfaithfulness toward her and lost her mind. She screamed at the top of her lungs, "You God damn corpse molesting cocksucker!" Dax looked up, but kept pleasuring himself He closed his eyes and looked back down carelessly.

Delilah ran into her bedroom and started destroying everything in her sight and path while cursing Dax. She lay in the middle of the mess that she had made. Suddenly, the door flew open with a bang. Dax stood in the doorway, covered from head to toe in blood. Delilah glared at him with a sinister stare. "Fucker!" she screamed as she lunged on top of him. She knocked him down, beating him viciously and cursing at him. He screamed back, but did not defend himself. He was starting to feel like he deserved every blow that she had saved for him. He let her beat him black, blue and bloody. He just pleaded, "Delilah, I love you. Why are you doing this to me? I love you so much . . . please . . . stop!"

"You fucking *liar*! You don't fucking *love* me! Our love has rotted! There *is* no love! I *hate* you! I love to *hate* you!" Delilah replied in rage.

"We love each other! I *know* you love me! We were *made* for each other!" Dax desperately replied

"I fucking hate you! I want you to die! Die, you *fuck* . . . Just . . . fucking . . . *die*!" Delilah verbally blasted in anger.

"Calm down, darling. Let's go on a date. I know somewhere we can go to ease your mind. I'll pick the neighborhood, and you can choose the house," Dax said with a warming smile. Delilah knew what he was hinting at, and wanted anything at the moment to sooth her mind. In a way, the act that Dax wanted to commit was a relaxing session of therapeutic foreplay and a prelude to rough make-up sex to them both. "We can try out our new masks," Dax said as he held up two black painted plastic masks. "I think they look better black. Don't you?" Dax asked. Delilah stayed silent and gave him a confirming head nod of agreement. "Go put on something comfortable and we'll hit the road," Dax suggested. Delilah went into the bedroom.

A few minutes later, Delilah returned with a solid black hoodie and matching sweatpants. Dax was now wearing a matching outfit to coincide with Delilah's. A wooden handle was sticking out of his pants pocket. He was holding the masks and video camera in one hand and a roll of tape in the other. He handed one of the masks to Delilah and they headed outside to the car.

"How about we head down to London Street? There aren't many street lights in that neighborhood," Dax said as he turned off of the main highway and into a residential neighborhood. Delilah nodded once more in a silent pact of agreement. They passed Deputy Rogers as he drove slowly down Nola Avenue, shining a bright spotlight down the street and in between the houses along the left side of the block. Dax drove through the clustered labyrinth of neighborhoods until he saw the London Street sign. He stopped at the end of the street and killed the engine. He exited the car and opened the passenger door for Delilah. He held out his hand and helped her out of the car.

They held hands and walked down the street until they reached the middle darkest center of the neighborhood. "Does that one look okay to you? They left the light on for us in the living room. That looks like an open invitation to me," Dax said. They walked up the driveway to 8650 London Street, and to the front door. Dax gave Delilah a kiss on the lips. They tongued deeply for a moment. Delilah finally showed Dax the heart drenching smile he had been waiting for all night. "I love you, baby" Dax said with a wink.

"I love you too, Dax," Delilah replied with a seductive lick on her lips. They put on the plastic black masks. Dax turned on the video camera, pushed the *Record* button and knocked on the door. "I'll get it . . . *Coming!*" a muffled male's voice yelled on the other side of the door.

Seventeen year old, Dennis Walden responded to the knock. His eyes grew wide with shock. As he tried to close the door, Dax stuck his foot into the house, extinguishing the attempt. Dax pushed open the door. He and Delilah entered the Walden home. Dennis turned around and ran toward the kitchen. Dax pulled the steak knife out of his pocket and threw it, stabbing Dennis in the back. He fell, face-first onto the floor. "What's going on down there?" Charles Walden yelled from upstairs. Dax walked up to Dennis and twisted the knife in his back, pushing it deeper as he zoomed in on the wound with the video camera. Before jerking out the blade, he stomped the back of Dennis' head with a jolting blow. "Sir, you may want to come down here! Your son had a little *accident!*" Dax yelled. Charles walked halfway down the stairs. Dax stood in the living room over Dennis' twitching body, wiping his blood from the blade of the knife. "Who are you? What have you done to my son?" Charles inquired. Dax looked over at Delilah. "Keep an eye on him," Dax said as he ran up the stairs after Charles.

Dax followed Charles into the bedroom where his wife, Katherine, was asleep on the bed. "*Wake* up!" Dax screamed. He punched Charles in the head as he lunged for the telephone, knocking him to the ground. Dax sat the video camera on the bedside table and cut the phone chord with the blood drenched blade of the knife. "Get up, we're all going downstairs!" he commanded. Charles tried to raise his head. Dax grabbed him by the hair, pulling him to his feet. "Get up and come with us now, or he fucking dies," Dax snarled. He put the knife to Charles' throat. "Okay, I'm coming, just please don't hurt him or my children!" Katherine pleaded. Dax smirked at Katherine. He grabbed the video camera and pulled Charles out of the bedroom by his hair. Dax dragged Charles down the stairs as Katherine followed in tears. They reached the living room where Dennis lied motionless on the floor. "It looks like you didn't have to babysit him too long, huh?" Dax remarked. Katherine began to scream and cry. "Dennis! *No!*" she wailed in an ocean of sorrow.

"Both of you *shut* up, and sit on the couch!" Dax ordered. "Go take care of the rest of the phone chords, and destroy any cell phones that you see," he said to Delilah. Dax handed her the knife and camera. He pulled the tape out of his pocket. Delilah nodded and left the room.

Dax taped Charles' hands behind his back and ankles together, and hogtied Katherine. He bit off two smaller pieces of tape and slapped them over their mouths. Delilah walked back into the living room and up to Katherine. She removed Katherine's wedding ring and placed it on her own finger. She held her hand in front of the video camera and displayed the newly ringed finger. Katherine began to scream as loud as she possibly could. "If you shut up, I'll remove the tape for one second so you can say your piece. If you scream, they will be your last words. I'll cut you into fucking pieces . . . understand?" Dax stated in almost a whisper. Katherine nodded. Dax slowly peeled off the tape, just enough for her to speak. In Dax's twisted way of thinking, it was an obscure form of additional physical torture. "Please, we'll give you whatever you want. You can take *anything*. We won't say a single word. We won't turn you in for what you-- did to our son," Katherine explained as she kept glancing to the front door. Dax resealed her mouth with the tape. "Thanks for sharing that. We didn't come here to take anything from you people." Dax paused for a moment as he and Delilah looked at each other. "Well, *yes* we did, but you won't have to worry about it. You'll never be able to get it back once we're gone," he replied. Collective tears streamed down Charles and Katherine's cheeks. The sight of Dennis bleeding before them added to the sadness, anger and rage that they were unable to express, even if they wanted to. Katherine and Charles both knew that something was about to happen shortly which instilled an equal amount of dread within them.

Dax lit a cigarette. He smoked it half way to the filter, and smashed the cherry against Katherine's eyelid.

"You bastard, don't hurt her!" Charles grunted beneath the tape-made gag. Katherine silently screamed in agony as remnants of the ignited ashes trickled down her face like tears of fire.

"Go check out the rest of the house to see if we're missing

anyone," Dax said.

Delilah nodded and left the living room with the video camera. She returned five minutes later. "No one else is in the house," Delilah said. She looked down at Katherine's and into her widened eyes. Delilah's identity as a woman had been blown. "There is a female's room here though. It's empty," Delilah added.

Dax looked down at Katherine and Charles. "Do you have . . . a daughter?" He looked at Dennis' lifeless body. "His sister, perhaps?" he asked.

Katherine tightly squeezed her eyes closed and shook her head from side to side. Sinus drainage and tears slithered over the tape on her mouth. She began to choke.

"I take that as a yes. Maybe we'll have the pleasure of meeting her as well," Dax said with a smile. Delilah looked at him with a sinister glare beneath the black mask. Dax could feel the animosity radiating through him from his other half. "Well, if not, we'll leave her a nice surprise . . . from us, to her," Dax stated. He walked over to Charles and put the blade of the knife to his hairline. He cut just deep enough to draw blood and slowly circled the blade around Charles' face. He bled down his face and neck. Charles shrilled in afflict, but his lips could not budge. "Would you like to finish him off, baby?" Dax asked.

Katherine rapidly shook her head and whimpered without uttering a word. She squeezed her eyes closed and turned her head as Delilah walked over to her helpless husband.

Dax handed the knife to her and stepped back, aiming the video camera at her with a euphorically childlike anticipation displayed in his body language. Delilah pulled Charles' head back by his hair. She placed the handle of the knife on the floor and lowered his chin onto the blade. She lifted his head and swiftly slammed it down, impaling the blade through his chin. Blood gushed all over Delilah's hand and the floor. She and Dax sadistically washed their hands in the grotesque fountain of flowing red.

Katherine could barely breathe. Her hope was draining as quickly as her husband's life.

"You can have her. Just make sure you kill her fast, so we can get the hell out of here," Delilah said as she jerked the knife out of Charles' neck and handed it to Dax.

He handed Delilah the video camera. He walked over to Katherine and looked down at her. Katherine looked up into the empty eyes behind the black mask and knew that her time was about to expire along with her husband and son's. She tensed up her body and prepared to take whatever horrible act that Dax was about to commit upon her flesh. Dax flipped Katherine over on her side. He took the knife and cut open her nightgown. He stuck the blade into her stomach and gutted her like a pig in a slaughterhouse.

Dax and Delilah stood above the three dead family members and looked down, relishing their accomplishment.

Dax and Delilah opened the front door. They looked back at the grizzly crime scene that they had created and put their arms around each other for a moment. In their minds, it was as if they were looking out over The Grand Canyon as a happy couple while breathing in the cool, crisp air of the scenery. They left the front door wide open and took off down the street towards the car. As they got inside, buckled up and started the ignition, another vehicle passed them. It turned into the Walden house. Eighteen year old, Elizabeth Walden could be heard all the way down the street as she walked into the house and screamed bloody murder. Dax and Delilah drove off into the night once more and headed to the comfort of their own abode.

Dax kissed Delilah passionately. He ripped off her fatality dyed clothes as she moaned in bliss. Dax tied Delilah to the bed and began to savagely enter her as they became one. They had wild intercourse for hours, fueled by adrenaline and their favorite rush . . . murder.

Delilah and Dax lay there holding each other and thought of all the yelling they had done at each other. All of the despair, the suffering, the self-mutilation, drug use, violence and abuse toward each other built up inside of them, like a time bomb waiting to explode. Delilah felt just as bad as Dax did about it. They hated to see each other hurt, but seemed to gain delight off of others' suffering in which they had induced by their own selfish volition.

Dax got the video camera. He and Delilah held hands and walked down into the corpse filled and blood drenched basement. The lingering reek of death and decay was swarming with flies throughout the room. The smell was totally blocked out of both of their minds, the only thoughts occupying their gray matter was each other.

Dax and Delilah found a comfortable corner and nestled themselves in it, facing each other. Delilah gazed into Dax's eyes. "I've waited so long for this. We'll finally be together forever . . .

just you and me," she said with a breath of soothing relief. She had always wanted a traditional wedding, just not in a church or court. This was the next best thing to her. It would be an eternal bonding of loved ones that no one could witness, but themselves.

Dax had waited for this moment as well. He looked her in the eyes. "I'm sorry for everything that I've put you though, Delilah . . . I'd fucking kill myself for you."

"I'd kill myself for *you*, Dax. I love you. I love you so fucking much," Delilah replied as they mentally locked deep into each other's eyes.

"I love you too," Dax replied with a smile.

There was true love between them, with no emotion added. They started to kiss passionately. They looked each other in the eyes once more. Dax turned on the video camera and aimed it at the two of them. The two tattered and battered love-bats picked up a pistol for each of them from the blood puddled floor. They raised the guns in the camera's view, placing the black barrels in each other's mouths. They waited for three seconds . . . and tightly closed their eyes . . . On a collective mental beat of "four," they pulled the triggers and blew a huge hole in the back of each other's heads. They lay there, together . . . dead, as one. Most of their headless, faceless, skinned and dismembered victims were scattered around them. Their slithering brains and skull matter crept slowly down the walls behind them. They were finally at peace . . . with each other and most importantly, the world around them.

"Dinner"
Stephen Cooney

Necessary Cold Ruthlessness

Timothy Frasier

The large room assaulted the senses with its mixture of normality and horror. At one end sat a man at a small wooden table covered with a red-and-white checkered cloth. A variety of wild flowers from the fields surrounding the camp were stuffed into a cracked white vase that sat in the center of the table. Along the wall, there was a modern gas cook stove. At the other end of the room, hanging upside down by his ankles from a chain hoist fastened to the ceiling, was a naked man. A section of his thigh was missing. The slow trickle of blood from his wound was swallowed by a drain positioned directly beneath the hoist. The man was unconscious and near death. The sweet smell of cooked meat lay heavy in the room.

Dr. Karl von Heidel, a small, 32-year-old, dark haired man stared balefully at the emaciated prisoner seated at the table. The plate in front of the prisoner contained a large strip of meat with a few potatoes around the edge, which he picked at tentatively with his fork, but never lifted to his mouth.

"Go on," von Heidel coaxed. "It is your only way to survive. If you refuse to eat, you will be sent to the gas chambers immediately!" He stared at the green triangle on the man's coveralls. He was not just a common criminal, as the green triangle signified. He was a German common criminal. Surely, he had surmised, the "beast" would be strongest in the five German prisoners he had requested after his miserable failure with the Jews and Gypsies. Now, after the failure of the first four, his hopes were waning with this man.

"I can't eat this," the man stammered weakly. "It is a sin to eat another man."

"You will suffer a horrible death! Save yourself!"

The man looked up at von Heidel with tears in his eyes.

"Take him away!" von Heidel ordered. Two of the four guards in the room grabbed the man and dragged him by the arms from the room. The other two guards removed the Gypsy corpse that hung from the chain.

Dr. von Heidel left the room and made his rounds before retiring to his quarters at 6 pm, where he ate a light supper. His assignment to Auschwitz had held the promise to be one of the milestones in his research career with its endless supply of humans available for research. Now though, it promised to simply highlight his failures. Dr. Josef Mengele had personally requested von Heidel. They had attended Munich University together and had become close friends there. Mengele had been fascinated with von Heidel's theory of Man's Inner Beast and the endless possibilities if it could be harnessed.

At 8 p.m., his rest was interrupted by a knock on the door.

"Dr. von Heidel, I have an important message from Dr. Frederick Krugar!"

"Enter."

The door opened and in walked a young man personifying the Furor's idea of perfection with his blond hair and pale blue eyes. Wearing black pants and a white shirt, his movement was precise, almost mechanical.

"I am Dr. Hans Wormal, a close associate of Dr. Krugar. I serve with him at the American labor camp" The young man clicked his heels and nodded.

"It is nice to meet you Dr. Wormal," von Heidel nodded his head but remained seated in his chair. "Where is the letter?"

"I have been sent with a verbal message. Dr. Krugar believes discretion to be good policy and sent me to you with this message. He knows of your search for the Inner Animal and has at his disposal the perfect specimen."

"I am intrigued...where are my manners? Please sit." He nodded to a second chair next to the wall. "Tell me more."

Dr. Wormal nodded and took a seat.

"Two weeks ago, a battle was fought near Keen. There were heavy casualties. Three days later, burial details discovered an American feeding on the dead. He did not discriminate, feeding on Americans and Germans alike. He was brought to the labor camp where we keep him in isolation. We've tortured him extensively for information, but he refuses to speak. The torture had no effect. In fact, it seemed to amuse him."

"This is fascinating! I must assume my dear friend Frederick is offering this man to me in order to advance my research."

"That is correct. He awaits your word. He also sends his thanks for your help in Berlin three years ago." The young doctor smiled.

Von Heidel returned his smile. "Tell him he is more than welcome. Thank him for this man he is sending."

Dr. Wormal frowned. "I don't know if this thing should be called a man. The guards simply call him *Kannibale*, I am very uneasy when I pass his cell. These are my words, not Doctor Krugar's,"

Von Heidel studied Wormal for several moments in silence. "Give my thanks to Dr. Krugar."

Doctor Wormal nodded, stood, and left the room.

Doctor von Heidel entered the room and paused. The American was seated at the table with his legs shackled to the floor. He wore a pair of red and white striped pants and nothing else. He was shirtless, revealing a powerfully sculpted upper body that was sparsely covered in coarse black hair. Though he was seated, von Heidel could tell the man was very tall. He appeared to be young, perhaps 20 years old. His complexion was extremely light, almost like that of an albino. There was even the tint of blue in his skin. He had the chiseled face of a Greek god with thick curly black hair that reached his shoulders. He carried an air of innocence until he turned to von Heidel and tore into him with his piercing green eyes, causing the doctor to flinch and turn his head. Slightly unnerved, he walked over to the wall near the subject where he could best observe. He had originally planned to communicate with him, but decided to wait.

Within moments, the door opened and two guards entered with a young Polish woman walking between them. She was naked and afraid. Her hair had been shaved in preparation. Von Heidel could see the shiny bare skin on her thigh that had been shaved as well. She glanced around nervously. One of the guards shackled a chain attached to a hoist to her ankles and yanked the chained violently, causing her feet to lift in the air and her head to smack the tiled floor, stunning her. After she was lifted upside down in the air, she regained her senses and began to shriek while flailing her arms in an effort to ward them off. After a few moments of her dangling upside down, one guard snatched her right arm and pulled it to the side while another guard slit her throat from ear to ear. Blood spurted from her throat as her body thrashed momentarily then lay still. There was a pleasing efficiency of motion to the process that denoted the countless times some variance of this task had been performed.

Von Heidel observed the lack of emotion on his test subject's face as the woman was killed. Even as she had dangled in pain and fear, Kannibale had remained passive, inert, blank. He sat now, watching as the woman's blood flowed down her face and poured from her shaved skull into the drain. The guard that had cut the woman's throat, now took the tip of his blade, circled her upper thigh and then down toward her buttocks. He then peeled the skin down slowly, revealing her lean thigh muscle. The guard sliced into it and traced out a piece of meat the size of a man's palm. He had been a butcher and his motions were practiced and effortless.

The thigh meat was handed to a second guard who took it to the already heated stove and placed it in a large, hot skillet where it began to sizzle. He sprinkled it with seasoning and turned it in the pan using a large three pronged fork. The smell of cooking meat permeated the room. One of the guards, a young man of nineteen, gagged as the aroma of meat got the better of him. The meat was still rare as the cook removed it from the pan and placed it on the prisoner's plate. Potatoes and a few carrots were placed around the meat.

During this process, Kannibale had evinced no discomfort, only mild curiosity. Now he leaned forward and inhaled. A strand of slobber slid from his mouth and onto the meat. It had been over a week since he had eaten. Without hesitation he tore into the meat with his fork, wolfing it down with reckless abandon. The vegetables were left untouched. He stared into von Heidel's eyes and then smiled ever so slightly. His lips and cheeks were shiny with the juice of the meat. A thin stream of red trickled from the side of his mouth. He looked at the woman. The blood had finally stopped flowing from her ruined neck. He ran his tongue over his lips slowly and then looked at the doctor.

Von Heidel was stunned and slightly taken aback. He had hoped for but hadn't fully expected this. "No," he said softly and paused. "Too much will make you sick. There will be more tomorrow." He directed his gaze to the guards. "Take him to the special room. He is to be treated well!"

As the guards led him away, von Heidel began to shake. He could barely contain his excitement. He considered finding Dr. Mengele so he could share his news with a peer, but decided to wait. How far could he take this man? He needed to know who this man was. When the time was right, he would extract all the information he needed.

On day two and three of Kannibale's participation in von Heidel's experiment, young male subjects were brought to the room, killed, and fed to the American. On the fourth day, another female was brought to the room. She was a beautiful redhead with a voluptuous figure. Marlina VanderGoff of the Gunderland Dance Troop had been arrested for hiding a homosexual friend. Von Heidel had pulled some strings to get her after learning of her arrest.

"I have met you before, Fraulein," von Heidel said as he stepped in front of her. "It was Munich, in the spring of thirty-six...if I'm not mistaken." She was nude but defiant. She stood erectly, her chest held out proudly and her eyes were full of fire. Her perfect breasts and hourglass shape filled him with passion. For just a moment he considered delaying her demise to enjoy her body first. He looked at the guards and he could see the naked lust they too were trying to hide. Kannibale, seated at his table as usual, seemed oblivious. He was salivating.

"I danced with my troop all across all of Europe and North America. Back before your Nazi cancer destroyed the civilized world." She spat in Dr. Heidel's face.

Von Heidel smiled as he took his handkerchief and wiped his face. "Now, that's no way to treat an admirer."

"What are you going to do with me?"

"This is simply a behavioral study, nothing for you to fear, Marlina. Do you see the young man sitting at the table?"

"Yes," she said as uneasily.

"We are going to observe his reaction as he consumes the meat we cut from your body. And, judging by your appearance, the meat should be quite delicious." He smiled at the woman while giving her time to digest his words.

Marlina began to cry and plead to no avail. It took three guards to shackle just one of her ankles as she thrashed about wildly. Giving up on the other ankle, the guard with the knife stabbed her in her right breast, causing her to collapse and draw into a fetal position. Her other ankle was quickly shackled and she was hoisted upside-down in the air. One of the guards cursed as he realized she had soiled herself and he had gotten it on his hand. He washed his hands, then took the hose and sprayed most of the feces off of the woman and down the drain.

Von Heidel took the knife from the guard and walked over to her. He slapped her lightly on her wet cheek twice and she opened her eyes.

Her face was framed in horror and she gritted her teeth as von Heidel placed the cold blade against the side of her neck and slowly cut her throat from ear to ear. Blood shot out from her severed artery in pulses, timed with her rapidly beating heart. Her body quivered as her blood and urine flowed into the floor drain. He handed the knife back to the guard who removed a chunk of meat with his usual skill and took it to the cook on the other side of the room.

Before the meat was done, von Heidel sent the cook out of the room and finished preparing it himself. He cut a sizable portion from the serving, a serving that had grown larger each day, wrapped it in a handkerchief, and placed it in his coat pocket.

Potatoes and carrots had been omitted from the Kannibale's menu since the second feeding. They realized he had hunger for nothing but meat. In just moments of von Heidel serving Marlina's cooked flesh to the young man, the plate was clean.

"I hope my cooking was up to your standards," von Heidel smiled at his own weak attempt at humor as he sat down at the table across from the man. He spoke in English with no trace of German accent thanks to a year of study in the United States before the war. He prided himself in not only learning other languages easily, but also mastering regional accents.

The man gazed into von Heidel's eyes. The doctor managed to hold that gaze for only seconds before looking away.

"Can you speak at all?" von Heidel asked. "Or are you deaf as well?" At that moment, a guard dropped a pan on the floor as he had been instructed. The young man looked quickly to the sound. "Ah! At least I know you can hear me."

The man smiled.

"What is it I should call you? Should I call you Kannibale?"

The smile remained.

"I would try to force the information from you, but I've been told those tactics would fail. Brutal methods generally work very well, so I use them. My preference, though, would be the carrot instead of the stick, as I am a civilized man. What carrot can I offer to you? What is it you would ask for so that I may hear the sound of your voice?"

The man stared into von Heidel, making him uneasy.

"I chose you, my strange friend. Do not forget that." He turned to the guards, "Take him to his room." As the guards reached the doorway with the man, von Heidel called to him. "You will speak to me before you leave this place, Kannibale!" He laughed as they disappeared into the hallway.

On his way to his quarters, Von Heidel went by the officers club and retrieved two bottles of beer. Once at his quarters, he sat down at his table and placed the beer to his right . Taking his time, he pulled the handkerchief from his pocket and placed it in front of him. Grease had soaked through the bottom side. Afraid of losing his nerve, he opened one bottle and drank it quickly.

Taking a deep breath, he un-wrapped the handkerchief and stared at the cold, charred meat. The grease had already congealed into white thick lard. He took his dagger and scraped away the hard fat and then sliced a thin strip of meat from the portion. He glanced quickly to the painting on his wall. It depicted a pack of wolves surrounding a traveler in the forest. A plaque beneath the painting was inscribed with the words "Necessary Cold Ruthlessness," a phrase taken from *Mein Kampf*. It had been a support and inspiration for the necessary cold ruthlessness that motivated his research. He stabbed the thin slice of meat with his knife, held it up, and looked at it. It glistened in the dim light of his quarters, revealing none of its secrets. It looked like pork or a lean slice of beef. He placed it into his mouth, almost carefully, clinically, and began to chew.

The meat had a sweet taste, but the texture was grainier than he preferred. Von Heidel stifled a gag as he began to think of the woman. Eight years ago in Munich, he had waited backstage after the show for her autograph. She had stroked his head gently as he bent forward and kissed the back of her right hand. He took a deep breath as he reminisced. His penis was erect and pulsing with excitement. He unbuckled his pants to relieve the pressure. Perhaps he should have had his way with her before he ate her. But no, it was this that excited him. It was thrilling to eat the life force of another human being. He was glad he had chosen her for his first meal.

He opened the other bottle of beer and washed the meat down. He cut a second, larger slice and tossed it into his mouth with his fingers. It tasted more like pork than anything he had eaten. He thought about her nude body. She really had been quite beautiful. In a different world, he knew he would have been trying to win her hand instead of eating her. Funny how things worked out he mused. He shuddered involuntarily and felt his gorge rising. He coughed and swallowed down the last of the beer.

He looked down at the handkerchief. About half of the meat remained. He sliced off another bite and ate it. The meat was toneless and dull. It was chewy and vile in his mouth. He determined he would finish it. He would eat this chunk of human flesh and then never, ever would he eat human flesh again. He picked up the last cold and slimy piece and put it in his mouth.

The next day, a male prisoner was brought to the room and shackled standing up. He was a big healthy man wearing blue coveralls. A laborer, von Heidel speculated. His men were not opposed to going into the city or countryside to find the specimens he needed if nothing suitable could be found when the boxcars were unloaded. In science, the ends justified the means.

"Why am I here?" The man asked angrily. "I'm no Jew!"

"Why you are here doesn't matter." Von Heidel said. It was these moments that he enjoyed most. "It is what you do while you are here that matters. That man at the table is going to try his very best to kill you just seconds from now."

"Why would he do that? I don't know that man! I've done nothing to him!"

"That is of no matter. He will try to kill you. If you manage to kill him, you will be set free. You have my word as a gentleman. My only advice to you is to fight like your life depends on it...because it does." Von Heidel smiled widely.

Four of the guards were armed with MP-38's. They covered the one, unarmed guard who unshackled the American. Von Heidel stood behind the guards, his right hand resting on the 9mm Lugar holstered on his side.

"Now my Kannibale friend, there is your meal if you want it."

The young man stood up and turned toward the shackled man. Von Heidel was in awe. Kannibale was easily seven feet tall, dwarfing everyone in the room. He slipped off his much too small shirt and tossed it to the floor. As he took two tentative steps toward the shackled man, his muscles moved like huge cables beneath stretched skin. In a sudden blur of motion, he moved across the room, snatched the man up, and slung him across the room and into the far wall. All the guards along with von Heidel were shaken. The man screamed and kicked at the American with bloody stubs while on his back. Von Heidel quickly looked back to where the man had been chained and saw both his boots still shackled with bloody bone peeking from the top. The man was violently ripped apart in just seconds with his intestines strung across the floor. Soon, a sickening sound filled the room as Kannibale fed. After a few minutes of feeding on the shoulder muscle, he rose up and pounded his victim's head with his massive fist, cracking the skull open with ease. He lifted the grey brain matter to his mouth and sucked it down, seeming to savor the taste as much as the total domination of another living creature.

Von Heidel left the room and went for a walk outside the walls.

The excitement of finding Kannibale had taken its toll on von Heidel. He was having trouble sleeping, and when he did manage a few hours, his dreams unnerved him. Whatever this man was had nothing to do with the experiments. He was too willing to do what so many would not, even at the cost of their lives. After his walk, the doctor retired to his room. It was near dawn by the time he dosed off.

Over the next week, both von Heidel and his guards became more comfortable with Kannibale. His was brought in unshackled and remained that way. Weapons were often propped against the wall. During one feeding, von Heidel sat at the table while his subject killed his victim. In moments, the doctor was asleep with his head lying on the table, propped on his crossed forearms. A sound woke him to find Kannibale sitting across from him with his hand full of bloody meat, reaching across the table toward him in offering. Rattled, the doctor jumped up and quickly glanced around at his guards, finding them all asleep. After that, he decided that if Kannibale was going to make an attempt on his life, he would have done it then. His trust of this man was uncharacteristic for him and he realized it, but he seemed unable to do anything about it. He began to feel that Kannibale was the one in control while he and his men were hapless prisoners.

At the end of the week, von Heidel changed protocol and had his men bring the victims in and shackle them before he and Kannibale arrived. Once there, he would send his men out of the room so he could observe his subject in private. It was then that the young man's sadistic nature began to reveal itself. With green eyes blazing, Kannibale would eat his victims alive, starting at their feet and slowly working his way to their calves, at which point all but one went into shock and died. One tough soul, a man of about fifty, held on till Kannibale reached his right thigh before he died of blood loss. Those that died too soon would send the young man into a tantrum. He would rip their bodies apart in a rage, then, as quickly as it started, it was over. He was his usual calm, controlled self.

The beginning of the week brought a surprise to von Heidel. He entered the feeding room to find Dr. Mengele sitting at the table with six guards surrounding him instead of a new shackled prisoner.

"To what do I owe this honor, Josef?" Von Heidel willed himself to stay relaxed as he joined his friend at the table.

"It seems the forays outside of the camp by your guards have brought much unwanted attention, Karl. After an investigation of my own, I was shocked to learn of your deviant behavior." Dr. Mengele sat with his fingers intertwined and pointed toward the ceiling. It almost looked as if he were praying.

"You know of my behavioral studies. You know as well as I that there are very few new arrivals at the camp that are suitable for my research. I needed healthy subjects to feed to Kannibale. He is the subject I've waited for all my life. We will learn much from this man."

"Ah! But this is where our problem arises, Karl. There is no Kannibale. There is you and only you. We are the Master Race, not savages. Your position does not entitle you to perform your barbaric practices against those who are not our enemy."

"I have watched this man kill and feed on his victims like a lion! Why do you say he doesn't exist? I can have my men bring him to this room now! Von Heidel was livid.

"We have interviewed your men and none have any recollection of this Kannibale you speak of. Two of your men reported your behavior to me directly. It seems that 'you' are the only kannibale in Auschwitz, Karl."

"This is nonsense! Is this some sort of joke? It is not funny!"

"It was also reported that you took some of the...meat, back to your room. Do you deny this?" Mengele's eyes bore into his.

"That is another false accusation!" Von Heidel's palms were sweating. "Where are my accusers? They watched this monster rip apart humans with his bare hands. I am a small person. I am not strong." Von Heidel was thankful he was seated. His legs trembled and he feared standing would be difficult. His bladder felt full. "How could I have done such a thing?"

"That is what I intend to find out, Karl. We must dissect you in the name of science. There is much information to be gleaned from you."

"No!" Von Heidel jumped to his feet but was quickly lifted by two guards and then slammed roughly on his back on top of the red and white checkered tablecloth. The cracked white vase full of wilted flowers crashed to the floor. A third guard leaned over and ripped open von Heidel's shirt, revealing a pale, hairless chest. Panic induced images flashed through mind, finally settling on one...Kannibale's impish, all knowing smile.

Von Heidel screamed as Mengele leaned over him, slipped a hypothermic needle between his ribs, and injected chloroform into his heart.

A voice whispered in von Heidel's ear the moment his heart stopped. It was an ancient voice dressed with the thin facade of youth.   "No   Doctor,   I   chose   you."
Mengele spent the next hour dissecting his old friend, cataloguing every organ. He took special care with von Heidel's brain. He weighed it and took measurements. It was sealed in a special container for shipment to Berlin where experts in the field would look for aberrations or abnormalities. As soon as he was finished, Mengele cleaned up and left for an early lunch.

Two days later, Mengele received a call that left him shaken. He reported to the head of the Auschwitz medical corps, Edward Wirths.

"So, what is the reason for this visit Josef?" Wirths remained seated. His voice was cordial, but his eyes revealed his disdain for Mengele.

"There was an incident today. The train carrying von Heidel's brain was attacked in the Sudetic Mountains near Hirschberg. Soldiers were killed and von Heidel's brain was taken."

"What craziness is this? Why would someone do such a thing?" Wirths stood up and glanced out of his window nervously and then pulled the curtains together.

"The witnesses said a crazy man with green eyes came from the rear of the train. He rushed to the courier transporting the brain and struck him with his fist, crushing his skull. He took the container and beat several men to death as he exited into the snow. The train stopped, but all they could find was the empty container and specks of blood and brain in the snow. The man's bare footprints led into an outcrop of boulders. It is there that they lost his trail." It was obvious that Mengele dreaded conveying this information.

"According to you, Doctor, the green-eyed man did not exist. You said the guards involved had no recollection of this Kannibale. Is there anything that you have failed to disclose?"

"Well," Mengele cleared his throat nervously. "It is true that the guards had no memory of this Kannibale. But there were other gaps in their memory. It was quite odd."

"Quite odd!" I allowed you to kill von Heidel in order to save us all the embarrassment of his actions coming to light. He was a

German citizen! I should have 'you' dissected and catalogued for your deceit!"

Mengele swallowed nervously.

"There will be no further mention of this, Mengele. Am I clear?"

"Yes."

"You are dismissed."

Seven decades after the horrors of Auschwitz had been revealed to the world, a naked man basked in the sun atop a boulder along the Appalachian Trail in remote West Virginia. The forest was deathly quiet, as if every living thing hid in fear. The man's nostrils flared as he dreamed. In one moment he feasted of the spoils of battle left by the Roman Legions. A moment later, he was tracking the Mongel hordes. As he opened his eyes, he remembered nibbling on the toes of Abel while Cain staggered away in shock with blood on his hands.

He sprung into a crouching position at the sound of a snapping twig, followed by the laughter of a man and woman. Every muscle in his powerfully built body was taut as he awaited the hikers to come into range. A fragrance tickled his senses, causing him to forget the hikers for the moment as he lifted his nose to the light breeze blowing through the pine trees. A smile crossed his lips and spread to his brilliant green eyes. War and pestilence was coming to this land. An epic war to end all wars lay on the horizon. The days of plenty were near. His stomach growled as he turned and bound off the boulder and onto the hikers below.

Diagra

Simon Critchell

Twenty minutes later he started to feel it. At first it was just an almost imperceptible flush. Over the next few minutes the feeling became more intense, so much so that he slipped into the bathroom to see if he could notice anything in the mirror. Sure enough the top of his chest was red. It didn't feel hot, but it looked pretty ugly.

He wondered where she was. He could hear her pottering around in the kitchen. He'd planned to slowly seduce her and surprise her with his newfound vigor and virility, but the desire was growing out of control.

He walked through the lounge and into the kitchen, where she stood, busying herself with dishes from breakfast. He loved her and had never stopped having desire for her, but the vision of her body and the god-awful clothes she hid it in had stripped away a lot of the carnality. He usually wanted to have sex because he loved her, not because the sight of her ass drove him wild with lust. Today it seemed very different. Her ass looked huge in the flowing baggy pants that she was wearing, but today the sight of it filled him with desire.

He walked up behind her and thrust the monster erection that he had between her flabby cheeks. He slipped his arms around her ample form, grabbed two handfuls of squishy breast and whispered into her left ear, "I've got something for you."

Karen jumped and gasped, quickly smiling to herself and thrilling at was wedged between her buttocks. She enjoyed the feeling for a moment and then turned to face him, grinning.

"You been watching porn on the web again?" She accused.

"Nope, just thinking about your sweet hole, darling!"

He grabbed her hand and yanked her away from the sink, his pole pointing the way as they headed towards the bedroom.

"I've got all wet hands, J." Karen playfully resisted.

Jensen ignored her and just kept pulling her along until they finally reached the bedroom. He spun her around and shoved her onto the bed.

Karen lay on the bed and let him get her clothes off as quickly as he could. He was being very strange, very dominating. It would have frightened her, but she was enjoying it. He hadn't shown her this kind of desire for decades. She pushed any concern away and determined to enjoy being ravaged.

Jensen had got her stripped and pawed at his pants to release his cock. He was finding it frustratingly difficult. It was so hard that it was straining the front of his trousers. He was so desperate that he started to try and tear his pants off, but they were stronger than he was. Finally through determination and a little bit of luck he managed to get the blasted button undone and his pants burst open.

"Fucking feel this!" He roared, grabbing Karen's hands and pressing them onto his weapon.

Karen was stunned by how hard he was, she was also shocked by his language. Jensen never swore.

He pushed her legs apart roughly and quickly got between them. He had no time for foreplay. He needed to get inside her. He lined up with her slit and thrust. Karen was thankful that she was excited and his aim was on, because he pushed his hips forward so hard and fast that he could easily have hurt her.

Jensen felt his cock force its way into her body. He felt the warm wet heaven of her pussy engulf him and it made his desire build even more. He grabbed her hips and started fucking her harder and faster than he'd ever done before.

Beneath him Karen gasped at the animal lust being dealt to her. His fucking was brutal and part of her was scared by it. Another more immediate feeling she had was the orgasm rocketing toward her. The cock pumping in and out of her catapulted her to an intense and incredibly satisfying climax that had her body shaking quite violently underneath him.

Jensen continued to thrust. He was humping so hard that he was bruising both of their pelvises, but it was not enough. He needed more. The desire was being overtaken by frustration and rage. However aggressively he fucked he could not get satisfaction. He started feeling a need to hurt her. He looked at her with a desire that was so intense it felt almost like hatred.

He didn't even question what he was doing. He had no control. His hands suddenly grasped her neck. She gasped and started fighting.

Using his hands on her neck and his thrusting crotch, he rammed her further up the bed, pushing her all the way to the beautiful carved hardwood headboard. His fingers dug into her throat and he started to slam the top of her head against the

138

wood as he fucked her. She tried desperately to scream, but was barely able to draw in a breath. The wood behind her started to turn red as her head was repeatedly smashed into it. She could feel the life being squeezed out of her as the man she loved continued to hump at her like a deranged animal. A few moments later the struggle faded away as blackness consumed her.

Jensen felt her slump, but all that did was enrage him more. He wanted her to struggle and now she wasn't even bothering to do that. He kept fucking and slowly dug his hands deeper and deeper into her neck. He felt the crunch in his hands and knew that he had stolen her life. He continued, squeezing and fucking. His assault on her continued for another hour, by which time her neck was pulped and his cock was red raw.

He fell back and slumped on the bed, exhausted.

Twelve hours later the phone rang. It stopped ringing before he properly got his eyes open. For some reason he felt absolutely exhausted and sore. He could feel Karen lying next to him, not by touch or from hearing her, just awareness of her bulk.

His crotch hurt and he let his hand move to it and explore. The fog in his mind slowly started to clear and he snapped his head in Karen's direction. The light streaming into the room from outside revealed the true horror of what he'd done and he started to scream as he threw himself backward off the bed. He landed with a thud onto the floor and crawled backward as fast as he could away from the nightmarish scene.

Suddenly every detail of what had happened rushed back into his conscience. He could feel her neck being crushed in his fingers; he could hear the sound of her desperate attempts to breathe. He could also remember the incredible pleasure he'd felt as her fucked her and even though he was lucid enough to be horrified by what had happened, he felt like a switch had been flicked in him.

He glanced over to the battered corpse of the woman he loved and wanted to vomit. He heaved as the magnitude of what he'd done hammered itself into his head. Yet, even as all that happened, he could feel the feint seed of arousal stirring. As he wept quietly and pitied himself he momentarily considered having sex with her again, even though he had a clear mental picture of how disgusting that thought was.

As he fought the conflicting urges a tiny seed of a thought struggled to grow. It was so vague and hazy that initially he tried to ignore it, but it nagged and worked at him, demanding attention, demanding to be uncovered, demanding to be fed. It eventually pitched itself against the self-loathing and the carnal desperation and it won. Jensen focused his entire troubled mind on the thought until it suddenly snapped into focus.

The pills!

He practically jumped up and rushed over to his bedside drawer. He ignored the tragic corpse of Karen with all his willpower and rifled through the eclectic mixture of useless crap that he treasured so much it had to be close to him while he slept. Among the knickknacks was the box of pills. He grabbed it and opened the packet to see if there was a consumer sheet with side effects inside. There was nothing, just two sheets of pills, with one missing.

It had to be the pill.

As he sat staring idly at the packet he realized that it didn't say Viagra on the front at all, it actually said Diagra.

What the fuck was in them?

There was nothing specific about what was in them on the packaging. He'd bought them online, but had a nagging feeling that they'd shipped from the city.

He rushed out to the rubbish bin and tipped the thing upside down, spilling rotten food and everything the food had leaked over and contaminated all over the ground. For a moment he didn't see the package the pills had come in and struggled to remember if it had been the week before that they'd come. But then he saw the stained corner of the parcel. He grabbed it and despite the putrid liquid that got on his hands, turned it over and around, hunting for a return address.

He found it. A small line that he knew he'd seen, across the bottom of the back of the envelope. *112 Kantal Crt, Newbridge.*

Jensen ripped the address off the packaging and stormed back inside the house, leaving the crap all over the paving by the bins. He rushed through his home, only stopping to put some proper shoes on and pick up the packet of pills sitting on the bed beside Karen. He grabbed his keys and jumped in the car. He sat for a moment in the driveway, copying the address into the GPS, then set off, letting the polite female voice tell him where to go.

During the 30 minute drive Jensen was not really there. He performed the function of a driver, but his mind was lost in a cloud of pain and horror. Even as he jammed on the brake when the traffic in front of him came to a standstill his mind played no part. His body was a robot doing what the GPS told it to do and the years of repetition operating a car had programmed it to do.

As he finally pulled down the dingy looking dead end that was Kantal Court he realized that he already had no recollection of any part of the journey.

Kantal Court was a rubbish littered alleyway off one of the main streets in what was locally known as Chinatown, a term that was considered racist and ignorant by at least half of the quite metropolitan population that lived and worked there. Jensen drove slowly, hunting for 112. He came to a door marked *110* and stopped the car, blocking the narrow road for anyone else that wanted to use it.

He got out of the car and walked past the stinking rubbish bins that sat between the *110* door and the next one. He got to the dirty red door and searched for a number. There was nothing, no number, no bell, just a sad old door with an old looking keyhole. Jensen crouched down and tried to peek through the keyhole, but it was blocked by something. He pushed against the door and it moved, quietly clicking open.

He slowly pushed the door open wider and heard a quiet invitation for him to enter.

Despite the anger and stress he was filled with, Jensen walked quite meekly into the strange little store that was 112 Kantal Court. The place was like an old fashioned apothecary. The walls were all lined with jars filled with liquids, herbs, pills and all kinds of other things.

Behind the long wooden serving counter was a friendly looking small old Chinese looking man, smiling at him.

Jensen walked up to the counter and slammed down the box of Diagra. "I want to know what is in these."

The little old man looked down at the box and then up at him with a frown. "Not for sale here." He said.

"I don't want to buy. I want to know what it is made of." Jensen insisted.

"I don't know it." The man said, shaking his head.

Jensen fished the torn strip from the back of the parcel out of his pocked and slammed it down on the counter. "I know this came from here. Don't try and pretend you don't know what it is."

"Oh! You bought online. I just send, not know what it is made." The old guy insisted, still smiling.

Jensen suddenly caught sight of something he recognized in a small pile of papers to his right. It was four sheets down and only the corner of the sheet was visible, but the ambiguous looking D at the start of the logo he could see was sticking out to him like dogs balls.

The old man followed his gaze and made a quick lunge for the pile of papers, but he didn't beat Jensen, who slammed the sheet he'd just snatched from the pile down onto the wood.

The only thing he could understand on the paper was the logo, Diagra. Everything else was written in Chinese, including some stuff in red that looked like a warning.

"This! What does this say?" He shouted, picking the sheet up and slamming it down again.

"I don't know, that Chinese, I'm not Chinese," he lied.

Jensen felt a rage take him over. It enveloped him in an instant and he shot his hand forward and grabbed the old guy by the neck, his fingers digging into the soft flesh.

"Don't fuck with me old man. I am having a very bad day."

"You racist! You think everyone here is Chinese!" The old man insisted as he struggled.

Jensen turned the man's head sideways and slammed it down on the counter by the sheet of paper.

He saw a metal spike further down the counter with a load of orders skewered on it. He pulled the man toward it by his neck. He grabbed the spike by his other hand and pointed it at the old man's eye.

"You have one chance to give me a straight answer."

"Okay, okay! I'm Chinese. It is recalled." The man said, recognizing that the ignorance card was no longer a viable one to play.

"Recalled? Why?" Jensen demanded.

"Contamination." The man said, "You want money back?"

"No I don't want money back! I killed my fucking wife!" Jensen bellowed.

The old man's eyes widened and he fought to think of something to say to placate the man who had him by the neck.

Jensen let the rage that he'd been trying to control take over. He plunged the metal spike into the Chinese man's eye and forced it all the way through to his brain. The old guy barely had a chance to react before he was dead. Jensen held him and hated him for a couple of moments before he let him go and the body slumped out of sight behind the counter.

He looked over to the packet of pills on the counter. They were calling him.

He'd killed two people. His life was fucked even though he knew that taking another Diagra would ultimately bring him nothing but anguish; it was all he wanted to do.

He quickly popped one of the blue pills out of the packed and downed it dry before he had a chance to change his mind.

He pocketed the packet of pills, turned his back on the counter and slipped back out into the street.

He needed to find someone to fuck before the pill kicked in properly. The burning desire to uncover the cause of what had happened to him was overtaken by a deeper, baser one.

He didn't bother with the car, he knew roughly where he was and he also knew that just a few streets away was the district locals liked to refer to as Grope Lane. He knew he would find what he was hunting there.

By the time he hit the red light district he was already starting to feel the flush. He knew he didn't have much time before he was likely to get out of control. There were several women loitering along the street, all waiting for punters to drive by and pick them up in their cars. Jensen briefly wondered if leaving the car behind had been a smart move.

Then he heard, "Want a date?"

He turned and saw the girl that asked the question. She looked totally drug fucked, but that didn't matter. His eyes went to her crotch and he wanted it.

He smiled at her. "Sure, you got a place?"

"Just round the corner." She said and set off ahead of him.

Jensen watched the skinny ass move as she led him down another dingy side street. Each step he took he could feel the need to fuck grow. By the time they got to the door of her rundown apartment building Jensen was fighting the urge to throw her down onto the street and ravage her.

They walked up three flights of disgusting, piss reeking stairs before getting to her door. As soon as she turned the key Jensen shoved her into the apartment. She desperately tried to demand cash from him as he ripped at her clothes.

She fought back. She was no stranger to violence, but he was far more powerful. It wasn't long before he had most of her clothes off. She was shrieking in his ear as he rammed his cock into her. He spared no thought about what she might be carrying in her body and blood. His cock pounded into her relentlessly. It was already the most brutal fuck she'd ever had and he'd only just started.

She clawed at him and ripped lines into his face and side.

His mind was almost completely focused on his crotch, but her thrashing and yelling was starting to aggravate him. He pulled his upper body back.

She got a brief look at his manic face and put even more effort into screaming.

Jensen gave her one quick and viscous punch to the throat, collapsing her windpipe. He went back to thrusting his cock in and out of her as she desperately fought for breath. He paid no attention to her struggle for life. She couldn't get any air and eventually went still and quiet under him as he kept fucking. He was nowhere near ready to blow and unlike with his wife he was glad this girl had stopped fighting. Her incessant screaming had bugged him.

While the noise she'd been making had bugged him, it had also troubled one of the girls working on the floor below. She'd crept up the stairs and peeked in to see what the fuss was about. As soon as she saw the struggle going on she bolted back down to her apartment and called Phillipe. They all knew the drill and depended on the guy to look after them.

Phillipe couldn't make money out of busted up women and he burst into BB's apartment to find Jensen violently humping away at her dead body.

Jensen turned his head to see who had just come in and came face to face with the barrel of a gun. He kept fucking, he couldn't help it.

A 9mm bullet smacked into his forehead at 700mph. The hollow-point spread as it smashed through the bone and little bits of metal shredded Jensen's brain before ejecting a good portion of it out of the back of his head. He collapsed on BB's skinny corpse, his cock still buried deep inside her and his brain matter and blood coating part of her face.

Phillipe pulled Jensen's body off her and rifled through his pockets. He was looking for money, a wallet, anything he could use. He found the packet of pills and shoved them in his pocket. It wasn't much, but he was going to need a good time after clearing up this shit.

Senhpi ez hrl Dmajld

(Coitus of the Damned)

Christian Riley

Editor's Choice Award Winner

She bathed in the colliquative afterbirth of the Underworld, sluicing her curvaceous features with erubescent gore. Scraping her nipple with a long fingernail, she stopped and went back at it. Baalat, Abyzou, Robber of the Mortal Infant, Serpent Seed, and Queen of the Damned—Lilith—pinched the rigid nipple between two fingers and gave a twist. She closed her eyes, moaned and smiled. She stood, ran a hand down her smooth skin and wet abdomen until she found her moistened and matted genital hair. She explored the dripping area with a finger, and then moaned once more, tantalized now by the clarion wail of the naked, tormented humans writhing in the pit next to her.

An impenetrable cloak of darkness obscured the surrounding walls of her lair, appearing as if Lilith, and her pool of carnage, and her trench of raveled mortals were suspended in night. But Lilith knew what lied beyond this black mantle, beyond her Walls of Pleasure, and beyond the Abyss itself. And she knew that on this night, he would come for her.

Nothing in the Underworld is absolute, save for absolute misery. To her size, the humans in the pit were minute, roughly the size of a large cock, (but not nearly the size of his gargantuan member). Yet those humans—if one could call them that— masticated against and within the Walls of Pleasure, beyond the darkness, were as varied in size as they were in posture. Or "completeness." It was this very structure, this fabric of woven limbs interlaced with gristle and bloodied sinew, splitting membranes and torn tissue, lost and wandering lidless eyeballs, headless and bodiless mounds of flesh each pulsing in harmony, or disharmony, to the breathing cadence of their charge—the Walls of Pleasure—where the embedded creatures had been eternally cutoff and suspended at the brink of ejaculation, teasing, left wanting, needing, craving, yet never finding... It was this structure that had whispered to Lilith his imminent arrival.

She had heard from these walls, which had heard from a transient Luciferge, who had heard from a Lost Soul that on this night, Orcus had been released. Lilith dug her finger deeper, pressed harder, moaned longer.

But how to prepare? The Queen of the Damned had over five-hundred years to get ready for this moment. She had concocted countless scenarios in her mind, and had devised numerous postures and postulations to accompany the impending string of time spent in thrashing exultation with the Punisher of Broken Oaths. She knew she would "make babies" on this night—hence, the pit of mortals at her side. And making babies brought with it the notion of motherhood; a concept that moved Lilith's black soul through time immeasurable.

Yes, *motherhood*: Lilith's forbidden fruit swaying high in the branches of a solitary tree, beyond reach yet seemingly so, the very apple lingering at the fingertips of Tantalus himself...

Lilith sighed. Nothing in the Underworld is absolute, save for absolute misery. She reached down and snatched a mortal from the pit. The human was male, his eyes bloodshot, yawning with horror. His mouth moved expeditiously, synchronized with the sounds of his language. She understood his words of course; variations of protests, and pleads for mercy. But these words were as heedless to Lilith's mind as a drink from the River of Lethe.

Still, she would kiss the mortal to assuage his suffering. Yes, she would do that. Pulling the creature to her mouth, his head the color and size of a cherry, Lilith pressed her lips onto his face and kissed, then pulled away. His eyes rolled to the back of his head and his body dithered, stunned from the great suction upon his cranium. Lilith then pressed her mouth to his groin and sucked. She gently probed his genitals with her tongue until she felt him stiffen—body and cock together. She felt his hands rest upon her brow. She felt his member grow rigid, a tiny barb or bramble at the tip of her tongue. His legs went limp as Lilith dug her tongue deeper into his crotch, his anus, licking and slurping his underside as if it were ripe fruit, until the little man groaned.

Knowing that she had now nursed his cock to the point of near climax, Lilith pitched the mortal off to the side, high into the air, before sliding back down into her bath. Yes; how to prepare?

She could wear something naughty. Lilith knew that a naked body isn't as seductive as one slightly concealed by thin garments. A simple white negligee perhaps, pressed to capacity by her ample breasts. She could even stain it with blood. Then again, Orcus might prefer leather.

And of course there was the swing; a little dusty from lack of use, but worthy all the same. Lilith could have her minions set it up next to the bed, where she would then climb in and wait. Swaying on her back, legs spread, pussy juiced with hunger; she would be an enticing morsel to any demon, let alone one who'd spent the last five-hundred years in mindless toil.

What the mortals on Earth referred to as "doggy-style," the denizens of the Underworld called "the ram." Lilith could lie in wait on the floor in this position, shoulders touching the ground, back arched low, her swelled cooch pushed up, begging. Orcus would enter her lair, find Lilith in the ram position, then promptly enter her, beginning an all-out assault of pumping and pulling. What's better than cutting to the chase with an irresistible offering?

Decisions, decisions, decisions.

She glanced down at the pit of mortals once again, searching for inspiration. There were fifty or so of the creatures, adults of their species, each plucked randomly from the world of the living. Presently, they were huddled together in a tight web of limbs, shamelessly expressing to each other their ghastly terrors.

Absently rubbing her nipples, Lilith observed the humans for several minutes. She concluded that her inspiration needed a little more intervention; she blinked her eyes and made it so. Amongst their howls and ululations, their incessant grovelings and squirmings, the captured mortals suddenly entered into an uncontrolled carousal of the flesh. Hands trembling, they reached for each other, groping breasts, testicles, hips and shoulders. They pulled hair, yet anxiously bit their own knuckles, eyes starring with crazed grief. They moved into various postures of copulation, sucked genitals, slavered their quivering lips and watering tongues over pubescent sap, stroked members, spread thighs, smacked thighs, yanked and thrust and mounted upon each other...all the while bawling with dread.

"Spare me the fucking foreplay, whore."

Lilith turned her head and smiled. "Orcus," she whispered.

A sudden, collective shriek emitted from the tangle of humans; standard announcement of the great demon's arrival.

"It's been a long time," continued Lilith, rising from her blood bath. "A very long time...my Lord of Pain and Suffering." She reached out and brushed her hand against his cheek, then stroked his goatee.

"Don't make me repeat myself, wretch." His hulking mass of muscles rippled as he unfastened clasps and buckles, releasing outerwear: flayed hides of indistinct origin, pauldrons of flame, vambraces made from bony arachnids, quick to scurry for cover upon hitting the floor. "Five-hundred years cracking the whip in the Fields of Punishment—bloody hell!"

"You did take an oath in His name, did you not?" Lilith stepped out of the bath, then strolled around her guest.

"Hmmf!" snorted Orcus. He ripped off his loincloth, and his massive demonhood sprang forth. "Hades is a fucking stickler. All I did was crack a joke to a bunch of Harpies over drinks, and bam!—Fields of Punishment."

"You've learned a lesson, then?"

Orcus flexed his groin muscles repeatedly and his meaty member bobbed up and down, stiffening into its full, two-foot length. "I'll show you a lesson, fiend." He grabbed her by the hair, she resisted, reached up and clawed his face and one of his horns, there was a brief struggle, then Lilith finally acquiesced and slid down to her knees.

"You promised we'd make babies." Lilith grasped his thick shaft with both hands, gently running he tongue up and down it, blowing softly.

"Am I not called The Punisher of Broke Oaths for nothing?"

Lilith smiled, then floated her fingers along Orcus' rigidness before sucking at his testicles. She reached a hand between his legs and dug her nails into his inner thigh, stroking the tip of his cock with the other, tongue working his genitals with fiery passion. She tasted a thousand years of anguish—the bitter and sour tang of salt and metal. Lilith reached down and scooped juices from her pussy, applying the sticky residue to Orcus' scrotum and cock. She sloshed her mouth over his cock and balls repeatedly until the taste had gone sweet, and then she smiled. Standing, Lilith said nothing as she pulled the great demon along by his wet erection, toward the bed.

Before lying down, Orcus stopped Lilith with a tug of her hair. He pulled up behind her, pressed his chest against her back, slid his cock between her legs, grazing her wetness and pushing through to the other side, where Lilith then reached down and seized it. "We'll make babies tonight," he said, "but it'll cost you." He glided his hands past her shoulders, smoothing across her large breasts until his fingers found her nipples. Then he squeezed and pinched, twisted and yanked while Lilith pulled up on his cock, jerking it against her clit.

"Anything," she whispered.

Orcus threw her on the bed, then lied down himself, rolling onto his back, his stiff member risen like the trunk of a tall tree. Lilith scrambled on top of him, straddling his face with her pussy, thoroughly taking his cock into her mouth. She managed half its length down her throat, gagging and spewing saliva, which she used as lubricant for her gliding hands and fingers. She caressed his pole with a firm grip, using long strokes and long pulls, up and down its great length while sucking his knob. Streams of spit periodically oozed from her gagging mouth, dripping down into lustrous sheens, polished by her working hands.

On Orcus' end, his nose and mouth took in Lilith's musky scent, sending bolts of lightning through his prostate, driving his cock to its fullest height. His tongue slithered out of his mouth like a snake, impossibly long as it entered into the cavity of Lilith's cunt. Slurping juices and slobbering his lips into her, Orcus feasted upon Lilith's moist tenderness until he felt her hips quiver. He pulled his tongue out, where it then split in half, becoming two slippery corkscrews. Now, Orcus drove one tongue back into Lilith's pussy, and the other into her anus, deep and wriggling, pushing and pulsing.

She came immediately. A torrent of yellow nectar rushed out of Lilith's pussy, bathing Orcus' face with a sweet flavor and pungent odor. At this moment, the surrounding darkness fled, and the Walls of Pleasure beamed in all its brilliant and gorgeous horror. Membranes bulged outward while arms and legs vainly reached forth. Hands flexed, mouths gaped open and screamed, the entire monstrous canopy of fibrous flesh and bone pulsed and echoed like a drum as Lilith and Orcus moaned in unison. Then the demon lord blew his nut-sack, sending a sticky stream of spooge high into the air, across Lilith's face, into her mouth, onto her back, everywhere.

This was just the beginning. Now, dripping with Orcus' hot seed, Lilith promptly spun around and mounted the demon's still-rigid cock. She engulfed it with her sodden pussy, and took the entire length into her, deep and delving. She sighed with each retraction, and groaned with each driving thrust. She fucked him with the fervor found only in a five-hundred year abstinence, clawing his chest, pressing her nipples into his mouth, ramping up and down his wet shaft, gripping his horns, crying with ecstasy after each rushing orgasm, one after the other.

When at last Lilith fell to her side, breathing heavy, Orcus sat up and roared with passion. "Now then, let us make babies!" Moments later, the mortals from the pit arrived, suspended in the air above the bed, a tangled cluster of panicking humans. The creatures screamed. They vomited, pissed, and shat. They jerked their heads back and forth frantically, driven by fear, watching with dread, apprehended by pure, raw evil.

Orcus pulled one down and stared at it; a female. He looked her in the eyes, grinning benignly, until she wailed. Then the demon lord howled with laughter, and began licking the woman with his tongues. Her guttural clamor and physical protests amused him. She became something of a toy for Orcus. He observed her breasts jiggle as she spasmed for escape. He watched the crevice of her crotch contort with each wriggle and waggle of her body. He pressed her against his cock, and snickered at her bulging eyes, then; at her limp figure as the creature passed out.

"Fuck me with that thing, already," begged Lilith, assuming the ram position. "You promised."

Orcus blew a spell onto the human in his hand, and the creature promptly awoke. "Wasn't a nightmare, my dear," he chuckled, and then the woman caterwauled violently before Orcus pushed her into Lilith's waiting womb. "Making babies!" he laughed, driving his pole in after the human.

Lilith grunted from the added pressure of having a human crammed into her cunt, but quickly "mothered-up," so-to-speak. She was making babies, and the very thought unleashed a flood of visceral ichor through her veins. *Yes! Motherhood! It was time! Give it to me!* She arched her back and craned her neck, staring as the demon lord's fantastic cock jam-packed her swollen vadge. "Put another one in!" she shouted.

By demand, Orcus snatched another human from the air and shoved it into Lilith. Then he snatched a third, fourth, and fifth, before bringing his throbbing erection into position. He noticed the last human to go in was making a break for it, attempting to climb out of Lilith's pussy. Slowly, comically, Orcus used the head of his cock to block the mortal's path. The demon obviously found great humor in toying with the horrified mortals, much to Lilith's impatience.

"Give it to me, you fucker!" cried Lilith.

Entertained still, Orcus slowly pushed his cock into Lilith, focusing on the tight squirm within. He felt little hands, little claws, and little teeth scratch and bite his knob. He felt frantic movements in the dark, as the mortals undoubtedly sought shelter from his freakish behemoth, the colossal trunk of pulsing meat there to squash them into oblivion. *No one escapes*, Orcus thought, as he angled his pelvis to-and-fro, ramming Lilith's inner walls—her own Walls of Pleasure—compressing, combining, amalgamating the helpless mortals into mangled kablooie.

Several minutes of pumping, and then Orcus finally came, sending an emission of creamy life into Lilith. The subsequent mixture of human carnage and demon seed within Lilith's womb coalesced into a coagulated package of flesh and bone. Orcus pulled his spent member out of Lilith as she rolled over onto her back. Her eyes flared open. Her belly grew. She spread her legs and cried in pain, and ecstasy. And, she pushed.

Seconds later, Lilith gave birth. Her baby was a disfigured bundle of flesh; oval-shaped, not unlike that of a large egg, a tousled and bloody lump with five crying mouths. She kissed it, smiled, then laid it to the side, sitting up again—ram position. "Babies," she moaned, emphasizing the plural form of the word.

Orcus stroked his cock, stiffening it, then began plucking humans from the air. Having observed the fate of their brethren, the creatures were now in an open state of scrimmage against the demon lord...much to Orcus' humor.

The game for him now, was how many mortals he could cram into Lilith's stretched pussy before one of them got out. A dozen in, and the last one managed to leap forth, down, and onto the bed, breaking a leg. Orcus laughed aloud. He snatched the panicked creature by its foot, then tossed it into his mouth, swallowing it whole before ramming his hard rod into Lilith's stuffed womb. There was a muffled cry that came from within, and a great moan that came from Lilith, and a terrible shriek that came from those humans waiting in the air, as Orcus drove it home.

And minutes later, Lilith gave birth once again.

The evening rolled on. Lilith and Orcus continued to fuck each other silly, using up the last of the mortals. And the "babies" were born. They were lined up on the bed; little baubles of gelatinous flesh, cooing and crying, and Lilith wiped tears of joy from her cheeks at the sight and sound of her new family. She felt a bloom of warmth spread throughout her abdomen, and her nipples tingled when she heard her little ones yammer. Motherhood was upon her, and although exhausted, Lilith was ecstatic.

Lying with her lover on the bed now, Lilith gently brushed Orcus' chest with her fingers. She kissed his shoulder softly, replaying in her head a few highlights of the night. She looked down at his limp and raw member, and took it in her hand, eager to suck it again for all that it had gifted her with. "You're a demon of your word, my Lord," she whispered.

At this, Orcus sat up and scooted backward, leaning against the headboard. He didn't say anything, just appeared to be deep in thought. From thin air, he produced a cigar and tankard of ale.

Lilith adjusted herself in response, lying now against his thigh, holding his cock against her cheek. She too was deep in thought. "We shall have to name them?"

Orcus rolled his eyes. "And the cost for making babies...is that they're all yours." He drained his tankard, took a long pull on his cigar before chucking it to the side, then climbed out of bed. Seconds later he was dressed and on his way out into the Abyss. He never even said goodbye.

Nothing in the Underworld is absolute...

Lilith sat on the bed, confused and dismayed. She never expected much from the Lord of Pain and Suffering, but her own feelings had her perplexed. To be so disappointed, yet happy at the same time. And was she happy? She had her babies now, and they were very much alive, wailing with hunger, a concert of chaos surrounding her. Which one to feed first? Lilith realized that she didn't even know *how* to feed her precious balls of joy. Each of them had several mouths, which were disfigured by layers of tissue, or distorted jumbles of teeth. She picked one up and pressed it to her nipple. The creature howled and tried to suck, but Lilith's nipple was too big, so she turned the bundle around, finding another mouth. It worked, the baby sucked hard, and Lilith felt a surge of happiness—until the little thing bit down. She cursed then laid the baby to the side, picking up another one. They were screaming something terrible, each of them, dozens of mouths gaping with angry hunger.

Lilith began to panic. The Walls of Pleasure surrounding her receded into darkness once again. The Queen of the Damned pulled her hair and shouted with frustration. Frantically, she gave another try at feeding them. Lilith picked them up one at a time, shoved her nipples into mouths, felt their suckling, then vicious bites. Their incessant wailing drove madness into her ears, her tiny crybabies with their never-ending hunger and unchecked tantrums, a bedlam from the bed causing a rush of anger, hatred, lunacy, and...

The last one in was Lilith herself. A bit higher now, the bloodline of the bath up to her chin, she closed her eyes and enjoyed the silence. She savored the press of warm liquid upon her entire body, then summoned a bottle of wine. She sighed, thinking about her night with its forays of lust, and her sultry emotions embedded with maternal longings. She felt a stir below her navel, an electric tingle in her nipples, and thought once again what it would be like. But thankfully, she felt her little ones wobble under the surface as she moved her legs, gasping for life of course while she smiled and drank her wine. Motherhood *indeed*.

"I'm Not Sorry"
Stephen Cooney

Just Take It

Robert Holt

"What exactly does it do?" The small red pill sat in my sweaty palm as the car bounced and rocked over the gravel road toward our hangout, a vacant shack at the far end of Carl's father's land.

"It is supposed to be like ecstasy," Jake said with a grin. Even in the darkness of the car I could see his teeth shining. How a guy that did every drug in the book was able to keep his teeth so fucking white is beyond me. "Only better!"

With that, Mallory began laughing. She had swallowed her pill a few minutes prior. I caught sight of her beautifully smooth legs from under her dress as she fell back against the window laughing. Jake quickly ran his hand from her calf up to her thigh and under her little hippy dress. "Just take it;" Jake looked from her giggling form to my eyes, "then we can all have some fun."

"Are you going to take one?" My question was directed to Carl, who was usually pretty level headed about what drugs he smoked, ingested, or injected, but it was Jake that answered. "Fuck yeah, man. I took one, Mallory took one, Dee took one, and Carl's going to take one as soon as he parks this death trap, right man?"

Carl nodded and looked into his rearview mirror. He was looking at Dee's cleavage in the mirror. I laughed as I realized this. It was so typical of Jake. The guy liked drugs and could get drugs. Because of this ability of his, he always had beautiful girls hanging around, but Jake was always more interested in hanging out with his friends. He used the girls to get us to share his drugs with him. Then we shared the girls. It wasn't a bad arrangement really. He bought the drugs, he brought the girls, and we all had a good time...usually.

"Is this going to leave me blunted tomorrow," I asked. "I have to work at my father's shop at nine in the morning."

"Jesus dude, you are killing me," Jake said, and Mallory broke into another fit of laughter. "If you are worried about it, just take half. To tell you the truth, this shit is new to me too."

I broke the pill in half. I looked at the two pieces and handed Jake the slightly larger half. "Cheers," he said and licked it from his palm and swallowed.

I put the pill on my tongue and tasted the strange, tingling taste. I swallowed.

The car came to a stop a few seconds later at the old hunting cabin. The girls hopped out of the car and held each other up as they laughed at the deplorable condition the place was in. Carl laughed with them, but I could tell he was embarrassed. "There is a pond out back that we can swim in later, I mean, if you want to," he said.

"Do you mean skinny dipping," Dee asked in a mockingly innocent voice that had Mallory literally falling over laughing. They were obviously high on something else too.

"That's right," Jake said as he hooked the front of Dee's blouse with his index finger and pulled downward. Her huge bare breasts bounced in their momentary freedom.

She slapped his hand away and scowled as she put herself away. "Asshole."

"Come on Dee," Jake said, "let us see your double D's."

She started laughing as she smacked Jake's hands away while he kept reaching for her breasts. She then stepped forward quickly, grabbed Jake by the ears, and forced his face into her tits. "This a close enough look?" She then fell to the dirt ground laughing beside Mallory as Jake made as if he had been struck stupid by her actions.

"Hey," Mallory suddenly said with a serious face. "He never took a chill pill." Her accusing finger pointed out Carl. I was relieved. Carl was the type that wouldn't point out that he was sober, and then the sneaky fuck would manipulate the whole group into doing whatever he wanted.

Jake strolled over to Carl and produced one of the little pills. "Come on man. Join the party."

"Yeah, don't you want to be cool," Dee said with a Valley girl smack of her lips.

"All your friends are doing it," Malory said in a voice made tinny through insuppressible laughter.

Carl smiled and swallowed the pill. He and I then went into the cabin. He instantly grabbed a broom and started sweeping the floors. I went around and dug out the old oil lantern and lit it with a match. After that, I threw a few logs into the fire place and got it fired up with a splash of lighter fluid and a few balls of crumpled newspaper. The girls then came in laughing.

"Cozy. Reminds me of Starbucks." Dee said, and Mallory began snorting she was laughing so hard.

A few minutes later, Jake came in, still zipping up his fly from pissing in the woods. He looked around. "No cops. No parents. No teachers. A couple good friends. A couple of beautiful ladies. A bottle of pills. This place is PERFECT!"

We settled down, sat cozily on the floor boards around the fireplace. We told stories and laughed. We told jokes and laughed. We made deep and difficult confessions and laughed. It was progressing as one of those legendary "Breakfast Club" type evenings where we all found common ground between each other. I learned things about my best friends that I had never known. Mallory seemed stricken with Carl, and Dee and Jake began pawing at each other before too long.

It was then that the drug kicked in.

I felt my cock begin to press against my zipper. I looked over at Carl, and his helmet was actually peeking out of the top of his sweat pants. I heard Jake moan behind me and I turned to see that Dee had hiked up her skirt and was riding him, pink thong panties pulled to the side to allow the entrance into her. I let out a little laugh and turned to point it out to Mallory and Carl when I saw that Carl was on top of her, thrusting away.

I stood up and grabbed my erection through my pants. I was desperate for something, anything. Jake then grabbed my shoulder. I turned toward him. He was completely naked now, and I could see the track marks pocketing his arms. His penis dripped seaman to the floor. "Your turn, brother."

I looked at Dee, and she was looking at me. She was on her back and using her shirt and skirt to lie upon. Her naked body was gyrating, and I could see a small droplet of Jake's jizzum leaking out of her. Under normal situations, I would have been repulsed and would have turned away. However, the drug pulsing through my veins made that impossible. I fumbled with the button on my pants, and then I fell on her. I thrust into her over and over and she ground into each thrust. She began screaming in orgasm, and it excited me further. I came inside of her, and as I did, she wrapped her legs around me preventing me from getting away or rolling over. She continued to grind on me. My limp penis threatened to slip out of her several times, but Dee did not stop. After a minute or so, I was erect again, thrusting again. She rolled me over and rode me in the reverse cowgirl position, bouncing and grinding.

Jake had been cheering us on, but now he moved in. Dee was ready for him. She grabbed his cock and began licking it. She took him into her mouth and down her throat. Jake was standing over my legs and was looking down at me, and we smiled at each other. He held his fist down, and I bumped it with mine. Jake

156

came in her mouth, I came inside her pussy, and Dee came again and again.

Never in my life had I ever had two orgasms back to back like that. The three of us laid there in an awkward pile. We all positioned ourselves in a way that allowed us to watch Carl and Mallory grind into each other. It took only a glance to tell that Carl was working toward his third orgasm.

"You go girl," Dee screamed to her friend, who replied with a grunt. Then Dee climbed onto me and stuck my half limp penis into her again.

"I think I am spent," I said, but she either didn't hear me or didn't care. She ground down on me, and I could feel myself expanding inside of her, getting deeper and deeper. Then there was a tightness inside of her and she dropped onto me and groaned. Jake had moved behind her and had put it up her ass. She continued thrusting despite the double penetration. Feeling the thrusting of Jake's cock from within excited me further, and I began to pulsate into her as fast as I could. I was like a hummingbird's wing. I was pounding into Dee so fast that she began screaming and didn't stop as orgasm after orgasm flushed over her and flooded out over me. I was so preoccupied that I failed to notice that Jake had slipped out of her ass. The shock as he penetrated my ass was devastating. Yet I couldn't stop thrusting into her.

Under normal situations, I would have not only pushed Jake away, but I very well may have killed the little shit. But the drug made me go along. I told him to stop, but when he didn't I just kept thrusting. The pain in my ass was intense, and I cried out in agony and ecstasy as I came again.

As I went limp, Dee dismounted and looked down at my still thrusting pelvis with Jake's dick shoved into me. "Looks like you boys have this under control without me." I cried up at her, but continued thrusting. She and Jake exchanged a high five as she stumbled over to Carl and Mallory.

Time on this drug became a mystery, and it could have been hours or seconds until Jake came inside me. Once he did, he fell down beside me and lit a cigarette. He took a drag and handed it to me. I took two drags, handed it back, and sat up to see what the other three were doing. They were a ball of limbs and torsos. It was as if all three of them wanted to simultaneously fuck and go down on the other two.

My head began to ache as if I was hung over. Jake got up and went to join in. He offered his hand to me. "Shall we join them?"

"No," I said. "I think I'm starting to crash."

"Get some sleep. I hear it is a rough landing."

This was the last thing I remember from the night. I fell asleep or passed out.

I awoke to sunlight shining in through the open door, and my cell phone producing a quacking duck sound from my discarded pants. Nobody else was around. When I moved to get my phone, the pain from my ass hit me. I lifted my balls and saw a small but significant tear in the skin and a massive amount of blood spreading across the floor from where I laid.

I cursed as I climbed to my feet and began dressing. I was moving stiff legged around the cabin. I looked at my phone and saw that it was nine fifteen. I was already late for work, and my father had been calling me every five minutes. We had only the one car here, and the walk back to Carl's house was over three miles away.

I found Dee and Mallory passed out in the back room. They were both sweaty and bruised. The room smelled of stale sex, but it was clearly not overly stale. Dee had her entire hand inside Mallory's pussy and Dee's ass hole looked like an orangutan's, puffy and swollen to a severe level. Seeing it actually made me feel better about my own pains.

"Do you girls know where Carl is?"

No response. I nudged Dee and asked again. She awoke momentarily and thrust her hand into Mallory a few times before passing back out.

I wandered outside into the blinding light of the sun. My head felt as if I had just been knocked out by a heavyweight, and the blazing sun did not help. I tried to yell, "Carl," but my voice did not carry further than my immediate surroundings. My ears were working better than my squinted eyes and choked voice though, and I heard something from around the side of the cabin. I went around the side with an awkward feeling in my gut. The sound was clearly human yet guttural and animalistic.

I saw the murky and algae covered pond first, then I saw Jake with his head raised to the sky and one arm holding onto a thin tree. He was naked and hunched down in the weeds. At first I thought he was shitting, but as I moved a few steps closer I saw Carl beneath him, lying face down and naked. Jake was thrusting into his ass. I stood stock still for several seconds, not knowing what to do, not knowing what was going on.

Suddenly, Jake turned his head and met my gaze. Every instinct I had told me to run, told me that what I was staring at was not human, told me that I was witnessing a brutal and savage rape. Carl was not gay, and even if he was experimenting, it wouldn't be with Jake, a known drug addict and womanizer. As the thought crossed my mind, memories of the previous night came back to me, and my swollen, still bleeding ass confirmed them. I am not gay, and I would never experiment with Jake, yet I had. And Carl was likely doing the same. The drug was a wild one, and it had made all of us do crazy, stupid things.

Jake was smiling at me and waving me over. I hesitantly limped over there. Jake never stopped thrusting as he addressed me, and when he did I realized that it was Carl that was making the groaning sounds. "How do you feel?" The question was delivered with such casualty that one would never guess that it was spoken while sodomizing my best friend.

"Like shit. You guys still at it, I see."

Jake looked down at Carl and then back to me with a broad smile. "You want a turn?"

He wasn't offering to dismount Carl, but to remount me. "No," I said. "I need to get going. I'm late for work."

Jake's face broke for a moment and a savage angry look came over him. "Bye," he said.

"We only have the one car."

"Just take it. We are fine. Aren't we?" He said this to Carl, who nodded.

I started to turn away, but then turned back. "Where are the keys?" Carl's eyes opened for the first time, and I saw how heavily bloodshot they were. His hand flopped out from under him and he pointed toward the lake. I followed his fingers and saw his pants lying on the bank, half submerged. I went over to them and held the dripping fabric up while I fished out the keys.

"Are you guys going to be alright?"

"We'll be fine," Jake said.

"There is no food here."

"We'll be fine," he repeated.

"Should I ask the girls?"

"Just get the fuck out of here!" He had the savage look again. I did not press it. I backed away and left in the car. I left with my best friend getting fucked in the ass by a drugged out maniac. I left four people in the blazing heat of July with no food or clean water and several miles from the nearest house. I want to blame the drug for my cowardice. I want to blame the headache, the stomach ache, the ass ache. But the truth is I was scared. And I left them to it.

After getting home, showering, and getting dressed, I got to work at my dad's shop over three hours late. He was furious at me, but he didn't say a word about it. He just gave me the orders to fix Mrs. Gaffney's muffler on her old Chevy. I slid under the car and assessed the issue. The pipe was cracked all the way through.

I was looking at the different tools and parts I would need, but my eyes kept going back to the cracked muffler, the hole, the slit. My cock started to pulse in my pants. My hands, lightly covered in motor grease slid down beneath my waist band and started messaging my penis.

I was on the verge of orgasm when my father kicked the soul of my shoes. "Are you sleeping under there?"

"No," I said in a choked voice. "I am just checking it out."

"You've been under there for over an hour. Get the fuck out."

I pulled my hand away, took a deep breath, and slid out. I instantly rolled to my side and stood facing away from my father to hide my erection. "Hey," he said, and grabbed me by my shoulder.

I glared at him over my shoulder.

"Jesus, boy. Are you okay?"

"I'm fine," I said. My voice sounded strange to my own ears. I sounded distant and ghostly.

"Take today to get yourself in order. We'll talk about this tomorrow."

I could smell fear on him, and it made my cock grow to have him afraid of me. I did not leave though. I went into the restroom there at the shop and finished my masturbating. Then I slept for several hours. When I awoke, I cracked the door and saw my father working under the hood of an ancient Volkswagen. I bolted out of the shop and into Carl's car. In the rearview, I saw my father walking toward me. I didn't hesitate. I drove off.

As I drove, I saw a pair of middle-aged women out for an afternoon stroll. They were overweight and neither very attractive. Despite this, my cock stiffened, and my instincts were to pull over and throw myself on them, to fuck them both until they turned blue.

I hit the radio on to distract me from my perversions. After a set of a few songs of the standard flair, the disc jockey came on:

> *"Pandemonium and mayhem has erupted throughout the listening region. Sex crazed teenagers on a drug known as Nymph. The drug deteriorates the brain to the point where Sexual impulses cannot be controlled. All listeners should be on guard for the next few days as this crisis is brought to bay."*

I swerved the car over and began searching the web on my phone. As music came on the radio, I shut it off. The local on-line news resources gave a wider scope of the situation. Rapes, murders, and overdoses were widespread throughout the Midwest. The drug was listed as causing a depravation of sexual morals and subsequent mania with a single dose, and a second dosage caused death. The drug was reported as factory made, and the reporter speculated that it was a form of terrorism from one of our countries enemies. I cursed the air as I read.

I tilted my head back and thanked God that I only took half of a pill, but at the same time my concern for Carl and the girls was raking me with guilt for leaving them. And Jake, he took a pill and a half, possibly even more that we didn't know about. Was he dead of overdose?

I sped toward the cabin. I hoped a police officer would clock me and follow me, but none did, and I didn't have the guts to call them, to confess my stupidity. I hit the gravel and dirt road that led to the cabin at full speed. Dust and gravel shot out behind me as the car shifted and threatened to fly out of control. I pumped the breaks to bring it back down to a manageable speed and continued toward the cabin.

I didn't see Mallory lying in the road, and I honestly don't know why. I may have been masturbating again, but I felt the jolt that the car took when I ran her over. I was later told that she had died of blood loss some hours before after being raped through a hole gouged into her back. I saw her in the rearview when I looked to see what I had hit, and my heart sank. Had I not hit her, I doubt I would have had the courage to do what I eventually did. I probably would have seen her condition and fled. Instead, I gunned it toward the cabin with the full knowledge that I was likely going to prison for manslaughter, hitting and killing a girl with designer drugs pulsing through my veins and all.

I stopped the car at the front of the cabin and jumped out. I wished I had a weapon of some sort, but I never took the time to locate one. I ran into the cabin, paying my hurt and swollen ass no heed. I burst through the door and sent a swarm of flies into the air. They had been feasting on the several puddles of blood on the floor; one of them had been from me. I stepped gingerly around the puddles to the door of the back room, where I had last seen the girls. Dee was still there, or what was left of her. Her head had been severed. I didn't need a forensic team to tell me that it had been used for sexual acts even after being removed from the body. The way the semen dripped from the corner of the mouth was a dead giveaway. In addition to the mouth, it also appeared that body had been raped down the bloody neck hole.

I stumbled back through the room in a panicked and sickened state, made worse by my irrational and horrifying erecting. I went out of the cabin and stumbled to the side wall where I bent and vomited. Upon raising my head, I saw Carl tied by his hands to a tree. Jake was standing in front of him, naked, thrusting. I moved quickly and quietly toward them, a feeling of terror coming over me with each step forward. It was all wrong. Carl's head was lulling forward, and resting on Jake's shoulder. They were facing each other. How were they standing, fucking, and facing each other?

When I was less than twenty feet away, a metal glint caught my eye, and I looked down to see a small garden fork; lying beside it was the shredded and discarded remnants of Carl's penis and testicles. I bent and picked up the fork. I had no hesitation, no reflection. I took several running steps toward Jake, the fork raised up like a battle axe from a Viking warrior. Jake turned toward me and the bloody sucking sound of the vacuum created from his withdrawing penis from Carl's body, from the place where his penis once hung was the anthem of my attack. It was the only sound I heard as I brought the fork down upon Jake's face, ripping off the front of his skull. The second swing sent the three metal barbs into his heart. The third swing I can't justify. It was vengeance, purely savage vengeance. I dug the metal prongs of the fork into his ass and I ripped upwards. His sexual organs were dug out, just as he had done to Carl.

I dropped the fork and spat on the corpse. I checked Carl but knew he was dead. From the cold feel of him, he had likely died shortly after I had left him that morning. I can only hope he had died prior to the mutilation and had not suffered.

I took my belt off then and attempted to hang myself from the same tree that still held Carl's body upright. Obviously I failed. My father and Carl's father showed up and cut me down. I was unconscious and near death, but I survived. I take medication to control my sexual urges now. I just pray that they keep working.

Sunset Lake

David Price

The sun floats on top of the lake, briefly, a giant red ball about to sink and submerge until the rebirth of morning. My reflection in the lake, flickering, wavering, distorted. Is that really me? Why did I do it?

My reflection in the lake looks back at me, into my soul. It answers me. *It was easy you just took the knife, pressed it against her neck and drew it ever so slowly, passionately across hear throat, savoring each moment like a lover's kiss.*

Clenching my fists in denial, I kick at the water. **NO!** It wasn't me. I couldn't have done it. A strong gust of wind passes by, the branches of the evergreens bending to it in succession like toppling dominoes. The surface of the lake is churning. Is it my rage? What have I done? Ripples on the surface; so many, so different, crisscrossing each other, crawling over themselves. Emotions are like that.

The knife, it slid into her throat so easily. It was so sharp and her flesh was so soft.

A short distance away, a mother loon dives under the water while her baby waits patiently for the meal she will bring back.

Don't say baby! There was no baby! Why are my hands so sticky? Tracks in the sand mark my passing, dark splotches near my footprints.

It's blood. You tend to get quite a bit of it on you when you slit your girlfriend's throat from ear to ear.

No! I would never do that. I . . . I didn't do anything wrong. The baby loon cries out, lonely. Its mother has not yet surfaced.

Killing your girlfriend is wrong.

I'm getting cold. I should have put on a jacket. A splash in the water near the shore, a big fish chasing little fish. I didn't kill anyone.

Just because you keep saying that won't make it real.

My reflection makes repeated stabbing motions, like Norman Bates in "Psycho." I look away and inhale sharply. The aromas of autumn fill my lungs. It wasn't supposed to happen this way.

I know.

The mother loon has surfaced with a fish in her beak. How long was she down there? I brought Stacy to the cabin because I thought it would be romantic, you know?

Uh-huh.

After Labor Day, it's so quiet and peaceful. The autumn foliage is fiery, wild, and explosive in its beauty. The lake is almost desolate. Nobody comes up this late in the season. We'd have it all to ourselves. It was a perfect place to ask her to marry me.

Heck of a change of plans, wouldn't you say? You know, with you killing her and all. Nevertheless, all things considered a good place to murder someone as well.

Shut up! It was going to be a long engagement, but at least we'd have a commitment to each other. I mean, I just got that scholarship to Amherst College. She was afraid that she would lose me. Four years at college is a long time, she said. I thought if we were engaged, She'd have nothing to worry about.

So why did she have to go and get herself pregnant.

A squirrel jumps from a branch, landing on another, sending a few pine needles spiraling downward.

That would have changed things. You would have to make a choice between her and school.

No, we were going to work it out somehow, but it would have changed my life. I would have had to take a part-time job, delivering pizza or something. Then things could have still worked out.

She was the problem, so you eliminated her, right? You attacked the problem the way dad always taught you to, face to face. He'd be proud.

No! It wasn't like that. You don't understand! We argued, but we made up. I bury my face in my sticky hands. Why is everything so sticky?

Yeah right.

The sun has sunken halfway below the horizon, like a red rubber ball melting into the playground on a scorching summer day.

Sniff, that was almost . . . poetic. You should consider majoring in English.

The crickets are getting louder. A bullfrog croaks nearby. Night is coming. I wonder how deep the lake is. How hard would it be to drown myself?

I can still see her face. Even though you were behind her when you cut her throat, her reflection was surprisingly clear in the porch window. There must have been just the perfect

164

amount of light. The look of horror in her eyes, the gurgling sounds she made as she choked on her own blood, these are the memories that will last a lifetime.

Stop it! Just get out of my head. I . . . I can hear the sparrows fluttering, chirping. They always come out at sunset. Footprints in the sand, my last impression. What was it Kevin said about drowning yourself? I don't remember.

I remember. "It isn't as hard as you think. When you dive in, drink all the water you can, then inhale as deep as you can. You won't have a chance and you'll sink like a rock."

Oh yeah, thanks.

Don't mention it.

I suppose I could take the canoe out to the middle of the lake. Even if there were someone else up here, after dark no one would see me out there. An empty canoe would wash up on someone's beach in the morning. It happens from time to time. Now, where was I?

You made up.

Right. That's the last thing I remember. We went to bed and . . . made up.

And then, early in pre-dawn hours Stacy got out of bed to get a glass of water. You snuck up behind her, took the knife from the countertop, and murdered her.

That's not what happened!

It certainly is.

I must have snapped somehow, I guess.

Yes sirree. That's the understatement of the century.

A small bat flies overhead, darting this way and that, diving close to the lake's surface, chasing mosquitoes most likely. Maybe . . . maybe I lost control, or sleepwalking! Yeah, that could be it. I was sleepwalking. I used to do that when I was a kid. It started up again at school. I loved Stacy. I would never hurt her on purpose.

The doctor prescribed Klonopin to stop the sleepwalking, so you couldn't have had an episode.

Water bugs glide across the surface of the water. The top of the moon has just appeared over the tree line, trading places with the fading sun. Daylight has almost vanished. Did this really happen?

Certainly did.

Maybe it's just a bad dream. The canoe rests on the shore, waiting for me, beckoning to me.

Look on the beach to your left. My reflection points. Ahh! What is that?! No, no, no, no, no.

It's her heart surrounded by a small pool of blood. Who does that? What is that anyway, some trademark for your new life as a serial killer?

A loon calls out again, as if bidding farewell to the setting sun, lonely, haunting. No, you see, this proves it wasn't me. Who could do such a thing?

A disturbed individual.

Exactly.

You.

NO!

Yes.

The moon just rose over the treetops. Looks like a pair of horns. What's that called, Devil's Moon?

And tonight All Hallows Eve, what a coincidence.

The crickets are singing louder. One frog croaks out, then another and another. Perhaps they're taking roll call. Something splashes in the water a few feet away, but it's too dark to see what it was now. I can never go back to a normal life after this.

You have a firm grasp of the obvious.

How could I have done something so . . . so evil?

It was easy, you just took the knife and . . .

Cut it out!

You already did that; her heart, remember? Just as she tore out yours.

No, no, no.

Oh yes.

Hand in my pocket, I feel something. Huh, look at this. I still have the ring. The stars are shining. There won't be enough moonlight to dim them tonight.

You won't be needing that ring anymore.

A train whistle echoes through the forest, the direction of its origin unclear, surrounding me and filling me with dread. I haven't skipped stones since I was a kid. Wonder how many times the ring would skip?

I wonder how many times her heart would skip.

Shut up.

Never know unless you try.

I clutch the ring, feeling its cold hard reality. This was my future, but now I don't have one. I push it hard into my fingertip until the small diamond draws blood. What have I done? The water had calmed down now, better for skipping stones, maybe even engagement rings. I pull my arm back, whip it forward and flick my wrist. The ring skips over the surface, one, two, three . . . wow, six times.

Not bad.

Hear the wind blowing through the tops of the trees. The sun is gone and the night creatures have welcomed me to their world. I wonder how deep the lake is?

What are you going to do, just paddle out there and drown yourself?

Yeah.

Don't forget to drink up.

I won't.

Good. Don't chicken out now.

The water's calm again. It's so dark.

Like polished black marble. Look closer.

I can see everything. So smooth, it doesn't even look like water anymore.

More like glass. Look closer.

A picture forming in the lake. It's me and Stacy. This is the drive on the way to the cabin.

I know.

Wait a minute, you can't make me watch this. It's going to happen all over again.

Light dawns on marble head. Look closer. The old wizards used to call that a scrying pool. We read that somewhere, didn't we?

No, I don't want to see this. Not again. It hurts too much. Please stop.

Remember.

"I'm so excited, Ryan." Stacy squirmed in her seat a little, delighted about something.

"I can see that. What's up?" I smiled, thinking about how perfect this weekend was going to be and how much I loved this girl sitting next to me.

"Nothing. I just have good news, that's all." Stacy flashed me a coy grin.

"Me too. What's yours?" There weren't many cars on the road. Few of the summer folk came north this late in the season.

"Can't tell you *now*," Stacy said in a teasing, playful voice. "I'm saving it 'til we get there."

"Oh man, I love it when you baby-talk like that. Turns me on, babe. That's okay, I'm saving my news for the cabin too. Your news can't be as good as mine." I smirked.

"I don't know. Mine is pretty great, Ryan." Her hand absently brushed against her stomach. I didn't pick up what the gesture meant at the time.

"Bet ya mine is better."

"What do you want to bet?" Stacy teased.

I made eye contact with her for a moment and saw so much love there that it almost sucked all the air out of my lungs. She was so awesome. "Hmm. How about sexual favors?"

"You are on, wiener-boy. Start limbering up those tongue muscles, because you're gonna lose." She flicked her tongue at me and grinned.

"Tongue muscles? Isn't the tongue one big muscle?" On the side of the road, three small deer stood like statues and watched as we drove by.

"Whatever. I know I'm going to win a night of my man doing what it takes to please me. A long night."

"You wish. I'm one hundred percent positive I'll win." I thought of the ring packed away in my duffle bag. I couldn't wait to see the look on her face and hear the squeal of delight when I proposed.

"Doubt it. I'm telling you, start doing tongue stretches." She illustrated this by touching her nose with her tongue and then going side to side and all around. "Come on, big boy. Practice makes perfect."

"All right, but your news is going to have to be phenomenal to beat mine. Maybe you should start warming up on a popsicle, just so you're ready for me."

"We have popsicles?"

I pointed backwards with my thumb. "They're in the cooler in the back seat."

Stacy unsnapped her seatbelt and reached back into the cooler. "Blue, yum, my favorite flavor!" She unwrapped it and licked it, teasing me. I could feel myself getting excited already. She stopped and pointed the popsicle at me. "*I* don't need the practice, though. You're the one who needs to do his tongue calisthenics."

"So you say. What would you like me to do if you win? Shall I trace the alphabet?"

Stacy thought about it for a moment, licking the popsicle, then, placing her lips around it, she took it into her mouth and pulled it out, again, and again, and again, driving me wild, getting me excited. "Pi," she said.

"Pie? What flavor?"

168

"Pi, the number." That popsicle didn't stand a chance against her. It was half-gone already. I wanted to be that popsicle.

"The num . . .? But Pi can be figured out forever!"

"Exactly." She smiled broadly. "You have a long night ahead of you. Get it, 'a head?'"

"I get it, but you're not going to. I'm going to win this bet."

"Start practicing. I have." She pulled the last of the popsicle off of the stick into her mouth and bit down, smiling and showing me her blue lips and tongue. She reached over into my lap and rubbed my erection. "You're gonna lose, buddy, and your balls are gonna be as blue as my mouth."

"I'm not worried. I got this easy."

"We'll see." There was such a light in Stacy's eyes as she turned away from me. She was so happy. I couldn't wait to hear what her news was.

What a memory. You two were getting along so well then.

Yeah, but it seems so long ago. When was it?

Yesterday morning.

Really?

Yup. She was still breathing then. Her heart was still beating for you. Not much of a chance of that now, is there?

Fuck you!

I guess her baby talk was a clue, huh?

I . . . I never thought of that.

You're welcome. It's what I'm here for. Look deeper into the lake. Remember . . .

As soon as we got out of the car, the smell of pine was so strong you could taste it. The cool clean air made you realize you're somewhere better, somewhere more powerful. I brought in our duffle bags while Stacy put the food away. She filled a wooden bowl on the counter with some Macintosh apples.

"So, what's this great news of yours?" Stacy asked.

"No way, you go first. I have seniority." I went over and turned up the thermostat. It was going to be a cold night.

"Are we going to go through that again? All right Pops, but you might want to sit down first." She patted her hand on a kitchen chair.

"Sit down, huh? Must be pretty serious. Did they make you head cheerleader at the community college?" I was trying to be funny, but sometimes I go too far.

"Asshole." She crossed her arms and turned away. "Now I'm not going to tell you."

"Oh, come on, babe. Don't be that way."

"Nope." Stacy shook her head. "You're not mature enough to handle this anyway."

"Am too."

"Are not."

"Am too."

"Are not."

"Am too, am too, am too, infinity."

She giggled, looked back and made eye contact with me. "Okay, I'll tell you as long as you take back that cheerleading comment."

"Right." I nodded. "I'm sorry, I take it back."

"'Kay. Here it is. You ready? I'm pregnant." She absolutely beamed.

Unfortunately, the expression on my face didn't match hers. I was a little shocked and a little confused, I'm sorry to say. "Preg . . . ? You mean as in 'with child?'"

"How else would I mean it, silly?" She frowned a little, and then her eyes welled up.

"Yeah right. That's great, honey. Just great." I ran my fingers through my hair.

"You don't look too happy." Her lip quivered a little as she said it.

"No, it's not that. I'm . . . you just caught me off guard, that's all. How far along are you?" I tried to fake a smile, aware that I was failing and making it worse.

"About eight weeks, why?" One tear rolled down her cheek. She had expected me to take this better.

"Eight weeks, hmm. I didn't notice when you missed your last period." It was difficult to make eye contact with her. Stacy could see right through me and into my soul.

"No you didn't. You were having too much sex to notice." Her voice had grown colder now.

"Heh. Yeah. So eight weeks still isn't too late to, um, uh, you know?" I regretted the words as soon as they came out of my mouth.

"I can't believe you would even think of an abortion!" Stacy yelled. Tears streamed out of both eyes now.

"I wouldn't! I mean, not if you wouldn't." I was such an idiot.

"No! We're going to be married someday, aren't we?"

"Yeah, of course we are. Hey!" Finally, a chance to save face. I went over to the kitchen table where Stacy sat, face down in her arms now, crying. "That reminds me of my news." I got down on one knee and pulled the ring case from my pocket. Opening it, I said, "Stacy O'Brien, will you marry me?"

Stacy looked up, tears smearing what little makeup she used and half-smiled. "Really, Ryan? Is this your good news?"

"It is."

She screamed in delight. "Oh my God, it's so perfect! Yes, I'll marry you."

"Guess it's too late to ask if you'll bear my children someday," I said with a smile, glad to have salvaged the moment.

"Definitely." She put on the ring and turned her hand this way and that, the way girls do. "Oh, it's so beautiful."

"I'm glad you like it. I love you so much, Stace."

"Listen Ryan," she said with a twinkle in her eye. "The food is put away. Why don't we go into the bedroom and decide who won the bet?"

"Hmm. Sounds good to me. But I think it was a wash. It evened out."

"You really think so! Why don't we both pay up then?" She winked, a devilish gleam that could only mean one thing.

"At the same time?" I said, my voice wavering a little. She was driving me wild again.

"Sure." She took my hand and lead me into the bedroom.

The water ripples and the scene vanishes.

Hey, that's not the end of the story!

I think we've seen enough.

But Stacy was still alive. Things were fine.

You really don't want to see yourself kill her, do you?

I didn't before, but you've brought me this far and I still don't remember what happened.

You had sex. You both fell asleep. When Stacy got up for a glass of water, you followed her, came up behind her, and killed her.

Why don't I remember?

Shock. Probably blocked it out.

Show me the rest.

It's really not necessary.

Show me.

No.

Show me, or I'll swim out into the lake and drown us!

Fine. You asked for it.

The lake reveals its hidden treasure, one last time.

We entered the bedroom and I took the duffle bags off the bed, throwing them on the floor. We stripped down, kicking our clothes into a pile in the corner. The kitchen light cast through the open bedroom door and caressed her perfect naked body. Stacy was athletic, having grown up with three brothers. She played ice hockey in high school and was an avid mountain biker. Her tight athletic body seemed to glow in the cabin's dim light. I stared at her, ready to explode, so hard it was almost painful. Stacy guided me onto the bed. I lay down and waited. She climbed up, straddling my face and I almost came before we even started. She lowered herself down to my mouth and swayed back and forth slightly, teasing me, revving me up some more. Satisfied, she placed her arms on the bed and crawled down the length of my body until I could feel her hot breath on my erection. She kissed it, and I quivered. She blew softly, whispering, "There you go." Finally, she took me into her warm, moist mouth. My eyes rolled back. I had to concentrate or I wouldn't last long. I did the only thing I could to take my mind off my own pleasure; I grabbed her hips and guided her down to my outreached tongue. I flicked my tongue before taking a long slow lick and then holding it there. Her mouth pulled away and Stacy gasped. She sighed and cooed for a few beautiful moments before bringing her head back down. The erotic circuit complete, she went to work, developing a rhythm this time. I matched her rhythm. I didn't know how to figure out pi, so I just counted and traced numbers with my tongue. She squirmed more every time a number ended in eight. We made love for hours before passing out in satisfaction and exhaustion.

After two hours of deep sleep, Stacy got up and wandered out into the kitchen, careful to keep quiet, even though I was out like a light. She took a glass from the cabinet and poured herself some water from the tap. She leaned against the porch window, looking out wistfully and sipping on her water, probably dreaming about our future together.

I rose and walked stiffly, like a marionette under someone else's control. My hand passed over the untouched bottle of Klonopin on the kitchen counter before I drew a large knife from the butcher block and crept up behind her. Did she hear me? Maybe, but what did she have to fear? She probably thought I would sneak up behind her and put my arms around her, kissing her on the neck.

Before Stacy knew what was happening, it was too late. I pressed the butcher knife against her neck and in one painfully slow but fluid motion, cut her throat. Stacy tried to scream but no longer could. Choking and gurgling, dropping to her knees, trying to hold in her own blood as it spurted from between her fingers, her mouth formed the word, "Why?" She collapsed face down, a pool of blood spreading across the knotty pine floor. Not content that she was dead, I rolled her over onto her back and proceeded to stab her over, and over, and over again. It was a hideous scene. Stacy's dead eyes stared up into mine as I carved her heart right out of her chest. My last act was to remove the engagement ring from her cold, dead finger.

I . . . I was moving like a zombie. My face was totally blank, with no emotion. Was I . . . sleepwalking?

Ding, ding, ding. We have a winner.

I had that problem as a kid. Stress would bring it on. Sometimes I acted out my dreams, especially the nightmares. It scared my parents pretty bad. I had an incident at school last week. Probably because I'm away from home for the first time in my life. I just filled a prescription for Klonopin yesterday, but I forgot to take it!

I know.

The pills were right there on the counter. If I had taken them, it would have saved Stacy's life.

Probably.

I had a nightmare after I fell asleep, but it wasn't that bad. I dropped out of school, got married, and got a job in a butcher shop.

You'd make one hell of a butcher.

This means I wasn't in control. It was a nightmare. I was sleepwalking.

Do you feel confident that excuse will hold up in a court of law?

It's *your* fault. You're my subconscious. You did it.

True, but you seem to forget, I AM you. You still did it.

Why did you do it? Why did you kill her?

I never really liked her and I didn't like the direction our life was heading. It's time to move on. Time for a change of scenery.

The police will never understand. I need to take care of this myself.

You're right. We have to remove the evidence and get rid of her body.

I clean the cabin extensively. Emptying both duffle bags, I put the knife and bloody rags in one, and Stacy in the other. She needs a decent burial.

What?

There's one of those little graveyards on the side of the road about a mile back.

Perfect, we can bury the evidence as well.

I load up my little blue Ford, get a spade from the shed, and drive to the little graveyard. It starts to rain. I dig for hours, the rain softening the dirt into mud, weighing it down and filling the hole with water. I'm covered in mud, but at least it's no longer blood. Not even the rain can wash me clean. Stacy needs an epitaph so I take out a pocketknife. On a nearby ancient headstone, I scratch in "Stacy O'Brien 1994-2013. She was my Juliet." The blade easily marks the soft, time-weathered surface. Sunlight creeps back into the early morning hours like a cheating husband sneaking back into his wife's bed. After saying a prayer, I drive back to the lake.

Why are we going back to the lake?

I have some unfinished business.

What?

You'll see.

Down at the beach, I load two concrete blocks and some nylon rope into the canoe.

Wait. I know what you're thinking. Stop!

I push the canoe away from the shore a climb in. Early morning mist clings to the calm waters of the lake. The nose of my canoe parts the dew. I forgot a paddle, so I use my hands. The lake cleans the mud and muck from my arms. At the middle of the lake, I bind my ankles with the rope, tying the other end to the concrete blocks.

Stop, stop, stop.

I can't let you do this again, ever.

I'll be good. I'll fade away. Just don't kill us.

It's too late for that. Much too late.

I hoist up the heavy blocks. The fine haze swirls around me. A dragonfly, still alive this late in the season, buzzes around me, curious. The canoe is still, motionless. The golden sun has just peeked over the tree line. A loon calls from blueberry bushes of the nearby island, perhaps the baby looking for its mother again. I inhale deeply, taking in the clean pine scent of my favorite place on earth, one last time. Heaving, I toss the blocks into the water, the loud splash breaking the perfect calm of the morning.

When the slack of the rope tightens, my feet shoot out from under me. My head bounces off the side of the canoe as the rope yanks me under water, the shifting weight causing the canoe to flip. I'm dazed by the blow to the head and gasp, taking lake water into my lungs.

Why? Oh why? We could have worked through this. Our life was just beginning.

At the bottom of the lake, my heart finally stops. Sweet stygian blackness claims me. My arms slowly rise up over my head, like a criminal who, after a long standoff, realizes at last that he must surrender.

On the surface of the lake, there is no evidence of my passing, except for the overturned canoe. The ripples in the water die down until they vanish completely.

I am dead, but I have a vision. In this vision, I am married to Stacy. We would have spent every summer up at the cabin with our two children and our big playful dog. The kids would have grown up here; building sand castles on the beach, swimming out to the raft, learning to water ski, playing fetch the tennis ball with the dog, and skipping stones. At the end of the day, we would have gone back to the cabin to cook hamburgers and hot dogs on the grill. After the sunset, there would have been popcorn, marshmallows, and stories told around a campfire. To end the day, I would have brought the family back down to the beach to look at the moon, constellations, and shooting stars, just like when I was a kid.

Far across the lake, the mother loon answers its baby's call. Quiet returns. Wind whispers through the tops of the tall pines, silently sighing "Welcome home."

Ashtray Kiss

Michael Lindquist

Editor's Choice Award Winner

Ashtray Kiss.

That was what he called her now. He had known every single little detail about her, but the years of ether and insomnia had taken most of that away. Including her real name.

Who was she? And what exactly had he done to her?

Whatever it was, it had gotten him sent to this place. Spending his days with drooling mumbling idiots, being restrained and force-fed every pill imaginable. Jonathan Watson, the fat, hairy, ugly psycho, would be stuck here in the Asylum of God-knows-where for the rest of his life. They still used ether here, for all the weird stuff they did to him. He wasn't a medical expert, but he was pretty sure they stopped using ether as an anesthetic long ago. Maybe the doctors and the staff just kept it for fun, since it could be a drug too. He had felt the effects of it many times. In the beginning, he had looked forward to that, even with the nausea that came afterwards. But now, he actually wanted to stay in reality, in his rotting and disgusting cell, because that was where he got to meet her.

Who else was he going to talk to? The other crazy people in here? The Shrink who just wanted to make himself feel better by getting some sort of breakthrough with one of the patients?

I got through to one of them! I reached him! I'm actually good at this!

No, the only one he wanted to talk to now was her. Ashtray Kiss.

The only time something even remotely interesting happened in here, were the nights when she showed up. The lights would go out, then came the hours and hours of insomnia, before he would feel that smell. The smell of cigarettes.

He remembered the first time it had come into his cell. Thousands of words swirled around in his head, merging and clashing, all at the same time, like a liquid dictionary. No sentences, no context, no meaning. He sat on the floor with his hands covering his face, hunched over like a broken statue.

At first, he thought one of the guards was passing by. But then the smell had entered his cell and gotten so strong he had to cough. It was like someone was right in front of him, blowing smoke in his face.

"You burned me, Jonathan," said a voice, as loose and thin as the smoke.

It was as if the smoke itself was whispering to him.

Talking smoke. That was a new one.

He saw cigarettes glowing in the dark. Five of them, close to each other. A bit to the right of them were another set of five. No. Not cigarettes. Fingers. They were fingers that looked like cigarettes. The tips glowed and thin smoke trailed from them.

"Who's there?" he asked. "Who the hell is that?"

A big cloud of smoke filled his vision and then seemed to pull itself together. It started to form some sort of human figure. A vague outline of a woman. Gradually more and more details, and then there she was. She seemed to be half smoke, half flesh, in a torn and dirty dress. Her skin was a pale, sickly mix of grey and green. Her hair seemed to be made of thick smoke, flowing out from the top of her head. Her eyes were just two burned-in black stains, as if someone had put out a cigarette in each socket.

This has got to be the ether. How much did they use?

"You burned me," said the woman.

"Burned you?" He didn't understand this at all. "Burned you, how? When? Who are you?"

Her fingers touched his arm, and left five burn marks seared into his skin. Jonathan winced and pulled away, but didn't scream. This couldn't be a hallucination. She grabbed him by the collar and pulled him violently to her.

"Kiss me, Jonathan."

Her lips seemed to be made of ash, crumbling at his touch, leaving dust on his lips. There was also a small sting of heat, like glowing embers sprinkled over his tongue. It felt like someone put out a cigarette butt in his mouth. And then came that taste. Her taste.

"You know that thing they say about kissing a smoker?" Jonathan had asked The Shrink the next day.

The Shrink looked like he suddenly snapped out of a daydream, as if he hadn't really been listening. As if all he did was just sit and nod and say "I see." or "How does that make you feel?" or "What do you think that means?" He seemed a bit surprised that he himself had to answer a question now.

"That it's like kissing an ashtray?" said The Shrink.

"Yeah. That's what it was like," Jonathan thought for a moment. "But all of her. Everything about her was just like an ashtray."

"She was like an ashtray? What do you mean by that?"

"I don't really know. She was just . . . never mind, forget it," said Jonathan.

"Who was she?" asked The Shrink.

"I think it was her. The woman I killed."

Jonathan realized he had forgotten her name. It didn't really matter anyway, did it? Now she was just a cloud of cigarette smoke disguised as a girl, with a kiss that tasted like an ashtray. An ashtray kiss. He might as well call her that. Ashtray Kiss.

"She said 'You burned me.' She kept saying that," said Jonathan.

"You almost sound like you don't know what that means," said The Shrink.

"Should I?"

"You remember what you did to her, right?" asked The Shrink.

"No, I don't, actually. All that shit you give me takes away more and more of my memories every day. I hardly remember what I did this morning, let alone years ago," said Jonathan.

"You burned her," said The Shrink.

"I burned her body?"

"No, you burned out her eyes with a cigarette," said The Shrink. "While she was still alive. Then you killed her."

The Shrink pointed at Jonathan's arm.

"What happened there?"

"My arm? What about it?" asked Jonathan.

"There are marks on it. Looks like burn marks."

He looked down at his arm and saw the five marks from her touch. If The Shrink could see them, they had to be real. That meant that she was real.

"She did that. She burned me."

After that, she started showing up every now and then. Sometimes her visits would be weeks apart, sometimes days, and sometimes there might even be two nights in a row. Every time she appeared, the endless stream of words in his head became just one word.

Burn.

Over and over and over again.

burn burn burn burn burn

Until it just became a nonsense sound without meaning, a sinister drum beat that didn't stop until she went away. But he didn't really want her to go away, did he? After all, it was the most interesting thing that happened here. Ever.

"You sad, pathetic little man," said Ashtray Kiss. "Just because I turned you down, you felt the need to put me through years of hell? Always looking over my shoulder. Checking the locks on the door every other minute. Waking up in the middle of the night at the tiniest little sound. Every time the phone rang I assumed it was you. Never once did I think it could be anyone else at first. I was always surprised and overjoyed when it turned out to just be my mother or one of my friends. One time, I actually screamed with excitement when it turned out to be a telemarketer."

"I'm sorry. I truly am." Jonathan was on the verge of crying.

"Do you even know what you did?" she asked.

"The Shrink told me. I couldn't remember it, but he told me."

"You don't remember my name, either."

"No."

"Instead, you gave me that ridiculous nickname," she said.

Even though her eyes where completely burned out and hollow, there was still some sort of life in them. Anger, pain and sadness, mostly. But he felt he could almost see something else behind all that. Something vague and hidden away deep in the dark. It felt almost like . . .

Kindness?

Pity?

Was there actually some sort of sympathy for him hidden in there?

No matter what she said or did to him, he realized that he had actually started to look forward to her visits. Sometimes he would catch himself fantasizing about fucking her. That was pretty messed up. Why the hell would he want to do that?

He longed for that cigarette smell. That luxurious fragrance of decay. It was like when you felt your girlfriend's favourite perfume, and you knew she was close by. Any minute now, and she would sneak up behind him. Put her arms around him. Whisper in his ear that she loved him. He could feel her breasts pressed against him, her breathing pushing them in and out. She would kiss his neck.

Of course, this was all complete fantasy to him. He had never had a girlfriend or even been on a date. The closest he had gotten was that time he was really drunk and had the guts to kiss the really drunk girl sitting next to him.

He suddenly realized that was her. Ashtray Kiss, or rather, the woman who would become Ashtray Kiss. That was how they met. He had forgotten that. Just like her real name, he had forgotten how they had met the first time. So that was it.

His first kiss.

His first physical contact of any sort with a girl. He had fallen in love with her at that exact moment. Right then and there, when their vodka-soaked lips met, and her smoker's breath had filled his mouth. He hated smokers, and had never smoked himself. If he would have had any sort of confidence at all, he would have been the type of person who coughed loudly as a demonstration if someone next to him was smoking. Even then she had tasted like an ashtray, but he didn't care. It was his first kiss.

They had talked some more after that, and then she had given him her phone number.

"What did that feel like? How did you feel at that moment?" asked The Shrink.

"It felt amazing," said Jonathan. "I mean, she tasted like crap, and she wasn't exactly good-looking, but it was amazing. I had never felt so good in my life."

It took him a week to find the courage to finally call her. Afterward, he wished he had never done that. She answered, he managed to stammer out his name and mentioned how they met in the bar.

She didn't remember that.

She didn't remember him at all.

So no, she didn't want to go out with him.

That was when it all started. How could she not remember? That lying bitch. Of course she remembered.

"How did that make you feel?" asked The Shrink, as if that actually needed to asked.

"What the hell do you think?" snarled Jonathan.

"I don't know. Tell me."

"I was completely destroyed. Furious. I wanted to rip apart the whole goddamn world. I wanted to kill everyone," said Jonathan. "She had given me hope. For one little moment, I actually believed that someone could like me. Maybe even love me eventually. I actually believed that. Then she took that away. I felt like the biggest idiot in the world. And I knew she was lying. I knew she had felt something too. She had to."

"So, why do you think she said she didn't remember, then?" asked The Shrink. "Couldn't she just have been really drunk? Maybe she was telling the truth?"

"I thought she was afraid. That she was ashamed to like me. That her friends would make fun of her for being with an ugly nerd like me," said Jonathan.

Even though she was kind of an ugly nerd herself, he still believed that. Deep down they were all like that, weren't they? Girls. Deep down, they were all like, or wanted to be like, the coolest prettiest cheerleaders in high school. The cool girls that smoked.

He wasn't good enough for them. And even if they did get together with him, they would never admit it. He would be a shameful little secret. They would hate the fact that they liked him. Absolutely despise the thought of maybe being in love with him.

"I wasn't ashamed of you, Jonathan. I really, truly, didn't remember you then," said Ashtray Kiss sincerely.

He looked into her cigarette-burn eyes and tried to find some indication if she was telling the truth. Completely pointless, he knew that. Whatever emotions he might see in there could just be pure imagination on his part.

"However, after a while I think I actually started to you like you in some weird way," she said. "I wasn't exactly a hot babe or anyone's masturbation fantasy. Guys didn't come up to me when I was in some bar or night club. Not even the drunk desperate ones just before closing time. But you, Jonathan, you treated me like I was the only girl in the world. Like I was special. And I think, deep down in the darkness, that I kind of liked that somehow."

Jonathan wondered if he would really have had the balls to do anything worthwhile if they had actually gone on a date. He couldn't see himself doing that. At least not while he was sober. He probably would have been to afraid to kiss her, let alone have

181

sex with her. That would never have happened. Lying there naked in bed and having to do whatever it was that you had to do. From what he had read, it seemed like there was about a thousand different things you had to know to be able to please a girl. He would never give anyone an orgasm. He knew that.

The yearning and obsession he had felt for her when she was alive was nothing compared to now. He craved her. He lusted after her. Every night she didn't show up was agony. Loneliness. Emptiness. Every single night that she wasn't there felt like that time she had told him that she didn't remember him, multiplied by a million. That feeling of pure heartbreak. That's what it was. Heartbreak. He really loved her. Not the girl she had been before, not the girl that he had stalked in life, but this one. This ghost. This swirl of cigarette smoke. Ashtray Kiss. It was her he loved now. Soon, the smell of cigarettes started driving him insane. Whenever he smelled it, he prayed that it wasn't just a guard smoking.

Maybe she felt the same way about him, because she started coming more and more regularly. Soon she would be there every night. It felt as if he had a secret mistress that snuck into his cell every night. This had to be the weirdest conjugal visits ever. A man and his smoke-girl. What a cute couple.

She reached out her hand toward him, but then changed her mind, realizing what would happen if she touched him. Maybe she actually did care about him?

"What was your real name?" he asked.

"It doesn't matter," she said. "I'm not her anymore. I really just am an Ashtray Kiss now."

She kissed him, and this time it felt strangely exciting. Her lips were still decaying ash and she still smelled like cigarettes, but it didn't matter. It was like when they had first kissed in the bar. She tasted awful, but he didn't care at all. She took a step back, her body phasing in and out of the smoke. Every time she appeared again, she seemed more and more . . . naked?

She stepped out from the smoke. Now she looked completely solid, like an actual human being right there in his cell. A naked woman. He reached out and touched her. She put her arms around him. It wasn't like someone blew cigarette smoke in his face this time. This felt more like a tiny little hint of incense.

"Burn me, Jonathan," she said.

This was so weird. Beautiful, but weird.

Thick smoke started to spin around them, like a tornado was forming with them in the eye. Her body glowed, turning into sizzling embers. It was as if a thousand cigarettes were burning him at the same time. Her body phased in and out, solid on moment and smoke the next. Jonathan could feel himself inside of her, feel his hands on her breasts, and then there would be nothing at all. The smoke from her breasts entered his mouth like milk turning to steam. Smoke rings pulsated out from them like shockwaves.

When he woke up the morning after, he could not remember what had happened next.

Did he have sex with a ghost made out of cigarette smoke?

Was she messing with him, toying with his emotions, to eventually break his heart and soul forever? That would only be fair, he supposed, considering what he had done to her.

"I love you," he said, surprising himself.

There was an eternity of silence, and then she leaned in close to his ear.

"And I love you, Jonathan," she whispered.

A soft kiss on his neck, and then she disappeared again.

After that, she did not come back for a long, long time. It might as well have been a lifetime. For Jonathan, it was back to the good old days of just being a drooling mumbling idiot with nothing to do. He tried to figure out why he had burned out her eyes. He felt as if he should know the answer to that. There had to be an answer. Was it because she was a smoker? Did he really hate smokers that much?

The cool girls at school, holding their cigarettes, laughing at him.

Was she smoking when she was on the phone with him?

Laughing with her filthy, disgusting smoker's breath.

Endless nights came and went, without even the slightest sign of when or even if she might come back. He couldn't think about anything else besides her. They had to start force-feeding him after he lost all his appetite. What was the point? Couldn't they just let him die? It wasn't exactly like they cared about him. The worst one was The Shrink, because he insisted on pretending to care. At least the other ones were honest about it. Letting him starve to death would just mean so much paperwork.

On the very night he would have given up completely, just as the final glowing ember of hope fell like the last grain of sand in an hourglass, he felt that smell again. That wonderful smell of cigarettes. And he could hear that word, louder and louder.

burn burn burn burn burn

He felt a rush of joy through his entire body as thick smoke surrounded him. She stepped out and they embraced. He loved the feeling of her glowing fingertips burning his skin, leaving marks that wouldn't heal or fade for years. Like getting a tattoo with her name. That's what it was. A mark of love. The proof that he was hers. Forever. Or was it just the way a farmer marks his cattle? Perhaps that was what he was to her. A possession, a beast of burden to order around.

"Do you want to be with me?" she whispered, seductive. "To love me completely, with your whole being?"

"Yes," he said, holding her as tight as he could.

"Then you know what you have to do, don't you?"

"No."

"Come on, you know," she said. "What's that word you keep hearing?"

Of course he knew what she meant. It was just so scary to say it out loud.

"Burn," he said finally. "I have to burn."

"That's right, Jonathan. You have to burn."

The next day he was supposed to meet with The Shrink, but that meeting would never happen now. Jonathan didn't want to talk, he just wanted to burn. Burn with her. Burn for her. He just couldn't figure out how. Understandably, they made sure that the patients didn't have access to anything that could be potentially dangerous in any way. Then he had a sudden thought of clarity.

Ether.

What about the damn ether they used on him all the time? In addition to being used as an anesthetic and a drug, ether was also highly flammable. He knew where they kept all of the containers, in the back of a dusty old storage room. Looking around, he noticed that there weren't any guards around now. He easily slipped in there.

Too easily. Maybe she was helping him along somehow?

"Please, Jonathan, do it," she whispered, as if summoned by his thoughts. "For me. Then we can be together forever. That's what you want isn't it? To be with me forever."

He picked up one of the containers of ether and looked around. There were nothing to start a fire with in here. He peeked out through the door, and still could not see anyone else around. The guard's desk caught his attention.

They all smoked, so there has to be a lighter or some matches in there.

In one of the desk drawers, there was a pack of cigarettes and a lighter. In his head he could hear that wonderful word, over and over. It filled his entire being, so strong and comforting that he didn't even flinch at the stench and taste of the ether as he poured it over himself.

burn burn burn burn burn

Hearing it chanted over and over was like listening to a choir of angels.

burn burn burn burn burn

He lit one of the cigarettes, and actually had time to take a long drag from it.

burn burn burn burn burn

He exhaled and smiled.

Burn.

Doing it for JRD

(Justice, Revenge and Deliverance)

David Eccles

Just how often has one heard the phrase, "There are no secrets in a town as small as this?" More times than one can count on one hand, I'm sure. Now, did one actually believe it, even once? I ask because in my town, I know that phrase to be a lie. And that's the truth!

We all have secrets. Little known facts and dark details about our sordid, grubby past that we would prefer to keep locked away in a steel-banded wooden chest and thrown overboard in the middle of the deepest ocean or buried beneath a thick layer of concrete at the side of the house prior to the new garage being erected, or even hacked into tiny pieces and fed to the local pack of hunting hounds. Maybe it's the kind of secret that the tax man would appreciate knowing?

From my perspective, discovering someone's secret is analogous to pulling the petals off a flower head. I like to strip away and discard the surrounding lies until all that's left is the truth at the heart of the matter, and when I see that truth I act accordingly, which isn't pretty sometimes, because I'm the kind of person who believes that the punishment should fit the crime and, although I'm not big on religion, let me tell you that when I act in retribution...it feels divine!

The very first time I felt the need to act on my impulses and the adrenalin rush I felt coursing through my body both during and after it was all over...it was like nothing I could ever describe with any degree of accuracy using just a single word.

It's as fresh in my mind today as it was on the day when I actually did the deed. The guy was slimier than the wet fish he sold in his fish and chip shop, ogling the teenage girls as they stood in line waiting for a fresh batch of chips to finish frying. To this day, I have no idea if he was Greek, Italian or Portuguese. Everyone knew him as Mario, because that was the name on the sign above the shop: Mario's Fish 'n' Chips. It made no difference that the sign had been there for over twenty years, or that the shop had had four different owners during that period, including at one point, a Sikh. Everyone who owned or managed the shop seemed to automatically inherit the name Mario. The townsfolk made sure of it, simply because the lazy bastards couldn't be bothered to remember the owner's real name, let alone ask what it was.

The shop itself was in a prime location, close to the local High School and situated on a corner plot on the high street, with a side road to the right and an alleyway that branched off from the side road that ran parallel to the high street, allowing delivery access to the rear of the shops which were originally a row of Victorian terraced houses. None of the houses had a garden at the rear; they all had stone-slabbed courtyards, and were separated by high brick walls topped off with pointed coping stones. Access to the rear yard of each shop was through a wooden gate, which were all identical, except for colour. These gates had a simple latch that could be operated by putting one's finger through a hole beneath the latch and lifting it up. If one was of a curious or voyeuristic persuasion, it was surprising just what could be seen through that hole.

Every day at lunchtime, and in the evenings too, Mario's shop would be surrounded by pupils from the nearby High School who would all loiter with their friends, desperate to spend their lunch money and allowance on just about anything other than school lunches, and having been a pupil there myself, I can understand their reasons for doing so: the food in the school "restaurant" was shit. I wouldn't have called it a restaurant or even a dining hall; it was more of a dying hall. If one had ever eaten there, you'd know just what I mean.

Despite protestations to the local Council about delinquent behaviour and the amount of discarded chip wrappers and burger boxes left lying in the street, Mario's shop continued to do good trade, with the man himself at centre stage behind the fryers, aided by his wife who was also of indeterminate Mediterranean origin, I assumed, and, in all fairness, was very pleasing to the eye, though I never saw her smile, ever.

Mario spoke in heavily-accented English, which made all the schoolgirls swoon. It seems to me that girls go weak at the knees as soon as they hear a language other than English. It made no difference that Mario was no oil painting to look at and could not be considered to be handsome, not by any stretch of the imagination. The man could read the ingredients on a shampoo bottle label and still have the girls creaming in their knickers, despite the fact that he was short and hairy, overweight, had two-day stubble and reeked of used cooking fat.

Night after night, he'd serve up soggy, greasy chips along with a double portion of innuendo to anything with tits while his wife who spoke no English stood by his side with a face like thunder. She may not have understood his words, but there was no mistaking his intent. Phrases such as "You ladies want a big sausage tonight?" and "I bet you girls like it with plenty of salt, yes?" accompanied by a wink always resulted in fits of giggling and flushed cheeks from fawning females, with the odd riposte of "Ooh, Mario! You dirty bastard!" being delivered by the one girl you just knew would be waiting in the alley at the rear of the shop after closing, hoping to hear that list of shampoo ingredients in a foreign tongue while Mario copped a feel of her tits, leaving her in the awkward position of trying to explain the greasy handprints on her school blouse to her mother when she got home and hoping that her father never got to hear of it.

Periodically, Mario's wife would take to her bed with a migraine and, during those periods, Mario would offer casual work to any of the local girls who were interested in making a few quid, with the added bonus of free food at the end of the night. Leanne Harrison was one such girl.

I used to follow her everywhere, and it wasn't only because I liked her; I suppose subconsciously I was learning to hunt, to blend in with the background and be completely inconspicuous. I knew her daily routine and only had to look at my wristwatch at any particular time of day to know exactly what she'd be doing, if, for some reason I wasn't shadowing her that day, after school was over. She was gorgeous; the kind of girl that every schoolboy fantasises about having as a girlfriend, and the kind of girl that schoolboys lie on their bed and wank themselves to exhaustion over.

When she began working in Mario's fish and chip shop, it was no surprise that the takings went through the roof. Every boy in town queued up just to be served by the statuesque blonde with the perfect smile, stunning green eyes, hourglass figure and a voice so sweet one felt she could talk a kamikaze pilot into turning round and going home. We all thought she was untouchable and that butter wouldn't melt in her mouth. Even I thought that and had resigned myself to the fact that she would never be mine. I was happy just to follow her, and to let my fingertips touch her hand for the briefest of moments as she gave me my change when she served me in the chip shop. Why did I not see it? I should have realised that there is no such thing as perfection. She had us all fooled.

I'm sure it was purely psychological, but the chips always seemed to taste so much better whenever Leanne was serving them. I'd called in to satisfy my need to see this stunning creature and load my stomach with whatever it was that I ordered when she'd asked me what I wanted. It was late, and I was the last customer before Mario decided it was time to turn off the fryers and close up the shop for the night. She'd given me an extra-large portion, and I had decided to wait for her and follow her home. I was waiting in the alley at the rear of the shop and was sitting on my haunches, leaning against the gate and cramming my mouth with chips that had sat for too long in the warmer. They were hard and crunchy, had too much salt sprinkled on them and a lot of them had sharp edges, but I didn't care. I figured I had between ten and fifteen minutes to finish my food before hearing the shop door locks engage, signalling that it was time for me to follow Leanne home. It didn't work out that way at all.

The whole length of the alley was in pitch darkness, so I noticed right away when the small outside light came on at the side of the rear door to the shop and light spilled underneath the gate. I turned to peek through the hole beneath the latch. Nothing could have prepared me for what I saw. It was my worst nightmare.

Mario stood on the first of two steps leading up to the rear of the shop with his trousers around his ankles, while the girl I had thought to be all sweetness and light and perfect in every way kneeled before him. He held her there, both hands wrapped around her hair, and the only sounds I could hear right at that moment were of Mario grunting like a walrus as he thrust his hips back and forth and Leanne greedily took his flaccid, greasy cock in her mouth, gripping his buttocks with both hands and working her perfect lips up and down his wrinkled shaft. Initially, I was of the opinion that Mario had somehow forced her into performing fellatio on him, but I had to re-evaluate my opinion when he let go of her hair and she carried on sucking him, and with increased enthusiasm.

I looked on helpless and dumbstruck as Mario fucked Leanne's mouth, until I happened to glance up and notice the twitching of the curtains in the flat above the shop. Mario's wife had been watching the whole time, but had done nothing to prevent it from happening. It made me wonder: was she so scared of him that she didn't dare say nor do anything, or was it that she had simply accepted the fact that the marriage was over and yet stayed with him out of convenience? Maybe it was a religious thing? Most Latin and Mediterranean types leaned towards Roman Catholicism, so divorce would be out of the question if it happened to be that she was a devout Catholic.

A loud metallic clicking sound brought me back from my preoccupied state, and I realised that I had unknowingly stood up and had operated the latch, pushed open the heavy wooden gate and was now in full view of all parties present. Mario's wife remained as still as a statue at her vantage point, whereas Leanne's head had immediately spun around to see what was happening, her lips making a smacking sound as Mario's member left her mouth. Upon seeing that it was only me and not her irate father coming to drag his daughter home by the scruff of the neck, she visibly relaxed and smiled at me; a look I regarded as being grotesque, because she had Mario's semen and her own saliva dripping down her chin.

Mario stood there for a second, looking drained, and not only of his semen. His deflated look turned suddenly to one of panic. He penguin-walked hurriedly into the shop, tripping over his trousers and he crawled, commando-fashion across the cold, tiled floor with his saggy, hairy backside in the air in a desperate attempt to flee from embarrassment. I wasn't too far behind, and found myself running after him. Just what a seventeen year-old boy was hoping to achieve rushing a man in his early to mid-forties I'm not sure. It was a compulsion that I was helpless to resist. As I rushed past Leanne, who still had that cock-sucking grin on her face, I lashed out with my right hand, catching her in the throat with the heel of my palm and instantly crushing her hyoid bone. That stupid fucking smile soon disappeared from her beautiful face and she collapsed to the ground, clutching her throat with one hand while reaching out to me with the other as if pleading with me to get help. I found it quite amusing really, but I had other business to attend to with Mario and so could not hang around to watch her silent death throes as she slowly asphyxiated.

Entering the chip shop, my heart felt like it was trying to burst free from my chest. The adrenalin in my system caused me to feel so very powerful; my senses seemed to be heightened enormously and coupled with the rage I felt at seeing the object of my desire debased and degraded in such a fashion before my eyes, I felt unstoppable, omnipotent. I could see Mario making his way towards the door which led to the stairs and ultimately to the flat above the shop. Less than two seconds later, I had snatched up a fish filleting knife from one of the worktops and was kneeling astride him. He had no fight in him at all; the weight of my body hitting him at speed had knocked the wind out of his sails. Acting on pure instinct, I took a hold of his greased back mop of dyed black hair, pulled back his head, passed the knife across his throat and pulled back in one rapid, smooth movement. The warmth of his blood as it spurted onto the back of my hand surprised me, as did the gurgling sound as it filled his throat and spilled from his mouth, but what surprised me most was the sharpness of the knife. Mario was really good at keeping his knives sharp, even if his chips were shit!

Throughout all my time in the rear of the chip shop, I kept my eyes and ears open in case Mario's wife decided to make an appearance, but she never showed which puzzled me. I calmly cleaned myself off in the sink and wiped off the knife and any surfaces that I thought I may have touched then I replaced the knife, hopefully from where I had taken it. The de-greaser that Mario used in the shop was wonderful stuff! There would not be a single trace of a fingerprint anywhere after I had gone, and as we had a coal fire at home, there would soon be no trace of Mario on me, either. I'd seen enough police shows on TV to know that I had to burn my clothes as soon as I got home, and I made a mental note to get up early and rake through the ashes and remove any metal fastenings that remained and to dispose of them on my way to school.

Leanne's body looked like a used and discarded sex doll, lying there twisted into a funny shape with her tits hanging out and her face covered in cum. She was pretty, but no longer beautiful. That certain "something" that made me desire her was no longer present. I knew it was time to go home. I had homework to do.

Needless to say, a huge police investigation took place, and their chief suspect was Mario's wife, obviously, but she was never charged due to a total absence of physical evidence, even though she had both motive and opportunity. The police were unable to complete the triangle, and to this day the case remains unsolved, much to my delight. The local newspapers and even most of the nationals ran the story for quite a while because someone who I believe must have been part of the investigation leaked certain details to the press; details that even I was unaware of. Leanne had died from asphyxiation after suffering a blow to the hyoid bone, and Mario had expired from exsanguination after having his throat cut, most certainly, but other post-mortem injuries had been inflicted, though it would be more correct to call them mutilations rather than injuries. Leanne had had her tits cut off and Mario was missing his balls and his dick. The items had been dipped in batter, deep fried and left on the serving counter at the front of the chip shop, wrapped in paper and sprinkled with salt and vinegar.

Mario's wife was really something else. It wasn't good enough for her that her cheating husband had died, along with his "bit on the side". She really did want her pound of flesh, so to speak, and I must say that I liked her style. That was fourteen years ago, and Mario's wife still runs the fish and chip shop. I call in from time to time and am always greeted with a smile and a wink from her, and I never have to pay for anything that I order.

That wonderful smile of hers gets to me every time. It's a smile that says thank you. Thank you for giving me justice; for helping me to get my revenge, and for delivering me from a life of misery. Hey, what can I say? It's all about doing it for JRD, and it's what I do best. I've had fourteen years of practice.

A Brief Held Beauty

B.T. Joy

Down at The Dive again, on Cedar Avenue, Aaron Madder eyed the mirror in the back john. He ran a thumb over the immaculately groomed line of his eyebrow; his sharp eyes contemplating every contour of his incredibly handsome face.

If anything he looked better than he had. The modern metrosexual look suited him. Not that he'd been anything less than attractive before. In the old days. Bearded as he'd been back then. But, nowadays, women appreciated the smoother look and Aaron had found, as the years progressed, that he'd been shaving, waxing, buffing and epilating hair from more parts of his body than he'd ever have thought necessary.

Still though, if you want to catch flies you've got to spin silk.

He ran his hands under the warm faucet and dried off. He'd been cruising The Dive for years now and it never took him more than fifteen minutes to find a girl.

He found this one sitting with a friend and had slipped into her peripheral vision; sitting by the bar while the two talked. He could always feel the hot throb between bodies when he'd picked the girl. He could sense her awareness of him. Her inability to hear what her friend was saying anymore. Her nipples hardening like tiny stones and her vaginal walls running with little rivers of pre-ejaculate.

Aaron grinned into his whiskey. Biding his time until the friend left.

"What was your name again?" His voice was silken. No trace of accent. Minneapolis born-and-bred. Though somehow touched by some recessive hint of exoticism.

His right hand, the one with the silver Quartz at the wrist, was stroking the back of the girl's right hand. She'd never been so easily close to orgasm.

"Anthea," she said. Trying to control herself. Trying to be sensible. "My name's Anthea."

"How could I forget," he smiled, honey-voiced, "that's a real pretty name."

"Listen . . ." Anthea said, "I never . . . I mean . . . I don't just pick up guys in bars . . ."

A sharp feeling like a wasp-sting cut into Aaron's chest. It was growing impatient.

". . . we could exchange numbers if you like . . . I'm free most of the weekend . . ." The girl was yammering on; and the pain in his chest, throbbing.

"You're very beautiful." He cut her off, "I'd like to take you home."

Anthea's neck and cheeks prickled. A guy had never been so confident with her and, though it should have offended her, in truth it turned her on even more. She hung there a moment; wavering over the dilemma. Then Aaron moved closer and took her warm face in the cups of his cold hands.

"Do you know what hell is, Anthea?" His voice and sharp eyes made her drunk.

"No." She answered hopelessly.

"Hell is a brief held beauty."

He brushed his thumbs over her beautiful cheekbones.

"We were both made perfect, weren't we?"

Anthea still couldn't believe the front of this guy. Now he was *perfect*? She should have up and left right there and then. But her body was vibrating like a struck bell under his touch.

"Hell is being so perfect," he whispered, "and letting it pass you by . . ."

There was a searing stab. Deep in his ribs.

"Please, Anthea," he ground his teeth ever so slightly, so as not to have her notice, "please, come home with me."

They'd only been sitting in The Dive fifteen minutes before they left together into the cloud-covered Minneapolis night.

Record maintained, Aaron smiled to himself.

They walked out over the greasy skids and stains of oil-seepage on grey tarmac; back to where Aaron had parked his metallic Toyota pickup. He opened the passenger door.

"After you," he said, as gallantly as he could with his guts churning up like a fucking meat-mincer the way they were.

Anthea looked at him a little cautiously. She couldn't believe she was doing this. She'd never once went home with some guy she'd met in a bar. For a moment she considered telling him so and leaving him standing there with his door in his hand. But then a feeling stirred in her again, just looking at him, a tingle, and an itch, deep inside her body.

Eventually she did what Aaron always knew she would; sliding into the passenger seat. These days picking up a girl was as banal as picking up groceries. Banal that was if he made it fast. Before the chest pains began.

Even as he pulled himself behind the wheel it started again; violent and more urgent than before.

Shit! He swore under his breath trying to ignore the sharp thrust in his heart. *I'm coming. I'm coming. Be patient.*

He set off as quickly as he could and he and Anthea did little talking. She put his brooding and his hurry down to horniness as she tried to relax into the sexual throbbing that seemed to emanate electrically from every muscle under his skin.

It was in this quiet tension that they drove up Cedar Avenue; passing the whiskey joints, service stations and pawn stores that clung to this part of Minneapolis like rust-brown barnacles to the hull of a long wrecked ship.

"Where did you say you lived?" Anthea asked.

"We're not far." Aaron answered.

They rolled by the weed-woven fences of the Community Peace Gardens. Aaron looked out indifferently on what could be seen of the park from the road. Last month two kids had been found in there. Her dress around her waist. His pants round his ass and his cock inside her. They were both sixteen and he'd used an old Swiss army knife to cut long lacerations in the flesh; just where her shoulder met her neck. He'd sliced at his own chest too and when the cops found them they'd both been sucking on each other's skin; their wet mouths red in the blaze of torchlight.

The young guy had attacked the cops; or so the papers reported. And the girl. She'd not even bothered to cover up; rising and squatting, bare legs and bare privates, mouth gory with her boyfriend's blood, snarling like an animal at the men who'd interrupted their midnight blood play.

They'd been booked up at the station on 4th Street. Indecent exposure in a public place had been enough to start with. But even Minneapolis' lax knife laws also threw the book at the kids for reckless use. Add to that police assault and resisting arrest and both had walked out with a hundred hours community service a piece.

According to later articles the court transcript from the local juvy was a weirder read than most pulp-fiction. It'd been the girl who spoke most. Seeming always stronger and more self-assured than the other. She'd told the judge that what officers of the Minneapolis Police Department had interrupted that night had been a *carnal ceremony* which should, in her mind, have been protected under the US Constitution as part and parcel of religious freedom.

We're disciples, she'd told the court. *Disciples of the Aluka Cabal.*

Strange, Aaron had remembered thinking, a little disinterestedly. *Young Jews aren't typical victims of these modern vampiric delusions.*

He looked at Anthea; truthfully, disinterested in women these days, and as disinterested in her as he was in the nocturnal sex-games of two barely legal fantasist fang-bangers. But he'd been lost in his own thoughts so long by now that he worried she might cool off before they reached their destination.

He couldn't risk any cock-ups. Not now. Not with his intestines shrieking with dull pain as they were.

"We're not far," he reassured her again, rubbing her wrist with his free hand.

Then turning back to the road.

"It won't be long now."

Moments later he pulled the pickup truck into 6th Street, where, by the shady, tree-lined sidewalk, he kept a little two-room apartment. The one where he took all the girls.

When they got into the apartment Aaron started in on her right away. He shrugged off his jacket and started undoing her blouse right there in the dark hallway. She had to be naked and ready as soon as possible.

"Whoa . . . let's take it slow." Her hands stopped his hands three buttons down; holding her clothes over her breasts.

He just stared down at her. His eyes were two spheres of shining topaz in the close darkness and for the first time she noticed the strange middle-eastern physiology of his fine-set features. Lost in his gaze she relented. Letting her defensive hands faint away hesitantly from her breasts.

Aaron took advantage; pulling the material down sharply over her shoulders and lunging hungrily over her. He pushed his jaw, hot with breath, into her giving flesh; biting hard at her uncovered cleavage.

"Hey . . ." she squirmed in his arms, "not so rough."

He raked his teeth softly, playfully, down the length of her breast; pushing away the lace of her lingerie with his mouth and beginning gently to suck on her erect nipple.

All the while his hands explored down below. Zipping down her skirt and letting it fall lightly to the hall floor.

She squirmed again. Part of her couldn't believe she'd let him get this far. How long had she known him. Twenty minutes. Half-an-hour tops. And now the guy was biting at her breasts and stripping her naked a foot and a half from his front door.

She felt his fingers graze the waistband of her underwear.

"Okay . . ." she pushed his hand away from her body, "I think we should slow down."

He looked at her like before. She felt it again. A wave of hot sexual charisma washed in from somewhere deep inside him; crashing against her, causing warm fluids to seep against the lace between her legs.

"We've got all night. And besides . . ." she blinked, her resolve melting a little yet again, "you've seen plenty of me . . . let's see what you're made of . . ."

Her voice hadn't been half as confident as she'd intended. Though the way she tugged at the hem of his plain black tee told him in no uncertain terms what she wanted.

Aaron breathed out like a thwarted animal; dispelling energy through his mouth and nostrils. The pain in his chest was growing immense.

She's here! He reasoned with it. *She's fucking here! Can't you wait a fucking . . . Shit!*

He rolled hard against the wall; his broad back crashing on plaster with a thorny crack and his right hand wrenching onto his throbbing chest.

"Shit . . . shit . . . okay . . . okay!"

The pain lessened; yet still remained.

"Are you alright?" Anthea touched his shoulders, wide-eyed and concerned "are you having an attack?"

He pulled his breath steadily back into a healthy rhythm then he grabbed her. Cupping her face in the chill of his hands. His face lurched sickeningly into hers and within moments Anthea felt it as his long, wet tongue rolled into her mouth.

"I'm fine," he wheezed, "I'm fine."

Then, starting to kiss her again, he reached back and tugged at the collar of his shirt; pulling it fluidly over his head. Just as she'd wanted.

He walked her backwards. Giving her no choice. Not stopping the constant rotations of his jaw as the jutting, red organ of his tongue stabbed again and again into the girls open mouth. He pushed her through into his living room. Pulling off her bra, breaking the strap, and throwing the tattered thing onto the laminate floors; scratched by a hundred pairs of high-heeled shoes.

He pressed her down onto the leather sofa; forcing his massive animal weight onto her slight frame.

"Relax," he whispered, "it won't be long now."

He grabbed her lace underwear with both hands and tore it away; leaving her completely naked under his heaving, sweating mass. Anthea was no longer having fun. There was something strange about that room. The one he'd dragged her into without her coherent consent.

Some dull noise was thrumming on the extremity of silence. The deep and brooding breath of something immense and immensely hungry hung in the air like a stinking pall.

Immediately she knew what the un-locatable sound was. It was the partner of the throng of sexual longing that had vibrated out from Aaron's chest that night at The Dive; like the irresistible pheromone of a wild and carnivorous plant.

His teeth sunk softly into her breasts again. She wanted to tell him *no*. She wanted to tell him to *stop*. But a feeling she couldn't explain held her down fast to the spot. She felt, and she didn't know the word at first, that she was almost *enthralled* by him; by him and, she knew now, by the weird and alien singing that bled like a bass tone through the empty room.

She looked up through the darkness at the nude, breathing heave of Aaron's chest. Her face shrunk back in disgust.

"What is that?"

"What?" he kissed her neck.

"On your chest . . ." she said, "that thing?"

There it was. Just above the light brown of his nipple. A series of letters; making two words in a language other than English. Hebrew, maybe. Yes. Hebrew.

"It's just an old tattoo," he whispered by the side of her face; she felt his blunt teeth clamp down on her earlobe.

"No it isn't!"

She shoved his heavy weight off of her and staggered away from the couch, the man and the horrible symbol on his labouring chest. She was so startled she hardly noticed her nakedness as she flicked the switch on the nearest lamp; partly illuminating the darkness around her.

The hungry noise of the room crackled oceanically in her head.

She stared through the new light, horrified, at Aaron's chest. She'd been right. It was never a tattoo. Those words. Those ancient Hebrew words. They'd been cut into his skin.

She couldn't tear her eyes away from that gory scarification. Scanning it as though trying to make sense of its bizarre meaning. The longer she looked the more terrified she became.

The wounds had been rubbed long ago with ink. From the outskirts of every dark letter a twisted confluence of black veins snaked back into Aaron's heart. And then . . . no . . . it couldn't be . . . was that thing on his chest . . . was it *moving*?

She swung her head away in revulsion.

"I want my clothes," she said, covering her breasts and genitals with both hands, "I want to go home."

The pain corkscrewed languidly in Aaron's heart. Just a reminder.

I know. He said to himself. *I know*.

Then turning the sharp topaz of his eyes on Anthea:

"Okay . . ." he said, "I'll just go grab my coat and take you back to The Dive."

He walked briskly out of the room. To collect his jacket from where he'd dropped it earlier.

"No!" Anthea called after him.

She'd been going to say she was going alone. That she never wanted to see him again. Not even to drive her back where he'd found her. But suddenly she became very aware of the vulnerability of her nakedness.

She moved out of the circle of light the lamp made and into the darkness around her. She followed him, out the way he'd gone, to the hallway. Picking up her skirt and blouse and pressing them to her chest. She'd been going to pull them on; open the apartment door; run out barefoot into the street and put as much distance between herself and 6th Street as she could.

There was just something wrong with this place.

But then she stopped. Aaron's jacket was gone. No sign of it where he'd dropped it. And no sign of Aaron either. The apartment was small but Aaron obviously knew it well and could have slipped off at any moment to the shadows of any other room.

Anthea retraced her steps. Holding her pawed and creased clothes close to her heaving chest. Eyes wide and terrified. As again, not knowing why, she entered the dark room.

The noise of deep, inhuman breathing filled her senses and for the first time she could locate the sound among the hanging silence.

Aaron had made sure to mask it with his massive body as they entered; horny and ready to fuck. The closet on the right side of the room. A tattered door of flaking white paint. And the breathing. The hot and hungry breathing that grated like an insistent sea upon the wood of the other side.

Anthea's naked feet moved involuntarily closer.

She didn't dare to blink as she approached the closet door; as she heard, in there among the breathing, the snarling sound of five thin fingernails running down the grain.

She turned, speechless with horror, and ready to bolt naked into the street if necessary. But her body was cut off and she screamed so hard her throat was grazed as Aaron's muscled arms wrapped inescapably around her body; pulling her towards that repulsive symbol that something other than him had carved into his skin.

"It's okay . . ." he clenched his teeth, trying to soothe her, "it'll all be over soon."

The last thing she felt before her body became entirely numb was the head of the syringe pushing its dirty snout up into the largest vein in her arm.

A double dose of ketamine surging like poison into her blood.

She woke only in snatches after that.

She's here.

Aaron was speaking.

Wait. Just one more moment. I'm coming. I'm coming.

She regained consciousness for long enough to feel her naked body cradled in his strong grip. To see her crumpled clothes strewn and messy on the stiletto scratched floor.

Long enough to watch as Aaron pulled open the closet door and released the hungry singing into the openness of the air.

She screamed silently and her waking eyes gave a violent flurry in her drugged skull. In the utter darkness, behind the closet door, she could barely make out the thing. But what she could discern was ugly beyond describing.

An odd assortment of broken limbs and old pieces of flesh. Two thin arms hung down from the ceiling, beckoning Aaron closer, and in the poorness of the light Anthea could just make out the strands of slobber on the black and circular immensity of the jaw that dominated the space; gaping, singing, aching to be fed.

Aaron shoved hard at her back; toppling her paralysed body like so much flesh and hair and bone, heavily into the closet with the thing; slamming and locking the door behind her. There was a vicious, wet, thrusting sound; like a single grubby fang piercing bloody meat.

Hell, Aaron thought. *Hell is a brief held beauty.*

Then he fell on his knees, as though in some carnal ceremony; pressing his beautiful face against the flaking wood.

"Please Friend," he muttered through the space between them and through the filthy sounds of satisfied drinking that throbbed from inside the dark, "please . . . keep me from hell . . . keep me in beauty!"

His manicured fingers scraped down the wood in desperation. He looked close to weeping. And then, in a wave of euphoric comfort, the pain in his chest stopped.

He smiled. Breathing hard in utter relief and pressing his face closer to the thing through the door.

Thank you, he grinned, *oh, my Friend, thank you.*

There was a sound from within. Like maybe Anthea's slowly draining body had started to kick and scream against the thing's hanging, corpselike arms. Then there was a sickly tearing and a spattering on the floor inside the closet.

Aaron bowed lower, as though to the thing, hunching down like a dog on the laminate and beginning to lick up long, red tonguefuls of the blood that crept out, slow and thick, from the space beneath the door.

Head Blown Out

David L Tamarin

It was when Vanessa asked me what time it was that things inside my head got out of control. I stared at the watch on my wrist, not understanding. Three red sticks spun around at different speeds, and they seemed to switch directions randomly. A dozen ancient Druid-like symbols surrounded the moving sticks. I started crying. "I don't know. I can't understand this thing. I think I'm confused, I mean. I mean. What?"

Not that I understood her question anyway. There are just a few people who know the truth, and the others are part of the lie. Some are aware, some are unaware, some are stuck in the middle. I was part of the few who recognized that her question had no answer and just begged more questions. What is time, how do you quantify a fluid moving existence, especially when time can slow down, stop, even move in reverse. There were a million different answers to her question, none were truly correct. Yet I was helpless to explain. Trapped.

I could not escape because I was trapped in this head, this mind, and could never get outside of it. I could never experience looking at myself with objectivity. I was and always would be a stranger to myself, possibly dangerous, never predictable. And in this way I knew the Universe would soon crack and split open under the weight of it own flaw, and then time would fly away like a freed dove and then space will be irrelevant when it stands outside of time.

We were headed for annihilation. There was nothing I could do, nothing I could say. My tongue froze, my mind went off like firecrackers, different thoughts and memories disappearing for eternity as I resisted defying gravity and floating into the great nothingness hidden behind the sky and the stars. My home.

I heard her mutter *Jesus Christ, I guess it's been 45 minutes* before I realized that she wasn't Vanessa anymore. She was Tanya, a woman whom I loved but never touched. I thought she was in another country. I was stunned, lusting like I've never lusted before.

"I'm finally gonna fuck Tanya." But she turned into a total stranger and I felt my stomach rise like when I start a rollercoaster. I want to get off the ride now but I can't I'm

trapped here I can't get off until the end of the ride that won't be for hours oh my god I can't stand another second I'll fucking jump if I have to. What is this place? This still cannot be Earth. I was no longer sure it had ever been Earth.

Then she (I don't know who she is now but she is supremely erotic, religiously
beautiful, and I wanted to deface her sacred alter, fill her church with my erect temple, celebrate Flesh Mass, stain her glass windows with a splash of blood and sex) was very close to me and in my face and telling me to sit down and her arm is on my arm. The lust comes back, overtaking my body which at the same time lost an element of reality in my disintegrating mind, and this new lust was of intensity foreign to me. In fact, these new feelings had me doubting my own reality. Had I become another person? But I was so erotically charged those thoughts simply dissipated into nothingness. I am questioning my existence on an intellectual plain but look down to see my cock in my hand, a beast getting bigger, growing from a baby to a hardened killer, older and rougher and harder. I'm standing there, and I'm jerking off. She starts laughing like a lunatic and then I see she transforms in some unthinkable way into Mike, my perpetually stoned room-mate. "What the fuck are you doing?" he asks me, hysterical. He looked like a man who just heard God whisper into his hear the fact that he did not really exist and should try to open his eyes to see who he is when he wakes up.

"Shit! I thought you were someone else."

"I hope it wasn't your mom."

"Tell me who you are." I grabbed his arm. Or his arm. Or its arm. It was a fleshy limb ending with a hand with five digits; that was all that I knew.

He pushed me off. "What the fuck are you doing?" Then I had a horrible sense of Déjà vu, of slipping into the past, of being caught in a time warp. I would be hearing that question for eternity.

What the fuck are you doing?

I looked around and felt like a newborn, aware only of my consciousness. I didn't know what I was. Time had just started moving and there was no past. I had no frame of reference. The words in my head sounded funny and started losing meaning. Am I in a graveyard? Is this a concentration camp? I was terrified and the fear and I became one.

Flesh isn't always Flesh. The Nazis intercepted an alien spacecraft. They learned how to travel time from the aliens. They didn't lose the war, they just moved it to the future and now they were going to get me and every other Jew and kill us all. I closed my eyes and I was stuck tight between other people, human-locked, unable to move in total darkness, suffocating as humanity crushed me from all sides and I hear the gas canisters falling and the hiss of gas and clawing at my face and screaming and I am being crushed by a gigantic pile of corpses, they suffocate me and violate me my chest hurts and I can't breathe.

The pain informs me that I live.

What the fuck are you doing?

Everything is shaking and I open my eyes and Mike is looking at me and his face has changed color and shape due his to the shock eating through his mind like hungry worms inside the head of a corpse. His eyes were monstrous, the pupils dilated like a full moon, his lips were blue, and I could read his mind. It was so easy, because I saw a little thought-bubble like they have in comic books hanging over his head and the words said "I need to get David some Valium."

I grabbed Mike and pointed at the thought bubble. "Look! Anyone who walks by can read your mind. David David David David valium valium valium valium get get burn get valium David."

Mike's back was turned and he got smaller and smaller and his legs pumped and soon I was alone in the graveyard. My place of comfort.

This must be where I'm buried. If I can dig myself up I can get back to Earth and stop this insanity. I dive down and start digging myself out of the hole I'm in. How did I get here? Covered in dirt. I must have been buried alive. Is this whole graveyard full of people buried alive like me? Arms grab me and pull me deep under the surface of the Earth where all is dark and dirt chokes and gags me and fear-monsters come to life from my skin and start drilling little holes to burrow themselves in. I feel myself become lighter as the blood rushes out of my body, out of tiny little holes that covered every inch of my body, and the blood flowed over me and flooded the dirt until I was caught in some demonic undertow that pulled me with such force that I lost control and started drowning, choking. I was sweating blood from everywhere, even my eyeballs which cried in agony like a roomful of tortured babies being used for medical experiments involving tolerance of pain and shock.

"What the fuck? Get over here!"

"This weed is wicked fucked up and-"

"Holy fuck! Somebody's coming out of that fuckin' grave!"

"Bullshit. Oh my god! That looks like Martian Dave. Hey!

Man! Are you all right? Do you need some help?"

I had been captured by aliens speaking in strange tongues. I could see their thought-balloons but the language was strange and unreadable like those symbols on my watch and it was like being deaf.

"Did he just climb out of a grave?"

"Is this a fucking zombie invasion?"

"Why is that dude buried when he looks pretty alive?

"Help!" I think and try to make that thought materialize out of my mouth. I look behind me at the thought-balloon and I can't read what I'm thinking. I became terrified and the symbols reddened. I knew these creatures could read my thoughts and I didn't know what I was thinking, what if I was thinking I wanted to hurt them, and they could read it? What would they do to me? I was badly outnumbered and was unaware of my own species or place on the food chain.

The symbols changed rapidly before me, still alien. The letters pulsated and throbbed like an unconscious drunk's bloated stomach. I was illiterate. I reached out to the letters.

Maybe I could hide my thoughts. I was naked, exposed. The humans made foreign sounds. Laughing at me? Discussing how to kill me and eat me? Seeing what scared me so they could fuck with me? I collapsed back to the Earth, not even knowing how I had returned to the surface from deep underground where I had lay buried like a mummy.

I could not take another second. My brain should kick in and shut down when something like this happens. I can't believe it's abandoned me. Left me alive to suffer. I was betrayed, forsaken. Is there not some mechanism in my mind that should be auto-destroying my memories to save me from my insanity?

I was coughing, choking on a cloud of smoke, an exotic beautiful smelling smoke that relaxed me and soothed me and comforted me. It told me I would be okay. It told me to ride out the storm. It told me the rollercoaster would eventually end, if I could just hold on, it would be tough, but I could do it. A guy who looked like Lemmy gave me a cup and I drank it down. It burned! Liquid fire set my stomach ablaze. "That'll set ya straight."

Lisa grabbed my arm. "Did you just drink all that Everlcear? You're already too fucked up. Are you okay? What's going on? What? You look real bad. You look fucking dying. Do you want to kiss me before you die? I know you've always wanted to, now is your last chance because I'm not a necrophiliac anymore. You want your hands on my tits and up my cunt, you wanna fuck me, you wanna make my pussy sore so I have to walk bowl-legged for weeks, don't you? You want your cock down my fucking throat. You want my tongue up your ass. You want me to suck you off so you can cum in my eyes and all over my face, don't you? Let me see if you're hard. You're so fucking hard! You fucking know you want me. Do you want me to pull my dress up and see if I'm wearing anything underneath?"

I grabbed her and we began kissing until she pushed me away to drink more.

"Aren't you going to pull your dress up like you said? I wanna see."

"Go away, you're fucked up. All right, here." She pulled her little dress up revealing her soft belly with the dolphin tattoos and her white and red striped cotton panties which she slid down, flashing me her pussy. She had dark pubic hair and pale flesh. She pulled her panties up and dropped her dress down. I was erect, I was practically bursting, I had to have her. I tried to grab her but she easily knocked me over.

The world spun in circles as she walked away.

I heard the other guys laughing and yelling and one said "Let's get the fuck outta

I was on Mars, in some hostile place, disconnected from my environment. I was out of control, totally out of control. I needed to get in control. I needed to get where I could be in control. I walked to Veronica's house. She lived by herself and she would be alone. I could go in and she would understand and I could be in control. I walked through a cartoon world, a video game world where I alone was flesh and blood. Was Ronnie flesh and blood? I would find out. Cars drove by but they weren't real to me anymore. I could see they were all empty. I was the last man standing. I stopped in front of a house and sniffed the air. This had to be her house. Three cars were in the driveway.

I pounded on the door until she opened it. But she wasn't Ronnie. She was some old lady with gray hair and a stern face. I could feel her wrath and indignation as she looked down on me. Ronnie lived alone so who was this?

"What do you want?" she asked me as the house pulsated. "Who are you? Who is Ronnie? Are you with the government? Do you think we are stupid? Waiting to die?"

I pushed past her into the house. She chased after me. "Ronnie! Ron! Come out here now. I need you! I don't know what is going on but I know you have the answers!" Then a young couple came out of one room and a confused looking kid came out of another room wearing his PJs and rubbing his eyes. The wife grabbed her kid and pulled it away and the elderly lady closed the front door. After giving the kid to her husband she approached me.

"There's no Ronnie here. You have the wrong address. I can't let you leave, but don't worry. You're lucky, I'm a former nurse, I can tell you need some help. I'm going to help you. And I will help you again when the punishments stop." She had brown hair and a hardened but pretty face with intense piercing blue eyes. "I want you to sit down on this chair." Her giggling should have scared me.

I did as she told me. Everyone else seemed to fade into the back ground. She sat down on the chair next to me and got very close to me. I looked at her and knew it was a joke! That was Ronnie underneath, in those eyes. I could see it. I grabbed her face and ripped at the skin, intent on seeing the real Ronnie inside. Arms grabbed me as I tore her lip and cheek and squeezed the top of her face tight and I punched until no one was grabbing me anymore and then I hit Ronnie to make her stop fighting back so hard and when she stopped shaking I ripped the skin from her face and even tore her throat out but I couldn't see the real Ronnie just beneath the skinless screaming face of a monster with no cheeks and big exposed teeth which I hammered and smashed as little bits flew in the air.

She stopped moving and I became aware of another presence. The child. His eyes were wide in disbelief. I put my hands around his neck and squeezed hard so no oxygen could get into his lungs. After going without oxygen for a sufficient time his heart stopped beating and he died and I let go and it fell to the floor with a THUD! I had taken the lives of everyone in the room. Was this a god thing? Where was Ronnie to tell me? I fell asleep, wondering, feeling my body sink into the couch as my brain turned to gas and went everywhere, as it became thinner, mixing in with the environment until there was no person left.

I woke up and set the house on fire. I cleaned myself in the bathroom as the fire got started and just made it out before the foundations started collapsing. *What the fuck are you doing?*

It was time to go home for the night. Well, by then it was morning. I was all set for another day on this planet. The drugs had worn off, but not the knowledge that I was in a foreign environment and my mission was to destroy these people. I walked with a smile, planning my next attack. My smile kept growing as I thought of my ancestors who were from some more complex universe.

That was the night I was born.

Old Tricks

Michael Zunenshine

"You down for the standard breakfast?" he asked her, scanning the restaurant to see if anyone would notice him pull out her chair.

"Don't know, what's the standard?"

"You don't know the standard?"

"I just said that."

"Oh, OK, sorry, well, I mean, just get whatever you like." He felt around in his pocket for some loose change to play with. She opened the extra-large menu and looked up and down the pages, flipping through them too quickly, he thought.

The waitress approached, "coffees here?"

"Please," he said.

"Can I have a cappuccino?" she asked.

"Yeah, sure, have whatever you want," he said.

"One coffee and one cappuccino. You guys ready to order or you need some more time?"

"I'm ready," he said, "but if you need more time—"

"No," she said, "I think I can manage."

"Shoot," said the waitress.

He began. "I'll have the standard, sunny-side up, bacon, white toast." He snapped his menu shut. She rolled her eyes and let the menu slip out of her fingers onto the table.

"I would like..." she trailed off for a second while the waitress watched them, "eggs benedict, with smoked salmon, and a fruit salad."

"OK, anything else?" asked the waitress.

"No thanks, we're good—"

She cut him off, "can I get a mimosa too?"

"A mimosa?" he asked.

"Yes, I'd love a mimosa."

"Yeah, sure," he said, and turning to the waitress, "and a mimosa."

"Just one?" the waitress asked.

The girl reached across the table to the boy. "Won't you have one too?"

"No, that's all right," he said, "I don't like mimosas."

208

The waitress flipped her pad shut, "OK, be right back with your coffees."

He noticed the waitress had an amused smile and it bothered him. Was their situation so painfully obvious, he wondered? Shouldn't breakfast waitresses show a little more tact? As a way to reclaim some of his pride, he checked out the waitress's ass to objectify her just a little. It was a small and pathetic victory.

"Last night was nice," the girl said.

"I'm glad you had fun."

"It was nice. Thank you."

"No problem."

"And thank you for treating me to breakfast."

"No problem, really. Not much for the standard, though, are you?"

"Nope. Definitely not."

"I could tell." He watched her shut her eyes and smile as a blade of sunlight cut across their table and struck her the face. Sparkling dust rose from her blonde, greasy hair and he focused on the paths of individual particles, trying to fix the moment, to lose himself in her effortless morning beauty. She was beautiful and he congratulated himself for bringing her home last night.

A bottle popped its cork somewhere off in the background, breaking the spell, and he started thinking about money.

Waiting for the food, their conversation was light and meaningless. He asked questions and she responded with short pleasant answers that went nowhere. He wondered if she was bored or was instead testing his capacity for boredom.

When their breakfast arrived, she spent several minutes considering her plate and rearranging the food on it. He stabbed his egg yolk and forked potatoes in his mouth and licked the bacon grease off his fingers and wiped his plate clean with toast. She neatly separated miniscule bites and lifted them carefully to her pink mouth with a downturned fork, using her four front teeth to pull the morsel off the prongs and closing her eyes as she chewed.

"Good?" he asked.

"Mmm."

"I'm just going to run to washroom." He got up and crossed the entire dining area to the washroom, conscious that she might be watching him, or might not be.

In the bathroom he rinsed his mouth out with tap water and blew his nose and patted sweat off his forehead and temples. He checked his cell phone but there was nothing new. He thought about searching her name on his phone's web browser or even looking her up on his mobile Facebook app, but realized what a lengthy stay in the washroom might seem like to her, waiting for him at the sunny table for two by the window.

Her eggs benedict were burst open but otherwise barely eaten. Her fruit had been picked at. Her cappuccino was still half full, but the little shortbread cookie was gone from the saucer. The mimosa had been fully drained. He looked out the restaurant window but saw only autumn foliage fluttering down the street. He took out his cell phone again; no texts, no missed calls, and he remembered they hadn't exchanged phone numbers. Accepting the circumstance, the boy considered reclaiming some of his self-worth by sitting back down and finishing her barely-eaten breakfast plate.

"All done?" The waitress was already grabbing at his empty plate and avoided eye contact.

"What? Oh, yeah, sure."

She cleared away the other plate and said she'd be right back with the bill.

The girl stopped by the window of a shop that sold cheap jewelry and makeup and hair accessories. An eyeless female bust stood on a column and absorbed her gaze. It was wearing an urban fedora, a variety of earrings up the whole length of her plastic lobes, non-prescription eyeglasses over her face and over-sized sunglasses on her forehead, and a simple suede choker with diamond-shaped rhinestones. The girl's fingers gently grazed her own neck as she considered each individual sparkling stone.

The sound of strained coughing sludge startled her and she jumped back a bit and held her chest. She would have tripped over the old beggar on the ground had she skipped right by the shop window. He was trying to endure his painful throat spasms and didn't notice her. A paper cup rested next to him with what couldn't have been more than one dollar in the smallest, filthiest change. His coughing changed into a private groan and a prayer as he looked up and caught her staring at him. He raised his cup and shook it at her, barely getting out the word, change.

Looking back at the display window, she saw her reflection on top of the cheap polystyrene bust with the choker. She looked back down at the old beggar and reached in her pocket. His mouth opened as he stretched his cup out to her. From her pocket, she pulled out a little shortbread cookie and waved it in front of his face.

Her apartment was all white walls and minimal decoration. The front door opened into the main room, consisting mostly of an antique-styled couch and coffee table set. The old beggar followed her inside and looked around the clean open space. She flung her purse over a heavy antique coat rack by the front door.

"Go on," she said, gesturing with her hands, "go on, go on."

He walked into the room keeping his hands close to his chest as she darted past him into the kitchen. He heard her rummaging with cabinets and fridge doors and playing with faucets. He sat down and stroked his dirt-grey beard and scratched the back of his neck and his scalp.

Her footsteps approached quickly and when she saw him, she snapped, "No, off the couch, off the couch." She came at him, stomping on the floor. He stood up, looking down at the cushion where he had sat to see if he left a stain.

She grabbed him by the sleeve and pulled him to an empty corner of the room. "Here," she said, "here," pointing down.

He bowed his head. She stood on her toes and started pushing down on his shoulders. "Sit."

His knees buckled and he gave in to her command and settled himself on the floor in the corner.

"Good boy," she said, "now, lie down." She gestured with the flat of her downturned palm to the floor. "Lie down, yes, good boy."

He slouched into his usual pose, typical of infirm street beggars. She smiled down at him like a proud mother. "You hungry?"

He was too confused to speak but he managed to nod his head. She left for a second and returned with a plastic dish that consisted of two connected bowls, and placed it on the floor. One was filled with water, the other with hard brown pieces with a strong earthy smell.

"Go on," she said, "eat." After some encouraging nudges with her foot into his side, he obeyed, picking up individual pieces of earthy bits and putting them in his mouth. He needed to suck each individual piece to moisten it enough before attempting to chew because of his rotten teeth and sensitive palate.

She watched him eat a few pieces but soon began feeling nauseous and turned away. He watched her lock the front door from the inside and do something with the doorknob.

She went into the bedroom and locked that door as well and fell onto her queen-sized bed with memory foam mattress and buried herself in decorative pillows and stuffed animals under her goose-down comforter.

The coughing pulled her out of a dead-black sleep. It had that echo caused by the tight quarters of ceramic walls. She tried for a few moments to sink back into the folds of night but the thick wet coughing sound started giving way to painful moans. When she finally heard the plastic seat back smack against the porcelain of the toilet bowl, she pulled the chord of her brass bedside lamp and shot out of bed with all the energy of a violent daybreak.

She didn't know if he would have the sophistication to lock the bathroom door, but either way she knew the lock to be useless against the slightest force. She pressed her delicate cheek to the door for one second, and then lifted her knee and pushed her way through.

He was squatting above the bowl careful not to make contact with the padded seat. His pants and long underwear and boxer shorts weren't at his ankles but caught just above his knees. Staring straight at her, his face was red and his eyes were wet and his mouth was open.

"No," she shouted, "No. Bad." She moved toward the squatting figure who responded with involuntary sounds of fear and incontinence splashing beneath him. Tightening her face at the nose and mouth, she grabbed a tuft of filthy long hair and pulled him off the seat. His pants prevented him from remaining grounded and he fell to the floor, staining its brilliant white surface.

"Bad," she went on, never letting go of his hair, which seemed to tear at rotten parts of his scalp. With a reserve of strength she pulled his head up and jerked his neck around until he was facing the inside of the bowl. She lifted her knee above the back of his head and came down with the full weight of her elegant figure until nothing floated above the brown water but loose strands of grey-brown hair. Somewhere to the side of the bowl his hand was flexing into fists and loosening itself. She counted this repeated gesture five times and then hit the flusher. The water swirled around the old man's ears and then his mouth and nose and finally disappeared down the hole. He gasped and she heard him suck in a mouthful of his own filth. His coughing was so strong he gagged and shook under her knee while she examined her fingernails.

She let up and he fell over to the side. When he looked up she was smiling down at him with a disciplinary look that told him he would thank her for this.

Her apartment building's entrance from the street didn't lead directly indoors but to a courtyard where the tenants kept their bicycles locked up and brought their dogs to relieve themselves when they were too lazy to take a walk. She led him to a corner of the courtyard right below her bedroom window. "Here," she said, and crooked her index finger, pointing it to the ground. The outline of the night sky was beginning to fade as the sun grew in the distance. She kept her finger pointed down and didn't take her eyes off of him. He pulled down his pants and long underwear and boxer shorts to just below his bottom. She tried to make out his penis among the ratty tuft of pubic hair but all she could see was a long hanging scrotum and she put her hand over her mouth to keep herself from giggling out loud and waking the neighbors.

They remained motionless as the sky turned a deep dull blue and the sounds of the apartment building coming to life reached the courtyard. She kept her countenance, knowing that if he saw that she was nervous about being discovered by neighbors, he might not respect her authority. She saw his knees shake and she hardened her features although her heart was warming up with the daylight. Finally, his eyes relaxed themselves and rolled just slightly upward as a delicate yellow stream drizzled beneath him. He shifted his feet to avoid the puddle and she broke out into a gorgeous smile.

Inside her apartment the daylight had spread across the walls and ceiling. She followed behind him inside while holding a piece of his jacket, jerking him back a little if he advanced before her too quickly. He started for the same empty corner of the room without looking back at her for approval. She stopped him and turned him around and took his face in her hands and gave him an approving smile. She touched his nose with the tip of her index finger and said, "stay." He watched her walk backwards until she was backed up against the couch and then dropped herself down on it. "Stay," she repeated, drawing out the vowel and rounding out the end of the word. She settled more comfortably on the couch, pretending not to notice him, but keeping him fixed in the corner of her gaze. He stayed.

"OK," she said brightly, and padded the cushion next to her. His mouth and eyes spread apart and he rushed to be at her side on the couch. She put her arm around him and folded his head into her lap and caressed his hair, repeating in long low whispers, "good boy, good boy."

All throughout winter these repeated gestures and commands were becoming second nature for both of them. They practiced the roles of the master pet relationship with alternating strictness, kindness, obedience, and an eagerness to please. Language was becoming less necessary as words turned into vehicles for primitive sounds with emotional and physical qualities. She recognized the signs of his body and served him with all the attention and immediacy she had to spare. His movements became quicker and his body more agile. A world was forming inside the apartment with it's own laws of recognition. Outside the apartment, her life went on as normal. She maintained relations with some friends and did satisfactory work at her part time internship and continued to receive regular money transfers from her parents.

One early spring night night she went out to a house party and was approached by a handsome intellectual who talked her ear off about his Master's degree in journalism. He was trying to redefine how we discuss the homeless so as to consider them not a problem to be solved, but rather to include them as a proper class in the socio-economic struggle. She went home with him and spent the night and after the sex she laid awake in his bed unable to fall asleep. On her way home the next morning, she went into the shop with the cheap jewelry and bought the suede choker with diamond-shaped rhinestones right from the neck of the polystyrene head.

He was asleep in the corner. His back was against the wall and his legs were stretched out in front of him just as she had first seen him on the street. She bent down and put the choker around his neck and his nose twitched a little so she kissed it to wish him wonderful little dreams.

Not bothering to wash herself after another one-night-stand, she slid herself under her goose-down comforter, being careful not to loosen them at the sides of the bed. They held her down, tight and warm against her memory-foam mattress. The smell of fresh linen mingled with the musty old man, and when she lifted her arm behind her head she could also smell the stale sweat of sex.

As if her salty skin acted like a lure, she heard him approach the bedroom.

The door began to open. She froze, lying on her back, trapped in the tight blanket. He stood in the doorway. His

214

posture was more upright than she had ever seen. Her breath felt ready to race away from her chest and she put all her energy into keeping it inside her. She heard the sounds of joints cracking and saw his right hand making a tight fist and relaxing itself over and over. Her lungs tightened and twisted themselves in her chest. He put a heavy foot forward into her bedroom. Her breathing almost stopped and his got louder as he kept advancing toward the bed. Despite the morning sun which was coming through her white lace curtains, a blackness crept up at her from all sides. She was reduced to the most basic of sensory perceptions. The smell of must and mildew and piss touched her on the face and down her belly and in between her thighs. One of his legs rose beside her and the weight of his knee came down on her mattress. Her delicate figure was shifted closer to the old beggar who was mounting with heavy and hardened breathing. She felt the second knee drop down beside her and a monstrous arm reach across her breasts, and finally, the head bury itself between her shoulder and neck, and his body relax. His facial hair around the mouth was wet with his spit and felt like glue connecting the two of them in bonds unspeakable outside their world of protection and dependence.

Her breathing became easier. She reached up and caressed his head, but there was no reaction. He was asleep and happy.

But it was a happiness he made for himself. She pushed him off and leapt from the bed and before he was fully awake she grabbed the bedside lamp by its neck and brought its brass base down against his head. He rolled over and moaned and shielded his face with his hands but she continued to bash his face through his hands and then the rest of his body.

After the cries turned into moaning and labored coughing soon there was no sound but the jingling of lamp bits and dull moist thuds. She placed the lamp back and went to the doorway. He was on his stomach and occasionally his torso jerked upwards in convulsions. She clapped her hands twice loudly and said, "off the bed.

"Come on, off the bed," she stomped her foot, "let's go, come on."

When she saw him reach for the edge of the bed to pull himself down, she said, "good boy," and walked out.

In the bathroom she started filling the tub with warm water. She looked in the mirror and then looked at her hands. Her palms had the imprint of the grooves from the lamp's neck.

She peeked out and he was standing, hunched forward, waiting between her bedroom and the bathroom. She smiled at him as she closed the door with her foot, barely mouthing the word, "stay." She stood up on the ledges of the bathtub and pulled down her panties and peed into the warm water. It burned just a little.

As the tub continued filling she opened the door and said, "come, here," and pointed to the ground in front of her. He obeyed and without further instruction also got down on all fours at her feet. She took a pair of scissors from the bathroom cabinet and cut his clothes off of him layer by layer, going up the middle of his back and down his chest and up and around the sides of each pant leg. Some bits of fabric stuck to his skin with blood. The smell of mildew and piss grew stronger. She had a hard time getting his pants all the way off and realized his calves were just as thick as his thighs as if he didn't have any knees. His skin was a mosaic of red blood and purple bruises layered over large, flaky white patches and raised maroon lesions. He was wearing watches on both wrists, and she removed them and put them in a drawer. Finally he was naked except for his shiny new collar. As she helped him step in the tub, she saw the gaps between his toes were long and came almost as far back as his toe mounds.

She washed him with her bare hands using soap foam from a pump dispenser. The water around him had transformed into a dark oily pool. She took extra care with his armpits and inner thighs and between the cheeks of his rear. She covered her fingers in toothpaste and opened her mouth wide to show him he should do the same. His gums were receded so that each tooth narrowed to a green-black point where they were attached. She rubbed her fingers gently over his teeth and gums and reached deep into his mouth across the back of his tongue. She twisted her arm and massaged his soft palate. His eyes stayed shut until her hand was out of his mouth.

She stood up and held out her hand as if inviting him to get up and dance. He took her hand for support and stepped out and she dried him with a clean white towel. She cut his hair and clipped his fingernails but his toenails were too thick and twisted to fit in her clippers.

When he was cut and dry, she pointed to the familiar corner of the living room and he curled up there and seemed to sleep. Gathering up his cut up clothes and sweeping up his hair and fingernails, she dumped them all into the tub with his soiled bathwater. She stripped down and kneeled beside the tub, staring into the dark clouded water. Glimpses of her reflected face were stretched and distorted by the moving grease pools gliding on the surface.

She stepped in the tub, sinking deep into the mild liquid until she was submerged to the chin. Fabric and hair clung to her arms as she moved them about making little waves. When she slid forward to let her entire head fall beneath the surface, she kept her eyes open.

The day was brilliant. She had been out walking for hours, letting anything from green lights to sun-dappled alleys guide her way. Stopping by a lilac tree, she plucked off a stem and put it in her hair, using her phone's camera app as a mirror.

A bicycle was riding by but stopped suddenly, kicking up dust. "Hey," someone yelled.

Frightened by the suddenness, she pocketed her phone and started walking away, pretending she assumed the boy on the bicycle was addressing somebody else. She heard his feet push off the street and come up behind her.

"Hey, remember me?"

"Oh," she said, "yeah, hi, how are you?"

"Fine, I guess," he said. He looked like he had just lost all the courage to tell her off for ditching him at the restaurant last fall. Now he didn't know if he wanted to be friendly. She took advantage of his pause to disarm him with her charm. "Isn't it a gorgeous day?" she asked.

"It's hot."

"It's gorgeous."

He leaned forward on his handlebars and swung his leg, squinting at her. "What are you up to?"

"I am up to ab-so-lute-ly nothing," she said, "care to join me?"

"Sure, I mean, what do you want to do?"

"Walk with me."

He didn't get off his bike but pushed himself along at walking pace next to her. She looked on ahead and up at the trees and all around, and he kept shifting his gaze from the ground to her face.

"You know," he said, "that wasn't really cool what you did to me."

She threw her head back and smiled and touched his shoulder. "Oh my god, I am so sorry, I totally forgot."

"What happened? I mean, did I do something?"

"No, of course not, you were wonderful."

"So?"

"Let's not talk about it, OK?"

"Sure, if you want, it's just..." he peddled in a circle around her, "...I was pretty pissed off."

"Why?"

He couldn't figure out her tone, which was too light, and maybe a little mocking. Mentioning how expensive the breakfast bill was seemed out of the question. "Well, it hurt my feelings."

"Oh, that's sweet."

He couldn't help but smile. That's, OK."

"Good."

"So... how about you make it up to me sometime?"

"What did you have in mind?"

"I don't know. Beers? I mean, I'm not saying you have to pay for them or anything—" but he regretted mentioning money. She didn't seem to notice.

"I don't drink beer."

"I mean drinks, you can order anything you want."

"Anything I want?"

"Yeah, sure."

They approached a lawn sale and she reached out to him to stop his peddling. Books, VHS tapes and DVDs rested with their spines exposed on a table, a sari blanket with rocks on each corner was spread out on the lawn and covered with old appliances and other random apartment decorations, and a cheap standing rack held a few sweaters and button-downs with cluttered wire hangers. A young bearded guy sat playing on his phone on the stoop behind his junk. He was wearing such a deep-cut V-neck shirt his nipples were almost exposed. "The table and the clothes rack are also for sale, if you want," he said, "but not the sari." As the boy on the bicycle ran his finger across the spines of literature and cinema, she touched the sharp point of a hanger with her ring finger.

"Have you read this?" He held up a book. She glanced at him and saw a thick mass-market paperback with a glossy embossed cover and then looked away.

"No," she said without smiling. He put the book back down in its original place.

On the sari blanket was a curious, little velour pouch of faded burgundy held shut with a drawstring. She bent forward and picked it up. Its contents clanked and shifted as she handled it. "Check this out," she said, tossing him the pouch. He caught it and tossed it up and down.

"Marbles. Cool."

"I like the pouch."

"Maybe you could buy just the pouch."

The bearded vendor spoke up, "pouch's for the marbles. Five bucks."

"I'm sure you could find some use for the marbles," the boy said, "maybe give them to some neighborhood children or something."

"That's sweet," she said. "Do you have any money on you?"

He reached in his pocket and pulled out a bunch of coins and tried to hand her exact change.

"Give it to him," she said.

He obeyed and handed the change to the bearded vendor.

"Thank you, that was sweet. I didn't bring any money with me today."

"That's OK; you can pay me back when we have that drink." He winced inwardly after saying this.

"As you like." She reached out for the sack of marbles.

"So... do you have a favorite bar?"

"Take me where you like to go."

"OK, yeah, sure, when?"

"Tomorrow night. Pick me up at my place?"

"Great, yeah, how about eight?"

"Nine. I'll text you my address."

"Okay."

They took out their phones and he gave her his number and she texted him her address. When he received the text he read it back to her and she smiled and nodded. He reached forward as if to touch her face. She flinched. He drew back. "The flowers," he said.

"What?"

"In your hair, they were coming loose."

"Oh," she said, and fixed them. "I love lilac season."

The sound of footsteps and keys woke him up and he scurried on all fours to the front door to meet her. She came in carrying a pouch and a small white box. He nuzzled his head against her leg for attention but she ignored him until she took off her sandals and set the two items down on the coffee table. Exhausted from her walk and a bit sweaty, she fell back on her couch, put her feet up on the coffee table, and fanned herself by tugging at her blouse. He waited by the door, watching her.

"OK," she said with emphasis. He came to her. She dug her fingers in his hair and shook his scalp with warm encouragement. "Who's a good boy," she repeated. He watched her stretch her toes one by one, and when she noticed his attention, she nudged his head toward her feet. He started lapping up the soles of her feet and up the sides. She giggled and teased him by prodding is face with her big toe, which he tried to catch with his tongue. She prodded harder and harder and he became more determined to catch her toe and it amused her to see him get frustrated.

As her giggling turned to a full laugh, he snapped and bit the arch of her foot. She stopped laughing and jerked her leg and kicked him against the jaw. "No." It was part of their routine of discipline and he obeyed without letting his feelings be hurt. She looked at him and sighed. "OK boy, want to play a game?"

He nodded, panting and licking his lips.

She opened up the little box. It was full of expensive pastries from the European bakery. His eyes bulged and he started sniffing at them.

"Stay," she said, and got up. She went over to the front closet and took out a man's winter jacket. It was a designer-style parka and seemed almost brand new. She took her purse off the coat rack and put it in the closet. She unzipped the parka and wrapped it around the coat rack and put the hood over the top, creating what looked like a tall hunchbacked figure with a black hole for a face. Standing behind the figure, she grabbed the rack by the base and leaned it forward at him, making deep, absurd growling sounds, "grrrrrr."

He looked at her and tilted his head, then couldn't help looking back at the pastries. She tried again to make the growling sounds, deeper and louder. He turned back to her, unsure if the sounds were actually coming from her throat, or somewhere deeper within her, or maybe they weren't even her sounds at all. His head kept tilting from side to side as she growled and jerked the coat rack towards him, but he wouldn't advance.

She put the rack down and picked up a piece of apple strudel. Taking a slow bite, she said, "Mmm," and chewed with emphasis. When she swallowed, she licked two fingers, then held out a third finger to him. He sucked off the sugary residue.

She held out the strudel to him and he started to leap toward it but she held it back at the last second. "Wait," she commanded, and returned to behind the coat rack and lifted up the faceless male figure again, making the same deep monstrous noises.

He let out a whimper.

She poked her head from behind the figure and said with her regular voice, sweet and encouraging, "Get him, boy."

He lifted his eyebrows and tilted his head. She advanced holding the figure, swaying it and growling, then popped her head from the side and repeated her sweet command. "Get him, boy."

He pawed in the direction of the figure but didn't advance. She swung it closer to him and the flaps of the parka brushed against his face. He whimpered and crawled backwards.

She slammed the figure down on the floor, took off the parka and flung it over his head, blinding him. "Stay," she commanded. He heard her reach for the pastries again, and something else that clanked like solid glass.

When she lifted the parka off his head, he saw her holding a broken piece of mille-feuille but she wasn't smiling. She came up to him slowly, then with one hand grabbed his jaw and the other stuffed the pastry into his mouth. He was confused by the delicious sugar until he chomped down on a hard piece of rounded smooth glass. He choked and spat it out. It was a marble almost two centimeters across, the diameter of a penny.

She wiped her hand, grabbed the marble, shoved it back in and held her palm over his mouth. He screwed his eyes shut and tears leaked from his crusted eyes and soon she felt his throat flex and release and a short burst of hot air from his wet nostrils.

"Again," she said, setting the parka back on the coat rack. As soon as she began making the low violent growling noises he turned and crawled quickly around the room. The figure chased him and lunged forward and they went around in circles. Survival instincts kicking in, he made as if to get up on two feet, but she foresaw this and turned the figure sideways, yelling, "No," and stabbed him hard in the back with pointed tip of the coat rack. His body twisted and fell. From the corner of his teary vision he saw her handle something flaky and march toward him. Before he could brace himself he was swallowing sweet puff pastry and breaking a brittle tooth on another marble larger than the first. He swallowed everything and felt the marble push the jagged piece of broken tooth down first, cutting against his throat.

He stayed huddled in the corner, gagging and spitting up sweet pastry flakes and salty blood. As she fixed up the parka again he pissed himself. As the warmth in his pants cooled, so did his blood.

When he heard the growling and saw the figure approaching, he met it with inhuman ferocity and a bloody hungry mouth. He almost took her down but she let go just in time to watch him tackle the parka off the rack and onto the floor. He clawed and gnashed and wailed while she watched him with pride and munched on some more strudel.

They repeated the lesson several more times while she consumed sweets and he swallowed a few more marbles when his attack lacked conviction. The floor was covered in vomit and blood and a few torn pieces of white fluffy lining fabric. Before putting him to bed and cleaning up she held him and fed him small bits of leftover pastries.

He looked up at her and reached forward to touch her face. She flinched, but let him continue. He fixed the purple flowers that were coming loose in her hair and then licked the tears that then fell down her cheek.

She knew the boy wouldn't be late. She even suspected he'd be lingering around the corner from her door at the appointed time so as not to seem too eager. Her buzzer went off at three minutes past the hour. So predictable, she thought, and bet that he would even apologize for being late.

Before buzzing him into the courtyard she raised the volume of the music coming through speakers attached to her phone. The perky indie rock tune woke the old man up from his sleep in the corner. He stretched his narrow body, naked on the floor, then scratched himself all over. When he heard the knock on their door he started moving around in circles and making low, uncomfortable grumbling sounds.

She called out through the door, "just a minute."

"No problem," the boy returned, eager and accommodating, like he'd wait outside forever.

She turned to the old man and called him over. He came to her feet and she crouched down and petted his head. "Who's a good boy, who's a good boy." She scratched behind his ears. "Mommy's going to put you in the bedroom, OK? Be a good boy and be quiet, OK? No barking, OK? Stay off the bed or else, OK? Mommy won't keep you there long." She grabbed his collar and led him into the bedroom, closing the door behind her.

Glancing around the room and quickly into a full-length mirror, she smiled. She opened the door. The boy took his hands out of his pockets and said, "Sorry I'm late."

"You're not."

"A little... what time is it?"

"Around nine."

"Yeah, I think it's a little after, anyways, sorry about that."

"Come in for a bit before we go?"

"Yeah, sure."

She moved aside and let him pass in front of her into her apartment. She watched him look around and run his hands through his wrists in a cyclical motion. "Nice place," he said, craning his neck to see nothing particular on the ceiling.

"Thank you," she said.

"Nicer than mine, I mean, you know."

"Is it?"

"Yeah, you were there, you remember."

"Oh yeah, Kind of."

He spun around to face her and slapped his sides. "So, shall we, or... do you want to have a drink here?"

"Let's get out of here," she said, "I just need to choose a purse." She opened the closet door.

"What kind of dog is he?"

"Oh you heard?" she said, staring into the closet, "just a mangy old mutt. I have a soft spot for those types."

"Can I meet him?"

"He's in the bedroom." She fingered the cuff of the hanging parka.

"So... can I go in?"

Slamming the closet door shut, she spun around and walked up to him with devastating determination. "You're not proposing to get a glimpse into my bedroom already, are you?" She smiled and took his arm.

"No, sorry, I didn't mean—"

"Let's get out of here, he's being punished and can't have visitors."

"Why is he being punished?"

"Because he's been a bad boy."

The old beggar was alone in her room for the first time. He was barely allowed in her room at all except for mornings when she would wake up and call him to the side of her bed. Once he thought of getting into bed with her but as he made to climb in she gestured for the lamp and then he knew better.

Now he dared to stand upright but still didn't dare to sit or lie down on the bed. She had a vanity in her bedroom and he stared at himself for a long time, examining inside his mouth and teeth, and then looked down at himself. The ground seemed very far. He opened her bedroom closet but didn't dare touch any of her hanging clothing. He paced from one end of the bed to the other several times. When he got bored of pacing on two feet he got down on all fours and continued like that. Time passed but he had no way of telling how much. There wasn't a clock in her room. He thought about it, and realized there wasn't a clock in her whole apartment. When he was a beggar on the streets, he wore a watch on each wrist. They disappeared along with everything else since he had come to belong to her.

He didn't realize he had been asleep. Suddenly his head shot up and he sensed their approach seconds before he actually heard them, talking, laughing, keys and doorknobs. He rushed the few short paces to the bedroom door and crawled in quick circles as they entered the apartment's main room.

Realizing she wouldn't let him out of the bedroom right away, he calmed himself and put his face to the door to listen.

"Wow." The boy's tone was playful. "Did I mention you have a nice place?"

"Shut up." She was giggling. "You're so not funny."

"Can I use your bathroom?"

"Of course."

"Be right back."

"The lock doesn't work, but don't worry, you can trust me," she smiled.

A door opened and closed and the beggar heard running tap water. Out in the main room, she put on upbeat music. He could no longer hear what was going on in the bathroom until the sound of a flush.

The boy must be back in the main room. "It isn't too loud for this hour?" he heard the boy say.

"Who cares," she said. "Hey, I have something for you."

"Really, what is it?"

"Hang on."

First, he heard the apartment doorknob being handled in a familiar way. Then, she went to the front closet. His heart paused and he pressed his face tighter to the bedroom door. Hangars jingled and fabric brushed. She spoke. "Don't ask why I have it, but I don't need it."

"A little warm for that this time of year, no?" the boy said.

"It's not for now, keep it, really."

"Looks expensive."

"It might have been, but it's a little used as you can see, even torn in one place."

"Whose is it?"

"Don't ask, but really, take it, I think you would look marvelous in it."

There was a pause, then the boy said, "are you sure?"

"Positive."

"It doesn't belong to someone? Some ex or something?"

"It's yours."

"Are you sure?"

"Yes." he heard her tone change. "It's just taking up space in my closet."

"OK," the boy said, reacting to her tone. "Thanks, I could actually really use it this winter."

"Good," she said. "Try it on, please."

Fabric rustling sounds for a few seconds, then the boy spoke. "What do you think?"

"Marvelous."

"Thanks again."

More fabric rustling but she spoke quickly, "don't take it off just yet, I like looking at you in it."

"Sure, if you like... So how about that night cap?"

"Is that really what you want now?"

"I don't know, what are you suggesting?"

"Wouldn't you rather," she paused, and he heard slow careful steps, "meet my dog?"

"Oh," slight disappointment, "I totally forgot, yeah, sure."

"Wonderful."

He heard her approach. Not knowing what to do, what instincts or rationale to follow, he crawled away from the door into the back corner of her bedroom.

She opened the door. The music got louder. He couldn't see the boy from his angle. She crouched down in the doorway, a dark silhouette backlit by the bright open space behind her. But he could hear her smile a dark smile that he was especially attuned to recognize.

"Here boy, come on."

He whimpered and pawed the floor.

"Come on boy, come meet Jared."

He tried to push himself further back into the corner. She came forward, slowly at first, then, when she was close, she quickly stepped forward and reached out and grabbed his collar. "Come," she commanded, "come see Jared."

She pulled him across the bedroom into the light. The boy in the parka took his thumbs out of his front jeans pockets and suspended his hands in front of him. His eyes and mouth contorted inward and he stepped back. His mouth barely moved but words slipped out, "what the..."

She came in between the two of them who couldn't take their eyes off each other.

"Jared," she said, "meet Scrappy."

The naked old beggar on all fours looked up at her when he heard his name. The boy stumbled backward with his hands in front of him and looked at her. "Holly, what the fuck..."

She bent down by the old man and put one arm around his neck and her other hand under his chin. "Scrappy," she said, "see Jared."

"Holly, I'm going to be—what the—"

"See Jared, Scrappy," she tightened her grip. "Grrrrrr," she started making the low and horrible growling noise."

The boy put his hand to his mouth and gagged into it.

"Grrrrr, Scrappy, grrrrr—"

"Who the fuck—"

"Scrappy, grrrrrr." She was kneading and gripping the old man's head and chin with increasing strength. "Get him, boy." She pushed him forward, but he dug his heels in the floor. She screamed, "Get Him Boy."

The boy turned and grabbed the doorknob but his hand slid right off. "Fuck," he yelled.

"Get Him Boy." She started pushing and jabbing the old man in the ribs, always making the horrible growling noise.

The boy wiped his hand on his pants and tried the doorknob again, then with two hands, then with the sleeves of the parka covering his palms.

She got up and swung her leg back and kicked the old man clean across the jaw. "Bad dog, Scrappy," she yelled. "Get him, Now."

The old man felt a historical instinct absorb him and he turned to face the girl. The boy ripped off the parka and wrapped a sleeve around the doorknob. The girl tried to summon all the violent hate from the room into her eyes and stare down the old man. The boy used his whole torso to lean against the sleeve-wrapped doorknob and screamed as it began to rotate under his weight. The old man started growling and the girl yelled, "Scrappy, No!"

The growling rose and became the scream of a man and the boy heaved the doorknob and the girl tried standing her ground but found herself stepping backward. The old man lifted a leg and put one foot squarely on the ground. The doorknob gave and the boy shouldered the door open and ran.

She kept stepping backward. The old man lifted himself up on two feet, tall, heavy, and hungry. She turned and ran to the bathroom and slammed the door shut and he kicked it open. She fell back in the bath and he jumped on top of her small and delicate body and she saw the horrible fangs close in on her face and felt her tender white flesh penetrated by strong and dexterous fingers like a new born kitten in the mouth of a greasy machine.

The day was hot and humid but nobody thought it was abnormal for a homeless beggar to be wearing a heavy parka. Shoppers and strollers made an effort to seem like they weren't making an effort not to stare. If anyone looked at him for more than a second, they would be struck by the fact that the beggar wasn't wearing any pants but rather several dresses and skirts to cover his legs under the parka.

He wasn't making an effort to ask for change or hold out his cup and didn't try to look too weak or hungry for sympathy. He just sat there, occasionally licking his gums and his lips. Every now and then he pulled up either sleeve of his parka to check the time on one of two wrist watches.

A young couple was approaching, walking a panting little fawn pug. The girl wanted to stop in front of the shop window to look at some cheap jewelry and hair accessories, while the boy, holding the leash in one hand, checked something on his phone with the other. The pug sniffed at the old beggar. The beggar looked at the dog and squinted his eyes at him. The dog looked up at him and for a moment ceased panting. The beggar slowly reached up toward the dog's face, but the couple started moving along and the dog was jerked away by its leash.

The couple walked away, jerking the dog every time it wanted to stop and sniff something. Scratching his neck under a ridiculously bejeweled collar, the old beggar watched them disappear, and smiled.

Sinister Desires

Michael Randolph

Enveloped in the hazy cloud, William took one last drag off the pipe before settling back in his favorite recliner. Squirming around, he managed to dislodge the spring jamming into his ass cheek. His vixen, Desiree, was staring back as he brought up the "Sinister Desires" web feed on his monitor. "Hey, babe."

Spread across the bed half a world away, her delicate skin brought unbidden images to William's mind as she caressed her clit. "I've been waiting forever. I hope you don't mind me starting without you?" Long black hair cascaded over her shoulders as she turned around to give him a view from the back as she fingered herself. "I do so wish you were here riding me right now."

"You're just a cam girl, Desiree. We'll never meet in real life."

Hurt, she stopped, flipping around to face him. "Is that all I am to you, a cam girl?"

"No, wait I didn't mean it. Don't stop!" Frowning, he sat up. "Sweetheart, don't be upset. You know how I feel about you. I just wish we could meet for real. You don't know how many nights I've dreamed about you."

"If you meant it, why'd you say such a terrible thing?" Glancing away, Desiree pursed her lips as a tear trickled down her cheek.

William's heart lurched seeing the pain he caused her. "Baby, please, I didn't mean it."

"Do you really want to meet? We could arrange it, if you're a good boy and do exactly as I say."

William took a deep breath realizing he'd have to pony up some serious money to make her happy.

She moved close enough to the webcam to fill the screen with her deep set black eyes. "You still have the pendant I sent you?"

"Yes," he replied.

"When you go to bed, make sure you have it."

"I promise I will. I'm sorry for hurting you. Can we start again?"

Sliding back across the bed, she opened her legs showing the soft trimmed hair just above her pussy as she started rubbing her clit. William took in the image of her full perfect breasts and slim waist, imagining pumping her pussy as she arched her back, gyrating against his hips. Smiling, she stopped. "That's it for now. I have to get ready for tonight." Before he could respond, the screen went black.

"What...No, come back!" he screamed. Pounding the table with his fist, William cursed as the glass pipe rattled off, breaking as it hit the floor. "Shit, what a fucking day!"

Stomping into the kitchen, he retrieved a spoon. "Guess I'm stuck with the old fallback," he grumbled, dropping some crack into it before heating the bowl. Inhaling deeply over the rising smoke, A jolt surged through his body.

The rush made him wobble as he walked back to his chair, sitting down he glared at the screen. *Dammit, I was looking forward to this night. Dumb bitch.* Picking up the pendant from the table, he fingered it, remembering Desiree's demand to wear it. *What a psycho.*

Ha, I'll wear it. When I see her again, she'll find out what I think about all the fuckin money I poured down the drain on this shit. Hazy, William leaned back drifting off to sleep.

Startled by a soft thump near his head, he cracked his eyes open, astonished as Desiree stood in front of him. Wearing just a pair of fishnet stockings gartered to a pair of open crotch panties, she leaned over him. "Are you ready, my sex slave?"

"Um . . . what?" Glancing down, he saw two perfect lips glistening with her juices. "God, you have no idea how bad I want your pussy."

"Just lean back and relax," she responded. Kneeling down, she opened his legs, rubbing his cock with her hands, bringing him to full erection, groaning as she pulled his pajamas off, watching her encircle his head with her fingers; he shook himself, hoping this was real and not a dream.

Dark endless eyes stared up at him. He realized only black shone from the sockets.

"What's wrong with your eyes?" He moaned as she stroked him.

"Shush baby, this is what you wanted, just stay still as I suck you dry." Long fingers curved around his shaft sending spasms deep into his groin with each caress. Pulling her mouth off the head of his cock, she whispered, "take a hit, it's all yours."

Glancing over, another glass pipe lay on the table, all ready. Lighting it, William inhaled the smoke, a strange haze fogging his mind. "Don't stop, I love it when you twist your tongue around the head."

"I know what you like. Don't order me," Desiree said. He jerked back, seeing sharp needle like teeth from under her lips surrounding his cock. "Settle down, I won't hurt you. This will be a night you'll never forget."

Unsure of what was happening, he sat still. *Please let this is a dream.*

Smiling, she engulfed him all the way to his balls, sucking and caressing him. Increasing the rhythm with her mouth, she grabbed his sack, digging her fingernails into the soft skin. Pain flooded into him, yet pleasure won.

He tried reaching out to grab her head, but his arms refused to move. Looking down, nothing held them, yet no matter how hard he tried he couldn't lift his hands from the armrests. "Desiree, what's happening? I want you but not like this."

Stopping mid-stroke, she raised her eyes, blood trickling from her lower lip. "You're not going anywhere, lover boy!" Standing up, Desiree looked down at him. "You've earned a just reward for the lavish amount of money you spend on me."

Turning around, her firm ass swaying as she moved behind him, William throbbed with the thought of being inside her. Glancing down, he noticed red welts stretching from the tip of his cock to his balls, shivering as she nuzzled his cheek. Goosebumps spread down his neck and arms. Her breath was as cold as winter. Frost formed upon his chest.

"Who" he started, but was interrupted as Desiree pressed her finger against his lips.

"I am your dream, your angel sent to fulfill every desire."

"Sex yes, but no pain," he answered, shaking his head. Gulping, William twisted his head upward. "Don't know what you are, let me go or I'll . . ."

"You'll what?"

"I don't want this, whatever you are."

Desiree slipped her hand under his shirt, bringing new cries of pain from him as she dug furrows into his chest. "You think it felt good every time you demanded I shoved a bigger dildo up my ass?

Sharp pain flared across his cheek each time she rubbed up against him. In the corner of his eye, he saw scales growing along her face. "Let me go. I swear I'll never cam with you again. Please."

"Begging won't help," she whispered. Pulling one arm from under his shirt, she pointed to the monitor. "Look, we're on webcam now. My friends want to see you suffer."

Tears ran down his cheeks, the fervent hope of this being a dream vanishing as she cut into his stomach with hooked claws. "You're just a cam girl, this isn't real," he mumbled.

Giggling, she moved back around to the front, kneeling down to engulf his cock again. Up and down she stroked him, the pain overridden by the sheer pleasure of her mouth squeezing him. Never in his life had he felt such pleasure from a blowjob. Unable to contain himself, he spewed his cum into her mouth, spasms rocking his body.

Exhausted from the orgasm, it didn't register at first when a voice came over the speakers. "Desiree, stop fucking around. Take the soul and be done with it."

Stunned at the command, William shook off his lethargy. Bound to the recliner, he jerked and bucked. "*My soul?* Get the fucking hell away from me."

"Master, I intend to," she responded to the tinny voice.

Raising her head, William saw the long scales covering her face. Pitch black eyes stared back, endless pits of depravity showing a soul held in thrall by evil. Flicking out between her sharp teeth, a forked tongue tested the air. "He isn't ready yet. Maybe if I fucked him good?"

"No, don't touch me," he screamed. "Help me, someone help!"

"No one's going to hear your pitiful cries. You've been dreaming about screwing my brains out. Here's your chance." She turned around, her firm ass swaying in front of him. "Isn't this what you dreamed of?" Sitting down on his lap, the pain melted away as her soft pale skin touched his. Backing up higher on his legs, wet rivulets of pussy juice ran between his legs as she mounted his cock, slipping just the head between her lips.

"Oh God all of it. I promise I'll do anything you say. Just let me feel the inside of you!"

Inch at a time, she swallowed him, her muscles squeezing his shaft with each clench of her legs. "How much do you want me, William?"

"I'll do anything, just don't stop!"

He felt a lightening of the force binding his hands to the chair with every stroke of her pussy up and down his cock. Free from the restraints, William reached around cupping her breasts in his hands, crushing her body against his. "Oh God, you're so tight. I never imagined you'd feel so good!" Lifting Desiree up, he set her on the floor, as she arched her back inviting him to keep pumping her.

Desire pushed back against his body. The need to cum inside, conquering his vixen, overwhelmed his mind. Pressing down on the small of her back, he thrust deeper in between her lips, feeling the head of his cock hit the wall of her vagina.

"Harder! Fuck me, William. Fuck me now before it's too late."

Stopping mid thrust, he glanced at the monitor. *Too late?* Silver eyes surrounded by a scaly elongated face stared back from the computer screen.

"My servant has claimed you. The less you resist the easier it will be."

Pain flared along is cock as he tried to pull out, releasing his hold; he slammed his fist across her back. Doubling over, blood ran down his legs. "Holy shit . . . fuck!" he screamed. Beating on her back and head did nothing. He collapsed across her, held in place by the pain as she gripped his dick.

"You promised my love. A few moments and we'll be together for all time." Turning her head as he draped himself over her, she flicked her tongue out, tasting the fear and terror oozing from his skin.

"Now," said the voice form the monitor.

"Yes, master," she responded, clamping down one last time. Blood flowed across the floor. Released, yet crippled William sprawled on the carpet. "Soon, my sweetheart, soon." Lying next to him, she caressed his cheek, her face returned to normal, smiling.

Darkness descended on William, his world dimming, Desiree's smile carrying him into oblivion.

Jarred by a car horn outside his apartment, William jumped up. Glancing around, he felt elated with no sight of the web girl or the face in the monitor. *Holy fucking shit, what a nightmare.*

Trying to shake the dream, he walked into the kitchen intent on making coffee and waking up. *I swear I will never do drugs or webcam ever again.*

Turning on the light, he froze. Desiree stood next to the sink wearing fishnet stocking and crotchless panties. "Hi, baby."

Like Windows to the Soul

Greg Chapman

They say the eyes are the window to the soul, but Michael Ford knew all too well that if you wanted the truth about a person, it was how they acted behind closed doors that mattered.

Michael pulled his overcoat tight around him as he walked along Spencer Street, his eyes keenly focussed on the steady procession of windows to his left and right. The freezing night air cut at his face, but he was quickly warmed by the radiance emanating from the houses around him. They were portals to a multitude of worlds of pleasure and if he was lucky, pain.

He slowed his pace and glanced at the façade of a grand turn-of-the-century gable. Through the faded lace curtains he could just make out an elderly couple watching a game show on television. He sighed and wiped his nose with the back of his hand.

Fucking TV – it's responsible for so much banality.

Michael knew people had no imagination anymore; no desire to speak to anyone. They were all simply too afraid to voice their opinions and arguments were completely out of the question. Yet, this was the show Michael craved. Internet porn had left him numb; in fact he now believed he was immune to its perversions, so all that remained for him to sate his appetite was raw reality. He needed to constantly replicate that pain from his past.

He scratched at his unkempt beard in frustration and picked up his pace. He turned left off Spencer Street into Kent Lane, a decrepit little short cut that would take him deeper into that part of the city where you could literally feel an upsurge in the crime rate. It was like stepping over a threshold into a room where everything was colder and darker than it was before. He hoped – no he prayed – that the treasure he sought was close at hand.

A knot of anxiety spread in his gut, but he welcomed it because it meant his next fix was fast approaching. He'd first experienced the sensation as a child on those nights when the silence was shattered by vile words and fear-induced screams. It was the only way he knew he was alive. He wanted to feel alive again tonight.

To live he had to remember; remember what it was like when his parents fought. It was the only way he could connect with the world, with anyone. He was raised on a series of tragic experiences that he witnessed from afar. No one bothered to teach him any other way.

Kent Lane ended where Cole Street began and it was in Cole Street that the possibilities became endless. From the cracked asphalt of the road to the filthy patchwork of brick apartments wedged together, this was Michael's Eden. He smiled when he saw the street was devoid of people, but crammed with vehicles. This told him that people were home, tucked inside and seemingly safe behind closed doors, unaware that anyone was watching. He stepped into the street's solitary phone booth, retrieved his binoculars from his jacket and waited.

Number 16 Cole Street was a two-storey apartment with five windows; the two on the ground floor revealing the lounge room and kitchen and the trio on the top floor providing a glimpse into the master and supplementary bedrooms. The apartment was home to a middle-aged couple and their teenage son and daughter. Michael didn't know their names; he didn't need to, but he'd observed them for almost six months now. Usually Number 16 became a hive activity just around dinner time.

Right on schedule, Michael heard the father's voice first; a booming baritone that resonated out into the street with the ferocity of a cannonball. Michael smiled and his skin flushed with goose bumps. It was going to be a great night. The father yelled abuse at his wife; a tirade that was more a volley of expletives than anything of substance. A moment later Michael heard the stomp of the man's feet on the internal stairs and he shivered with delight.

The father recommenced the abuse once he reached his son's bedroom. Michael looked upward to the boy's window and adjusted the focus on his binoculars. The boy was lying on his bed, earphones in to block out the outside world, like always. Surely the boy knew by now that it was pointless; that his father would simply barge in? Michael saw the boy's bedroom door swing open, saw the boy flinch beneath his father's imposing stature. Michael listened intently.

'What the fuck are you doing?' the father said, 'you lazy little turd!'

The boy never got a chance to speak. His father gripped him by the hair and dragged him from the room. Michael moved to the left side of the phone booth and peered into the second window on the top floor – the daughter's bedroom.

When father and son entered, she was quickly on her feet – a good little soldier girl. The father thrust the two of them together and they huddled, cringing with terror. Michael licked his lips and pressed the binoculars closer to his eyes. He didn't want to miss one frame of what was about to happen – what happened almost every night.

'You two fucking disgust me!' the father told them. 'You make me sick!'

With his enormous hands, he gripped the backs of their necks and brought them even closer together. Michael could see tears rolling down the girl's cheeks as brother and sister came closer and closer. The pervert felt his cock stir in his jeans.

The girl and boy came closer, the pair simply dolls in their father's hands. Their noses touched and they tried to pull away, but this only served to anger their father more.

'You're filthy!' he said, 'Filthy little children!'

The father's hands slid up to the backs of their heads and pushed their faces together until the boy's lips locked with his sister's. Their passion became a survival instinct because they knew that if they didn't do what their father wanted, he would surely hurt them.

After a moment of yearning, the father released them and the siblings stood like statues of shame, neither daring to move, or utter one word. The father, his face now slack with inebriation and arousal, promptly walked to the window, checked the street and drew the curtains.

Much to Michael's dismay, the show was for their eyes only.

He waited a minute before stepping out of the booth. Regardless of the outcome, he still had many mental pictures to take back home. The moon was a looking glass and he worshipped it as he walked, thoughts of Number 16 Cole Street looping in his head.

As he turned back into Kent Lane however, he caught something out of the corner of his eye – a figure, lurking, looking straight in his direction. He stopped to get a closer look at it, but it was gone, swallowed by shadows. He smiled anew, further aroused by the concept of a voyeur observing another.

Who watches the watcher?

He let out a hearty chuckle and walked the rest of the way home.

Cold pizza and cola – the perfect meal for the insomniac.

Michael would never freely admit he was of the nocturnal variety, but when he spent most nights trawling the streets for the private lives of strangers, he could hardly argue.

The meagre salary he pulled in as a freelance website designer was enough to pay the rent and put food in his fridge, but it left little for much else. Fortunately, his only non-work-related hobby didn't require a car.

He devoured the last of the pizza and stared at the screen of his laptop. He was trying to complete a page for a real estate agency, but he couldn't focus; the knots of anxiety twisted more frequently than usual and the urge to venture out into the night was strong. Instantly he recalled the sexual theatre that played out in Number 16 Cole Street. He checked his watch: 12:48am. He turned to look out his front window to the darkened street.

Maybe just a quick walk; an hour can't hurt, and who knows what you might find?

No, he told himself. *You've had your fix for one night.*

He walked to the window and reached up to pull the curtains closed when he caught a shimmer of movement in the street. His apartment was on a corner and a bright tall street light illuminated a great deal of the neighbourhood and sometimes, if he was really lucky, he didn't have to leave his home to get a good show. The single nurse across the street was fond of lycra and running, but he'd never dare to "follow" someone who lived so close to him. Could this be her returning home from work?

He squinted to better study the silhouette and he thought that it had a weight of familiarity about it. It was definitely a person; tall and lithe, wearing dark clothing and – were they sunglasses? Whoever they were stared straight into his home – at him. Michael drew the curtains and headed for the front door to go outside and investigate.

When he opened the door and stepped out onto the lawn, his mystery observer was nowhere to be found. Michael jogged up to the kerb, looked left and right, desperate for any sign of them. He thought of the stranger he'd seen earlier on Cole Street and wondered if it could be him – or her. Again he was enamoured with the possibility that he had a secret admirer. He stood on his front lawn in the dark for a moment more, hoping to see that same someone creeping away in the dark. Just a glimpse; that was all Michael wanted, but he went unrewarded.

He retired to bed wondering why the stranger would be wearing sunglasses at night.

Searing pain woke Michael at dawn.

He tried to open his mouth, but it wouldn't part, his tongue pushing and sliding helplessly – and painfully – against the inside of his lips. Fibrous threads ran vertically along the inside of his mouth, like a train track made from flesh. He was unable to sit up and when he turned his head to determine why, he saw his hands had been tied to the bedhead. He screamed, but the sound was unable to escape. Panic set in when he saw a figure wearing sunglasses standing at the end of his bed.

Oh fuck – it's him.

The stranger, hands clasped neatly in front of him, was wearing a filth-covered black hooded sweatshirt and black jeans, but it was his face that drew Michael's terrified gaze: pale, a thick lumpy, old horizontal scar instead of a mouth. Over his eyes was a strip of tattered burlap and black 80's style sunglasses.

Fuck! What's going on? What's this fucker doing in my house?! What's he fucking done to my mouth!?

The stranger raised a finger to his non-existent lips to shush him, then let his arm fall slowly to his side.

Michael felt something tugging at his mind, digging; like a splinter pushed further into a wound.

Please do not blaspheme. The voice was inside Michael's head.

Fuck! What the fuck are you doing?!

The stranger shushed him again, but this time Michael heard the distinct shush in his head.

You must clear your mind of all obscenities Michael – silence is the key.

Michael hesitated. He didn't know what – or whether – to think. But he needed to know who this stranger was and why he had hurt him. *What do you want?*

The stranger sat on the end of the bed and Michael flinched.

You are looking in the wrong place, the stranger revealed. *You look, but you do not see.*

What am I not looking for?

You do not see, Michael.

What the fuck do you mean!?

The stranger stood then and returned to his pose at the end of the bed.

God gave you two eyes to see Michael; two lips to speak; two ears to hear; two chambers in your heart so you can love. Yet you have wasted them – the things you see displease Him, the words you speak hurt Him. You do not hear Him when He calls to you, and you stopped loving yourself many years ago. He sent me here to help you.

I've watched you for a long time Michael; watched you watching them. You have sinned over and over and worse still you've watched countless other sins being committed. The evils of the world are not for entertainment Michael. They must be stamped out and we will silence them – one soul at a time if we have to. My Brethren are scattered across the globe fulfilling His New Gospel. We are His Shepherds and every one of His sheep will return to Him in time.

I followed you here and waited for you to slumber. I found you here and began the ritual. I'm afraid I had to inject you with a derivative of valerian root to ensure you did not wake while I silenced you. Working with needle and thread is very delicate work after all.

Michael could plainly see the stranger was psychotic; the very definition of insane. Yet how could the insane communicate via thought?

God, the stranger intoned. *God makes it so.*

Please – you have to let me go!

Silence Michael, you must hear me, the stranger continued. *You must listen to Him and I have silenced you so He can speak to you. I too was once like you – naïve and rebellious, without guidance. When my brethren came to silence me I railed against them, but over time, their notions of Silence, Patience and Grace overwhelmed me. It was beautiful and it will be beautiful for you too.*

Michael pulled on his bonds and screamed soundlessly, his mouth burning like fire.

How is this fucking beautiful! You've mutilated me!

The stranger pulled down the hood from his hairless head and removed his sunglasses. His calm composure set Michael's heart into a frantic rhythm.

Perhaps you need to see to believe Michael? Many of us were the same – we had to see Him to believe in Him. He is here amongst us you know. The Second Coming happened in secrecy. Maybe if you are willing you will be taken to Him and see Him for yourself. Until then, this will have to do.

Michael watched as the stranger unravelled the narrow band of burlap from around his eyes, his right hand whipping around and around, slowly revealing the horror below – two hollow sockets, eyeless and all-seeing. The pervert's screams and cries were muted.

Silence, Patience and Grace – that is all that matters Michael. If you look, you will see, if you wait, He will come and if you listen you will hear His voice.

No! No!

The stranger approached him and took a small instrument in his hand. Michael stared at it just so he didn't have to bear witness to his captor's eyeless visage. The instrument of rusted steel was like a pair of scissors with rounded ends – ends designed to pry things open. Before Michael could react, those ends were curling around his right eye.

Nooo!

The fresh scar that was Michael's mouth almost split from the force of his screams as the stranger removed the eye from its socket with the care and attention of a surgeon. With the optic nerve still attached, he placed the eyeball upon Michael's heaving chest so he could see his own face, contorted in agony. Within a few moments, the left eye was out and resting beside it. Michael vomited bile, but he could only swallow it back down. He could see his own misery unfolding in his features.

Then the stranger spoke to him one final time.

Before you can truly see, you need to look within Michael and perhaps in time you will find the patience to behold all of His wonders. Goodbye Michael, we'll meet again soon.

Michael screamed and thrashed like a madman; piss flooded his pants. The question "Who Watches the Watcher?" stabbed at his psyche relentlessly until finally, exhaustion took hold. He watched himself fade away into darkness, a sense of bliss washing over him and, just like the stranger promised, there was Silence.

Tais Teng
Cover Art

ABOUT THE AUTHORS

K. Trap Jones is an award winning author of literary horror novels and short stories. With a strong inspiration from Dante Alighieri and Edgar Allan Poe, his passion for folklore, classic literary fiction and obscure segments within society lead to his creative writing style of "filling in the gaps" and walking the line between reality and fiction. His debut novel THE SINNER won first place in the Royal Palm Literary Award within the Horror/Dark Fantasy category. He is also a member of the Horror Writer's Association. More information can be found at www.ktrapjones.com

Ken Goldman, former Philadelphia teacher of English and Film Studies, is an affiliate member of the Horror Writers Association. He has homes on the Main Line in Pennsylvania and at the Jersey shore depending upon his mood and his need for a tan. His stories have appeared in over 665 independent press publications in the U.S., Canada, the UK, and Australia with over thirty due for publication in 2013. Since 1993 Ken's tales have received seven honorable mentions in The Year's Best Fantasy & Horror. He has written four books : three books of short stories : YOU HAD ME AT ARRGH!! : FIVE UNEASY PIECES BY KEN GOLDMAN (at Sam's Dot Publishers and an all-time top ten bestseller at the former Genre Mall); DONNY DOESN'T LIVE HERE ANYMORE (a book of five short stories released by A/A Productions in print, Kindle, Nook, and download formats); STAR CROSSED (an e-book of five short stories released by Vampires 2 Publishing Company, available as a download and in Kindle format from the publishers site and from Smashwords); and a novella, DESIREE, (published by Damnation books, available in downloadable eBook from their site, while print and Kindle editions are available at Amazon.com); Ken would be famous except for the fact nobody seems to know who he is. However, he looks forward to the day when he and Stephen King are called to the dais and someone asks "Who is that guy standing next to Ken Goldman?

"William J Fedigan's style is all punch - no fluff. Fedigan is Rocky Marciano in print. You've just stepped into the ring with one of the best." --Dan Fante

J. Daniel Stone is a 25-year-old writer born and raised in New York City and is an affiliate member of the HWA. He does not eat meat, believes in equal rights and absorbs as much art and science as he can. His work has been reviewed by respected horror websites such as Horrornews.net, who said his stories are "lush and ultra-violent, thus which successfully invokes the great horror literature of the 1990's" and Hellnotes, who deemed his work "Psychologically Insightful." His debut novel, *The Absence of Light*, was published by Villipede Publications.

Shaun Avery is a crime and horror fiction fan with a particular fondness for satirical horror, especially the media-skewering kind. He has won writing competitions and has stories accepted for numerous magazines and anthologies. This is probably not the last time he will tell a tale that mocks the world's obsession with fame.

Jason Hughes grew up in Texas. He has been a lifelong fan of the Horror genre for thirty-six years and counting. He likes to keep his writing on a level of realism with everyday people that are placed in horrific situations. He graduated *The Tom Savini's Special Effects Make-Up Program* in 2004 and still does Special Effects today. Jason is the Editor of the anthology *Moral Horror*, available now in stores everywhere. He is a contributing Writer for *The Houston Examiner, Beyond the Dark Horizon* and Writer/ Reviewer for *Horrornews.net*. His writings can be found in such anthologies as *Nocturnal Illumination, Ladies and Gentlemen of Horror 2010, Bleed, They Will Come, Quakes & Storms, Southern Haunts* and *Bigfoot Terror Tales Vol. 1* along with *Twisted Dreams Magazine* and *House of Horror Magazine* among others. He is also a multi-published (and transferred to audio) Poet. Jason was chosen as one of the top ten best Horror Authors of 2009-2011. He has written screenplays for Mudd Miller Films/ Rebellious Cinema, Sick Flick Productions & American – International Pictures (released *The Amityville Horror, The Town That Dreaded Sundown* and much more). He is also a Drummer, t-shirt Printer, Sky Diver and avid Supporter of *The West Memphis Three* (www.wm3.org).

Chris Riley: With fifty story acceptances in less than two years, as well as a recent Honorable Mention at L. Ron Hubbard's Writers of the Future Contest, Chris sees no end to his writing addiction. His stories have been published in numerous magazines and anthologies, including *Underground Voices,*

Cover of Darkness, Bete Noire, The Absent Willow Review, Residential Aliens, and *Bards and Sages Quarterly.* You can reach him at chakalives@gmail.com, or at his crappy blog; frombehindthebluedoor.wordpress.com.

Timothy Frasier is a novelist, short story writer, and poet. His work appears in several James Ward Kirk anthologies, Static Movement anthologies, and literary magazines. He lives in Western Kentucky with his wife, Lisa, and their German shepherd, Chief.

Roger Cowin currently lives in Centerville, IN with his wife, Barbara and their pack of vicious Yorkies. His poems have been appearing in journals around the country for over 25 years. Most recently his work can be found in *Sunstone* and *Indiana Horror 2012.* His first collection of mainstream poetry, PASSING THROUGH DARKNESS is now available from Amazon.com in paperback and Kindle.

Mathias Jansson is a Swedish art critic and poet. He has been published in magazines as The Horror Zine Magazine SNM Horror Magazine, Dark Eclipse, Schlock, The Sirens Call and The Poetry Box. He has also contributed to several anthologies from Horrified Press as Just One More Step, Suffer Eternal anthology Volume 1-3, Hell Whore Anthology Volume 1-3.Homepage: http://mathiasjansson72.blogspot.se/

Sydney Leigh hails from the North Shore, and when not writing horror or dark fiction, can be found teaching English to unsuspecting youths. Between her love of animals, cooking, film, music, photography, and nature, she is never at a loss for a creative outlet... or inspiration. Her best friend is a Border Collie, and despite holding degrees in English, Psychology, and Graphic Design, she spends most of her free time doing her teenage son's laundry. Her short fiction has appeared in various anthologies which she hides from her husband so he can sleep at night.

David Price: I have been published in the anthologies Dangers Untold and Tales from the Grave. I also have an essay coming out in the anthology Real People, Real Phobias. Most recently, my novella "Dead in the USA" was published by Third Cove Press. I am an active member of the HWA and the New England Horror Writers and I am also on the NEHW Board of Directors.

Shawna L. Bernard is a freelance writer, graphic artist, and editor who sometimes masquerades as a tiger named Hobbes. She spends her time creating everything from bucolic poetry and photo essays to dark fiction and horror under the guise of her literary double, Sydney Leigh. Her work has appeared in magazines, anthologies, and on bar napkins across the country. A native of Massachusetts, she also trains dogs, rehabilitates wildlife, and always keeps a bag packed for spontaneous road trips with her imaginary roommate, Ted.

David Eccles: Born the son of a trawler-man, I spent my childhood reading comic books and classic science fiction novels, always dreaming that I'd be a writer someday but doing nothing about it until after I'd wasted half of my life sweating inside an electrical domestic appliance manufacturing plant, then working for an engineering company assembling and testing safety return valves for pipelines and finally working in the security industry as a security guard and bouncer at rock concerts and night clubs. It was only after giving up my job to take care of my invalid father that i finally took the step to start a blog and to write. I have collaborated with a number of other writers and authors on a couple of projects, and shortly my story "All Sunshine Makes the Desert" will feature in a collaborative e-book anthology with an apocalyptic theme, entitled "Echoes of the Wasteland", the proceeds of which will go to charity. Roy James Daley, author and owner of BOOKSoftheDEADPRESS.com was the first to give me a break and he featured a short flash fiction story of mine entitled "The Teeth Police" www.booksofthedeadpress.com/2013/03/flash-fiction-by-david-eccles.html I'm currently working on a submission for the Neverland's Library fantasy anthology, more short stories and my debut novel, which, because of all the story ideas i keep having has been sidelined for the moment. Incidentally, my story "Doing it for JRD (Justice, Revenge and Deliverance)" was written as a homage to JRD (James Roy Daley) for giving me that first break and showing my work on his website.

B.T. Joy is a Scottish poet and short fiction writer. Originally from Glasgow, he has also called London and Bridge of Weir home and has travelled widely; working in the USA on farms and ranches and hitchhiking, camping, climbing and sailing both there and in four other continents. Since gaining a First Class Honours degree in 2009 B.T.Joy's short horror fiction has appeared with Static Movement, Flashes in the Dark, MicroHorror, SNM Horror Magazine and Surreal Grotesque, among others. His poetry has also been widely published and in 2012 he was a nominee for The Ravenglass Poetry Press Competition. Having received a Postgraduate Diploma in Education in 2012 B.T.Joy currently teaches High School English in Renfrewshire.

Michael Zunenshine is a native Montrealer who has spent the last few years earning a living writing professionally for others. Recently he has abandoned professional writing to focus on his own creative and critical pursuits. A selection of his earlier work can be found at thenormalmachine.com.

Michael Randolph is a horror writer and poet currently residing in San Antonio Texas. When not crafting new horrific stories and poem, he works in aviation and facets gemstones. His work has appeared in Burial Day books, and Dark Eclipse Magazine.

Brigitte Kephart, as a child, thought creating imaginary worlds to play in, or escape to, was a gift from the divine. Sometimes she played in gardens full of tulips; other times were filled with dark tomblike spaces and her imagined heroics of escape. Raised in Indiana, her debut short story "Sanctuary" appears in the Barnyard Horrors anthology and "Fair Play" can be found in the Sex, Drugs and Horror anthology.

Greg Chapman is a horror author and artist from Central Queensland. His novellas *Torment* and *The Noctuary* were published by Damnation Books in 2011. His latest, *Vaudeville*, was published by Dark Prints Press in July 2012. His fourth novella, The Last Night of October will be released by Bad Moon Books on Halloween 2013. His fiction has appeared in Eclecticism, Trembles, Morpheus Tales, Bete Noire and Literary Mayhem. His comic book illustrations have appeared in Midnight Echo, Decay and Andromeda Spaceways Inflight Magazine. He also illustrated the Bram Stoker Award-winning graphic novel *Witch-Hunts: A Graphic History of the Burning Times*, written by Rocky Wood and Lisa Morton, published by McFarland in May 2012. Find Greg on the web at http://darkscrybe.com

Max Booth III is the author of True Stories Told By a Liar and They Might Be Demons. He is the editor in chief of Perpetual Motion Machine Publishing, the assistant editor of Dark Moon Digest, and the fiction editor of Kraken Press. He is also a committee member for the Horror Writers Association. He currently resides in San Antonio with his partner. Follow him on Twitter @GiveMeYourTeeth or visit him on his website www.TalesFromTheBooth.com.